W9-CBS-970

THE PROSECUTOR

Books by Magdalen Nabb

DEATH OF AN ENGLISHMAN
DEATH OF A DUTCHMAN
DEATH IN SPRINGTIME
DEATH IN AUTUMN

THE PROSECUTOR

Magdalen Nabb
and
Paolo Vagheggi

ST. MARTIN'S PRESS
New York

 For information, address St. Martin's Press, 175 Fifth Avenue, New York, N.Y. 10010.

Library of Congress Cataloging-in-Publication Data

Nabb, Magdalen, 1947–
    The prosecutor / by Magdalen Nabb and Paolo Vagheggi.
    p. cm.
    ISBN 0-312-01497-X : $16.95
    I. Vagheggi, Paolo. II. Title.
PR6064.A18P75 1987 87-27456
823'.914—dc19 CIP

First published in Great Britain by William Collins Sons & Co., Ltd.

First U.S. Edition

10 9 8 7 6 5 4 3 2 1

Although no reader of this novel can fail to be reminded of the kidnap and murder of Italy's premier Aldo Moro in 1978, it must be emphasized that this is a work of fiction. The characters and incidents are entirely fictitious and no resemblance is intended to any living person.

PROLOGUE

'Sound all right?'

'When is the sound ever all right in this barn of a place. We're still working on it. Any problems up here?'

'Take a look.'

The telecamera panned over the pin-sized heads of the vast crowd far below and then swung to the right to zoom in on an island of empty space.

'You're getting that light cable right across your frame on this shot. I'll go down and see if I can get it shifted. Give this lens a cleaning, will you? You've got a hair in the gate that's showing up on the monitor. God, it's freezing up here! You can tell it's November. I'm off.'

The cameraman switched off the power and cleaned his lens carefully. Then he backed into the shadows to smoke a furtive cigarette before switching the power on again. The music began and arc lights flooded the empty space where the cable had been moved back out of his line of vision. He panned over the crowd for a few minutes before swivelling back to the right. The space was now dotted with tiny red and black figures. Such general sound as reached him was muffled and confused so that every now and then he had to glance down at his cue card propped on a marble ledge beside him: *Sermon – M.J. Lazurek – 18 minutes*

He zoomed in on the plump black and purple figure that rose and came forward to the microphone.

'From the gospel according to St John: "Believe me, the time is coming, nay, has already come, when the dead will listen to the voice of the Son of God, and those who listen to it will live. As the Father has within him the gift of life, so he has granted to the Son that he too should have within him the gift of life, and has also granted him power to execute judgement, since he is the Son of Man. Do not be surprised at that; the time is coming, when all those who are in their graves will hear his voice and will come out of them; those whose actions have been good, rising to new life, and those whose doings have been evil, rising to meet their sentence." '

'Lousy,' murmured the cameraman. The speaker's voice was clear and slow but it was obvious that there would be too much echo as everyone had expected. Well, it wasn't his problem.

'On this All Souls' day when our prayers are for the faithful departed, let us remember particularly in our prayers the soul of our brother in Christ, one who is no longer with us because he sacrificed his life for the common good. The Gospel says, "those whose actions have been good, rising to new life, and those whose doings have been evil, rising to meet their sentence". Those whose actions have been good . . .

'Ten years have passed since Carlo Rota departed this life but we have not forgotten him. He remains with us in our hearts. We remember his constant dedication to his work as a statesman, we remember him as an exemplary husband and father, we remember him when still a young man, a student of Law, already committed to the defence of the Faith against the grave threat of Communism and its evils.'

Those whose doings have been evil . . .

'We remember him also when, during those sixty long days as a prisoner of the Red Brigades, he kept his spiritual integrity, his moral force, his faith in God, totally intact. The letters he wrote from that cruel prison demonstrate his strength, the strength of a man who refused to the last to betray his immortal soul.'

A brief burst of sunshine sent a beam of amber light through the window behind the high altar and the cameraman shifted to take advantage of it, though the full effect was spoiled by the arc lights. The shaft of colour was doused as suddenly as it had appeared. It was probably raining again. He didn't return immediately to the speaker, who provided little in the way of visual interest, but moved slowly down past the two cherubs clutching their gold and black crown to rest on the gesticulating figure of St Ambrose, whose dramatic attitude and swirling gold draperies were better matched to the sententious words than the chubby little Monsignor who was pronouncing them.

'Let us remember the words he wrote to his family during those dark days: "I die a Christian," he wrote, "in the great love of a family that I shall watch over from heaven."

'In the ten years that have passed since those words were written the fight against this terrible organized violence has never ceased, yet many of those responsible for that dreadful deed, and for whom we invoke God's mercy, are still at liberty, still free to try and corrupt the young with the false ideals by which they justify their violence.

'There are young people among us who may well remember little or nothing of what happened on an April day all those years ago when, after the cold-blooded slaughter of the young men of his escort, Carlo Rota was abducted before the shocked and disbelieving eyes of the people of Rome. But it is to those young people, for whom that day may seem just one more episode of history, that I say beware! Beware false prophets and false ideals. Beware above all the end that justifies the means. It is on your constant vigilance, on your strength and righteousness pitted against those forces of evil still at large among us, that the future peace of the world and the defence of the Faith depend.

'Those of us who as adults lived through those days of tension, of horror, of disbelief, who still hold in our minds the image of that shattered body abandoned in an automobile, abused and scorned even after death, cannot help but remember the lesson that Carlo Rota taught us, the example of a man who made no pact with the devil and his agents, who refused to save his own life at the cost of humiliating the

State he had helped to found on Christian principles, a man who asked for nothing and gave everything. This lesson of course, selflessness and meek suffering is one we must learn and transmit to the young who are always and everywhere in danger from the Godless and the violent!'

He was right about one thing, thought the cameraman whose nose was beginning to run: It *is* freezing up here. Quick pan over the crowd again . . . He should be finishing any minute. And there's still the rest of the service to get through . . .

In the cameraman's opinion, his perch on the balcony just under the domed ceiling of the apse of St Peter's was probably the coldest place in Rome.

CHAPTER ONE

As always when he awoke in the morning, Lapo Bardi was fully conscious the moment he opened his eyes. The luminous dial on the clock showed five minutes to seven. He could have switched off the alarm, given that he never dropped off to sleep again, but instead he lay still on his side, his left arm crooked under his neck, aware of the fact that dining in a restaurant the night before and finishing the meal with a cognac was the cause of a queasiness which would be unlikely to wear off completely before evening, and then only if he avoided any further irritation to his liver. No alcohol then. And at eleven o'clock he had a wedding to go to. The alarm clock gave a faint click and he swiftly reached out his right hand to stop it before it started ringing. In the same movement he switched on the bedside lamp, sat up and flung the covers aside. His feet touched a silky Persian rug, luminous in the pool of soft light shed by the lamp. The rest of the large study in which he had spent his nights for the last eight years or so was in almost total darkness. At least half the heavy volumes of law that filled the bookshelves had been his father's. The divan in the study had always been kept made up for him since he often worked late into the night when he had a case in court.

Since the time of his affair with Giovanna he had never presented himself in his wife's bedroom. He would have considered it indelicate. Not that there had been any drama. Laura had not reproached him, never so much as mentioned it, never made a scene, though she must have known the reason or she would hardly have accepted his absence without comment. He considered himself fortunate and, in gratitude, treated her with scrupulous gentility during the brief periods he spent at home. He never inquired what she did with herself when he was away, confident of her discretion. Sometimes he was away for almost a week at a time and he spent more hours working through case notes in the back of his car on some interminable motorway than in this room.

It was to avoid disturbing Laura that he showered and dressed almost noiselessly in the bathroom that communicated with his study and her bedroom, opening and closing the door very softly and taking up the Beretta 9 and keys from his bedside table without the faintest click. With the Beretta in place in its holster, but still in shirtsleeves, he left the study and went downstairs to the kitchen where he drank two glasses of mineral water and prepared himself some coffee. He did it meticulously but very swiftly, not because he was in any hurry but because he preferred to avoid the cleaner who let herself in with her own key at eight. Once he had returned to the kitchen before leaving for some reason and had found her finishing what coffee he had left in the pot and smoking a cigarette. Probably she always did it, and though it didn't bother him one way or the other he had been faintly embarrassed by the way she had turned quickly to the sink to hide the cup from him. He wasn't even sure what her name was, Marisa or Milena or something or the sort, a slight girl with fair, almost colourless hair. She must have been sickly because he had on a number of occasions found his wife doing her work because she was away ill. He poured out his coffee quickly and took it back upstairs and switched on the reading lamp on his desk where he intended to read through some case notes as he drank.

Luigi Gori, terrorist. A small fish, but small fish might have contact with bigger ones and this one had decided to repent and collaborate in the hope of getting himself out of prison. He had also decided that he wanted to tell his story to Lapo Bardi, the most prominent Substitute Prosecutor specializing in terrorism, and the first thing Bardi intended to ask him was why. Not that he hadn't a good idea. Years of interrogating terrorists had taught him that most of them, excepting a few charismatic figures, were insignificant youngsters without brains or talent whose only hope of making themselves important was by attaching themselves to the Red Brigades or some similar group and working their way up to the privileged position of being allowed to shoot down a perfect stranger in cold blood. And most of the ones who 'repented' on being caught continued their pursuit of significance by getting the maximum amount of attention from the authorities for their story.

Luigi Gori. Florentine. Aged 28. Arrested two weeks ago on October 19th at the Florence railway station while buying a ticket for Rome. Now in the prison of Sollicciano where Bardi would start questioning him in less than an hour's time. A small fish.

Beyond the double shutters a church bell was striking eight. Bardi drained the last of the coffee and contemplated the photograph on the identity form. A squat, unprepossessing face, moustache, tiny round glasses that gave an intellectual air. The only job Gori had kept for more than a month was as a hospital porter.

The door from the bathroom opened.

'No!' snapped Bardi without raising his eyes, mentally damning the cleaner who should have known better than to come near his study at that hour unless the door on the corridor was ajar to indicate his absence.

'It's me . . .'

Laura was standing in the bathroom doorway, her blonde hair still tangled from sleep, barefoot and wearing some sort of half-transparent robe.

He raised his head so abruptly at this unprecedented intrusion that she unthinkingly pulled the flimsy robe closer over her breasts. It was years since he had seen her fully undressed and that tiny protective gesture made his eyes stray against his will over her body as if a perfect stranger had suddenly presented herself half-naked.

'You're up early.' He looked down at the file again to prevent his eyes from straying like that, conscious that this and the tone of his voice made the comment sound like a rebuke.

'I wouldn't have disturbed you but last night you came in so late . . . I was thinking about Sylvia's wedding . . .'

'What about it?'

'I thought – she is your chief's daughter. I thought we should arrive together.'

'Out of the question. The most I can say is that I'll put in an appearance at some point. I have to be at Sollicciano most of the morning. They'll send a car here for you and I'll make my own way there.' He still didn't look up. There was something almost indecent about reacting like that to your own wife. He was irritated with himself for not being in command of the situation, the one thing he couldn't tolerate . . . A date on the second page of the file caught his eye: 1976, the year Gori joined the Red Brigades, two years before the Rota abduction . . . He hadn't meant to be abrupt but she had surprised him. He ought to say something kind or at least polite . . . Without taking his eyes from the file, he groped for a cigarette in the wooden box on the desk, broke it and lit half of it, a quirk left over from a long-forgotten attempt to give up smoking. 1976 . . . The face of Luigi Gori stared back at him sullenly. An expression typical of post-war working-class youth, pampered inside the family and underprivileged outside it. A lethal combination. He wasn't concentrating properly, no doubt because of Laura's interruption. A pleasant remark, that was what he meant to see to and what was spoiling his train of thought. But Laura had gone. He hadn't heard the door close. Well, they would see each other at the wedding.

He got up and went to open the inner and outer shutters, letting in the noise of the sluggish morning traffic. The November day was still darkish and grey. It was raining quietly and steadily and there were little pools of water on the gravel drive leading to the front iron gates. Below the window the big leaves of the magnolia were shiny and dripping, lit by the streetlamp that was still on outside the high railings. Some of the shutters were open on the villas across the avenue and parked cars were starting up to join the stream making for the city centre to the right, leaving little clouds of exhaust smoke hanging over the wet pavements. There was never room for Bardi's car to park when it arrived at that hour and he was punctilious about being ready and waiting in the entrance hall exactly on time. Another fifteen minutes. He closed the window, slipped on his jacket and began pacing up and down the room with the Gori file in his hands. There were no specific charges apart from the standard 'Participation in an armed group'. Joined the Red Brigades in 1976. Nom de guerre, 'Piero'. And Carlo Rota had been abducted and then murdered in Rome in 1978. The biggest and best organized operation the Brigades had ever undertaken and it had been planned in Florence. At that time 'Piero' couldn't have been more than a messenger boy. A small fish, but even so . . .

Bardi lit the other half of his cigarette, still pacing. It had to be handled carefully. Let him talk. There was nothing they wanted more than to talk about themselves, to be understood, to cut something of a figure, too, while remembering to put in how much they regretted it all here and there.

The traffic outside was picking up speed. Impatient horns punctuated the general roar. Bardi glanced at his watch, stubbed out the tiny cigarette and packed the file into the overnight case that went everywhere with him because of emergency calls which often took him away to some prison at the other end of the peninsula at a moment's notice. The files on all his current cases were packed in one side, spare clothes, ammunition, cigarettes and medicines in the other. He spun the combination locks and took the case downstairs, leaving his door ajar.

At the foot of the staircase, the girl was removing the silver from a big mahogany sideboard in the dining-room on the right. From the oil painting above her head Bardi's father in his judge's robes gazed sternly and serenely out of the open door. A scene that seemed to Bardi to have been repeating itself exactly for all the fifty years he had lived in that house. No, not exactly. On the rainy mornings when he had been leaving for the *liceo* with his bag of schoolbooks it had been his father himself who had watched him go from the little office on the opposite side of the hall. Nobody had used that room since he died. Other things had changed too. The daily woman had taken the place of the couple who used to live in, the man acting as his father's chauffeur. They had left when the old man died. Laura hadn't wanted people living in and he had no use for a chauffeur himself. And that, he thought, slipping a raincoat over his shoulders and choosing an umbrella from the mahogany stand in the gloomy light of the hall, was another thing that had changed. No one had ever challenged a judge's authority in his father's day. He'd had no need of the armoured car and two-man escort arriving at the front gate now. Bardi shot the portrait a wry look and opened the front door to meet the challenge with relish.

'Good morning. You can remove his handcuffs.'

When Gori was freed the two guards stationed themselves on either side of the steel door and the prisoner came forward, offering his hand to Bardi who shook it briskly.

'And your defence lawyer?'

'I wish to renounce the presence of a lawyer for the defence.' Bardi received this formal declaration with a satisfied nod.

'Sit down.'

The small room was windowless and bare except for four upright chairs and a table where Bardi's case lay unopened next to a typewriter. If Gori had decided to talk without a lawyer present, Bardi had also decided to do without his registrar. The fewer people present the better. The two faced each other across the table for a moment in silence. Gori's face lacked the defiant sulkiness of the photograph and his glance shifted uneasily before the keen gaze of the Substitute

Prosecutor, who had the air of some predator toying with a prey he wasn't sure he cared to devour. Their silence was punctuated by the clanging of distant doors and raised voices distorted by echo. Gori flinched slightly at each sudden noise. Without comment Bardi slid a sheet of paper into the typewriter and typed rapidly: *I wish to renounce the presence of a lawyer for the defence.* After which he pushed his chair back slightly and relaxed in it.

'Why me?' The question was sudden and sharp but Gori must have been expecting it.

'You're the best there is.'

'A double-edged compliment?'

'No. I've heard about you. You're the best. The only one who could understand –'

'Understand what? That you want to get out of here and that making use of the new law on repentants is about the only way you'll manage it? That shouldn't be difficult for anybody to understand.'

Gori's face darkened. He was offended. What had he expected, some sort of father confessor? A communion of souls? A man to man chat? Bardi gave no quarter but he wasn't the sort to make use of anyone's illusions, however convenient it might be to do so. And Gori's illusions had already been made good use of or he wouldn't be where he was.

'Tell me whatever you wish to tell me, but remember that I'm a Prosecutor for the Republic and that you're trying to put yourself on my side, not the other way around. That way we can at least hope to understand each other.'

The sullen expression of the photograph was there now. Gori's short fingers tugged nervously at the ends of his moustache. His round face was stubbled with some days' growth of beard. When he spoke his voice was jumpy but very subdued.

'It's not true what you said, that I just want to get out of here. You get time to think in prison . . .'

'You've only been here two weeks.' Bardi's bright eyes

showed a faint trace of amusement. It was lost on Gori, who was too absorbed in himself to notice it.

'You can think a lot in two weeks on your own. I know now that everything I did was a mistake and I want to tell everything whether I get out of here or not. We've got to put a stop to it all and this is the only way I can help. It's all been a crazy mistake and we're beaten, we can never win, I realize that now.'

Bardi noted the anomalous use of 'we' without comment, more concerned that he was going to have to spend days listening to long-winded speeches of self-justification in the hope of hearing one or two useful facts. Gori and his like were quite self-centred enough to believe that the 'Repentants' law had been created for the good of their souls rather than as an insidious and increasingly successful means of dividing and destroying militant groups.

'Let's begin in 1976. Who recruited you?'

'It didn't just happen like that. Things started before . . . the trouble was I was out of work, if I'd had a decent job things would have gone differently for me . . .'

Bardi resigned himself. 'Then tell me how it did happen.'

'It was a time when everything was going badly for me. Not just because I was out of work, we had problems at home as well because our flat had been sold to a new landlord and we'd been given notice to quit because he wanted it for his daughter. Everything would have been all right if we'd been able to buy it ourselves when it came up for sale.'

'You must have had first chance, given that you were tenants.'

'We did but we couldn't afford it, especially the deposit. My dad was due to retire in a couple of years. We could have managed if those shits he worked for had agreed to give him the lump sum due to him when he retired, but they wouldn't. And he'd worked in that shop all his life, since he was twelve years old. If you saw the amount of money they turn over in a big fancy place like that right in the centre. I was livid with my dad, I reckon he was a right mug, he should have forced them.'

'He could hardly have been in a position to do that.'

'No, he was in the same position he'd been in at age twelve, a pathetic underdog. And he was the only one there who really knew the business inside or out, not like the owner who'd inherited it and didn't give a damn. When my dad started work they still used to make saddles, now it's all fancy bags and stuff, but he's the one who knows about leather and they treated him like some kind of shop boy. That's when I decided I wasn't going to be a mug for anybody. It's the same story if you work in a factory.'

'Have you ever worked in a factory?'

'No, but I know plenty of people who have. Anyway, I decided that nobody was going to take me for a sucker all my life so I could finish up with nothing like my dad. That's why when I met some people from a local left-wing group who were for starting some militant action I was dead keen. I'd never been interested in politics – some of the group, the ones who were students, used to go on about it to me and a few others. They'd give us talks to try and make us more politically aware and I suppose after a bit we got into it, though I didn't have any really clear ideas myself, I was just pissed off with the system. In some ways what we did was serious but at that stage a lot of it was for kicks, especially burning cars and stuff. I got a lot of satisfaction out of it because I was flaming mad about what had happened to my dad. I think a good few of the others were like me, a bit confused, but we never talked about it. The student types were more serious, but when I look back on it now that I know more about politics and armed struggle, they didn't understand anything. They were always on about educating the people. Educating the people my foot. All they ever did was cause the local police a pain in the neck. They couldn't educate the people because they didn't even know who "the people" were, let alone understand them.

'Later on when I joined the Red Brigades I learned a lot. It's not enough just to cause chaos. Every action is supposed to cause more people to join you, otherwise it's a waste of time. The sort of thing we did then didn't encourage anybody to join us – like occupying houses. We did a lot of that. People would hang around you, all for you, because they wanted you to occupy a building or a flat for them. Then, once you'd done it and they had somewhere to live they'd be back into the system as fast as their legs could carry them. Afterwards they wouldn't even speak to us in the street, never mind join us. They didn't give a sod then for the struggle for Communism. Even though I didn't have any clear ideas about politics myself, I could see after a bit that what we were doing was stupid. I just went on doing it because it was something to do, a way of kicking back at the injustice of the system. I was good at it, as well. It wasn't long before I was organizing actions myself. In those days we used to follow what the Red Brigades were doing and I'd model myself on them, only on a smaller scale.'

'Did you have any direct contact with them?'

'No. We had to follow what they were doing through the newspapers. A lot of it seemed to belong to another world because it had to do with factory workers up north, and Florence is different. We had different problems, especially housing and unemployment. The only thing we had in common was anti-fascism. We used to beat up fascists, people of our own age mostly. It was easy enough because we always outnumbered them. Even so, it was dangerous because if you were caught at it you were bound to finish up inside. That's why a lot of the group eventually dropped out. They started preaching about non-militant struggle but underneath they were just scared. Some others dropped out because they got jobs. First chance they got they were back into the system. In the end, because of the split between militants and non-militants and other people dropping out for their own reasons, there were only about six of us hardliners left. Can I smoke?'

Bardi nodded, watching him. Gori's hands were trembling slightly but he had stopped reacting to the background clangs and echoes. Finding that there was no ashtray, he dropped the spent match surreptitiously between his knees and then inhaled deeply.

'There was one who dropped out – not out of the movement altogether, he was one of the non-militant lot . . . it's rubbish that non-militant stuff . . . Even so, I respected him because he had brains, he was an Assistant at the University, and because he told me that his real reason for his decision was that his wife was pregnant. You can't blame somebody for that. His wife was great as well, beautiful-looking and a real lady, I saw her once. He was the only one of the intellectual lot that I ever talked to much. The others talked a lot of rubbish, especially the younger students. He used to give me stuff to read as well –'

'His name?'

'Bandini, Aldo. I hope he won't get arrested because he's dropped out of the movement altogether now, but that's for you to decide . . .'

Bardi was typing. When he stopped he asked: 'What did he give you to read?'

'Mostly Red Brigades manifestoes, and books on the history of Communism. I'd never read anything like that before. I'd never been interested in books but this stuff was different because it was real. Anyhow, that was how I first got to really thinking about politics, because of him, and when he went over to the non-militant group we still kept in touch. We used to meet sometimes for coffee in a bar in Piazza San Marco, near the faculty where he worked, and I'd tell him what was going on. By that time the few of us who were left were spending more time arguing about what to do than doing it and I was pissed off. Then one day – it was the November of 1975 and it was freezing cold and pouring with rain – we went for a pizza together at lunch-time. I was even more pissed off than usual, especially as I was wet through because I needed an overcoat and I had no money. I told him I wanted to break away from the group and find a bigger one where there was some action. He didn't say anything at first but then after, when we were having a coffee, he said if

I was serious he could put me in touch with the Red Brigades. I said I was dead serious but I didn't believe him because even though he used to give me all their manifestoes I didn't think he knew any of them. Looking back on it now, I can see that there was no reason why he shouldn't have known somebody but then it didn't seem possible. For us the Red Brigades weren't real people. We used to follow everything they did and talk about them all the time but it was like you'd talk about films or something. They'd pulled off all these fantastic actions and none of them had ever been caught, nobody had any idea who they were. For us it was like they had magic powers, they were so mysterious in those days. Imagine anybody knowing them. So when Bandini said he'd put me in touch with them I thought, "He's talking rubbish like the rest of them after all, the cretin. Put me in touch with the Red Brigades!" When I left him I was laughing to myself but I was disappointed as well, because up to then I'd really respected him, and what with being fed up with the rest of the group I thought to myself, "Now there's nobody." '

He was trying to catch the ash from his cigarette in his cupped hand and then dropping it on the floor anyway.

'But he did put you in touch with the Red Brigades?'

'Not right away. I never thought about it again after that day but I got more and more fed up with the group. We hadn't done anything concrete in months, nothing but argue. So I stopped going to meetings because they were a complete waste of time. There'd been a lot of rows at home as well and that was making me depressed.'

'Did your parents suspect what you were up to?'

'No, never. They'd never have thought of a thing like that. They don't know anything about politics. My mum doesn't believe it even now that I've been arrested, that's how good she is. The rows started because all that time I was out of work, and because I was never at home they thought I was out looking for a job but in the end they realized I wasn't. At first I'd make up stories about going for interviews and not taking the job because the pay wasn't enough or because there were no prospects. But then I couldn't be bothered making stuff up any more, I was too taken up with other problems, especially when the group began to split, so once I lost my temper with my dad and told him straight that I hadn't been looking for any job, that I had better things to do than waste my time looking for somebody who'd be willing to exploit me the way he'd been exploited. And it's true, that, even though I shouldn't have said it in front of my mum. She had to go out to work all the years she was bringing me and my sister up and she's never once had a holiday because he didn't earn a decent wage. I told him I'd be ashamed of that if I were him. After that there were rows every day and when we weren't rowing we didn't speak at all. There was just my mum and my sister trying to keep the peace but at bottom they always took his side just because he was working and I wasn't.

'Then my brother-in-law who's a ward orderly got me a job in the hospital where he works. If things had been going better I'd have told him where to stick his crummy job, but the way things were I was sick of all the rows and I thought, "What the hell," and I took it. To tell the truth, I didn't mind the thought of it all that much because I had this idea that there was something good about working for your sick comrades. Rich people go in private hospitals and this was a state one. It wouldn't be like being in a factory where everybody's getting ripped off, from the workers to the customers who buy their rotten capitalist junk. Only, when I got there I hated it. I couldn't stick the smells and people whining and grumbling night and day and being ordered about all the time by blokes who thought they were somebody because they'd been stuck in the same dead-end job for twenty years. I'd shoot myself first. There was this old chap I used to have to work with nearly all the time who used to make me sick, he had such dirty habits. There was one thing he used to do, he used to shut himself in the toilet with a newspaper, take his shoes off and sit there for about twenty minutes doing what he had to do and smoking and reading. Then he'd come out and carry on working without even washing his hands and if you have the bad luck to go in after him it was enough to make you sick. Next news he'd be chatting and joking with the patients as he wheeled them round. They thought he was great, always one for a laugh, always cheering them up – if they'd known he'd just come out of the toilet without washing his hands they might have thought differently. If it hadn't been for him I don't think I'd have minded the job so much once I'd got used to it. Some of the patients were all right.'

'In any case you stayed on there. Go on smoking if you wish.' It was preferable, even in that airless room, to the constant moustache-tugging.

'I only stayed on because that was when things started moving with the Red Brigades. When you first get taken on as an irregular it's better if you have a job so as to seem as ordinary as possible. Then nobody suspects that you have any other life. That's the only reason why I stuck it in the hospital as long as I did, that and the fact that I needed money. Irregulars don't get paid and they're expected to provide their own arms. That costs money. I kept on working as a porter until I became a regular.'

'Go back to your recruitment. How was the contact made?'

'It was when I'd been working for about three weeks. I got a phone call from Bandini. It was a bit since I'd seen him. He asked me to meet him at the bar in Piazza San Marco because he had something to tell me. I didn't think anything of it. I'd come to the conclusion by then that he was all hot air and he'd been missing having somebody to show off to. But I went anyway. It was my morning off – I worked shifts – and I suppose I was bored. I hadn't seen any of the group for weeks and the job was getting me down, too. When I got there, there were two men with him and I knew as soon as I saw them that they were from the Red Brigades. They were just like I'd imagined them. Faces as hard as nails and dead serious.'

'Who were they? Their names?'

'One was Li Causi, though I didn't know that then. The other one I never saw again, he was from a different column and I don't know his name, that's the honest truth. He was a cousin of Bandini's, that was how it had worked. And that was another reason why when the group split Bandini had gone with the non-militant lot. I found that out much later. He was a sort of talent scout for the Brigades, so he couldn't get into anything too conspicuous that might get him arrested. But the other reason, his wife being pregnant, was genuine as well, I still believe that. When this meeting was actually going on I was too excited to think straight. It seemed like a miracle that these two should have come just to see me. The other one, not Li Causi, had come down from Turin. I know now that that's always the way people are recruited, it was normal. But I was flattered. All I kept thinking was, "This is it, the big time. Somebody's taking me seriously at last." If they'd told me to go out in the street and shoot somebody right there and then I'd have done it. They were impressive, the way they could talk. They asked me a lot of questions about politics and I managed to answer well enough because by then I'd studied a good bit. I told them I'd got fed up with the group I was in because half of them were too ignorant to plan actions that had any purpose to them and the other half didn't want any action at all. I was a bit embarrassed about saying that last bit because of Bandini being there listening – I didn't know then about him being a scout – but he didn't say anything, just nodded, and anyway I wasn't going to risk missing a chance like this just to be polite to him. They asked me how much I really knew about the Red Brigades and that was all right because I'd read all their manifestoes. Then they asked me about what actions I'd been in. Mostly I told them about ones that I'd planned myself. I saw them look at one another and then one of them, Li Causi it was, said I was obviously capable of organizing the right sort of action but that the scope was too narrow, that their target was the State, not just fascism which was only a superficial manifestation of the problem. He said you couldn't bring in communism just by fighting fascists, the State had to be destroyed. It was too much for me to take in just like that. They went on explaining things to me for a bit but I suppose they could tell that I was still thinking in simple terms of fascists against communists.'

'Stop a moment.' Bardi began typing again, writing down about a tenth of what had been said. Neither of them were any longer conscious of the noises of prison life beyond the heavy door or of the two silent figures guarding it.

'Go on.'

'When we parted they told me I should keep on studying and that they'd be in touch. After that they sent me stuff to read regularly and bit by bit I began to understand the full scope of what they were trying to do. For the next three months I felt great. Something was going to happen at last. Of course I know now it was all a mistake and I'd chosen the wrong path. My dad used to be for ever saying, "You have to learn to compromise in this life, the best is the enemy of the good," and stuff like that. But I was an idealist, I always have been. I have to really believe in what I'm doing, that's my trouble. In those months I was really happy. I didn't even mind doing my shifts in the hospital. I got to cracking jokes with that old pain-in-the-neck I worked with and he started saying, "That's more like it, you're getting into the swing of things now. I knew you had it in you once the rough edges wore off." And all the time I was thinking, "You're a smelly old fart who doesn't even wash his hands when he's been to the toilet." But I kept smiling. The minute I got home I'd start studying . . . Do you mind if I –'

'Go ahead.'

Gori's hands no longer shook as he lit another cigarette. He was fully absorbed in his story.

A series of clangs suddenly started up, getting nearer and louder. A look of annoyance crossed Bardi's face. It might mean an interruption.

'Go on,' he said quickly.

'After about three months they came to see me again and we talked. This time I was better prepared. I'd read everything they'd sent me and I understood why the target had to be the State. I could see they were satisfied with me. They looked at one another like they had that first time but this time Li Causi said to me, "If you want to fight, arm yourself. We'll be in touch." '

Footsteps were echoing along the tiled corridor outside. One of the guards shot the spyhole open.

'Urgent telephone call for the Substitute Prosecutor.'

'Mr Substitute? I have the Chief of Police on the line. Hold on, please.'

'Bardi? Thank goodness we've found you. I've already called your home and the Procura.'

'What can I do for you?' Bardi was looking at his watch. Only twenty minutes left before he had to leave if he was to catch even the tail-end of the wedding, and for what good twenty minutes would do now that he'd been interrupted he might as well call it a day.

'I want you to stay where you are until I can send you a heavier escort. We've had a warning that there might be an attempt on your life.'

'Really. Yet again. Who from?'

'It was an anonymous call, about an hour ago. I want you to –'

'I think you know my feelings about anonymous calls. They'd be shooting a magistrate down every twenty minutes if they could all be taken seriously.'

'Even so, considering the case you're handling –'

'If you mean Gori, he's hardly in that category. If he gives me a couple of names I'll be lucky.'

'You're interrogating him now?'

'I was.'

'Then I don't think we can take the risk of ignoring this call. I'm sending you two cars immediately.'

'I have my escort with me and I'm leaving almost at once. I'm already late for my next appointment.' Bardi's bodyguards were carabinieri and he trusted them absolutely, they'd been with him for years. They wouldn't welcome any officious interference from the police and neither did Bardi, who had no desire to have two conspicuous police cars trailing through the city with him.

The Chief was getting het up.

'I know you dislike this sort of thing but I can't take the responsibility of ignoring a warning in times like these, surely you realize that!'

'Of course I do. Well, send them along if that covers you, and if they arrive before I leave, well and good. If not, the responsibility will be mine and you'll have done your duty. Don't worry about it.'

And they won't arrive before I leave, Bardi thought as he hung up, if I can help it. Blast the man, he's like a mother hen.

As soon as the guards unlocked the door to let him back in he saw that the damage had been done. Gori started nervously at the noise. The floor below his chair was strewn with cigarette ends and his hands were trembling again. There was no point in going on. Without sitting down, he jerked the paper from the typewriter and stowed it in his case.

'What's happening?' Gori had the look of a child about to be abandoned.

'I've been called away. We'll go on another day.'

'Wait! I wanted to ask you . . . it won't get out that I'm talking to you? Because if it does . . .'

'Nobody's going to make an announcement about it. But it will get out sooner or later, you know that.'

'They've killed people in prison before now. I shouldn't be here, I should be in a special prison. I wanted to ask you –' Gori started to his feet. The guards moved forward immediately with the handcuffs. 'Wait . . .'

'My dear Gori, there's nothing I can do or say at this

moment. No doubt you'll eventually be transferred.' He shook Gori's hand. The palm was wet.

'You don't know what it's like to know you're under sentence of death for what you're doing even though you know it's right!'

Bardi raised an eyebrow. 'I think you and your friends have done your best to see that we do know what it's like.'

'That's not the same thing, it's not personal.'

'That's a great comfort. Anyway you're safe enough as long as nobody knows.' He nodded to the guards and left the room, still inwardly cursing the Chief of Police.

Even from a distance it was evident that Poma and 'Mastino', waiting in the car, were arguing violently as usual. Poma, with his flamboyant black moustache was gesticulating fiercely. 'Mastino', a fair-haired northerner whose nickname meant mastiff, was staring stolidly ahead and making the occasional ironic remark, his favourite way of tormenting his southern colleague. They thought the world of each other and of their charge, who treated them like the sons he'd never had.

As soon as they saw him they announced in unison:

'We've had a radio message –'

'I know. Let's get out of here before they arrive.'

'We shouldn't,' Poma said, starting the engine happily.

'Ah well, no doubt we misunderstood their message.' Bardi settled tranquilly into the back of the Alfetta and they raced out of the couryard. The two lads resumed their argument which seemed to be about women but to take in politics and racial prejudice with a side argument involving food. It was starting to rain and Poma switched on the windscreen wipers as he talked. Against this familiar background noise Bardi opened his case, put on a pair of tiny rimless glasses and made one note on the Gori file. In small neat script with a slim gold fountain pen he wrote the name of Li Causi.

CHAPTER TWO

'We-want-to-see-the-church!' persisted the small plump woman doggedly.

'No,' repeated the elderly Marshal of Carabinieri just as doggedly, 'you can't.' Rain was dripping from his black hat and collecting in rows of droplets on the wrought-iron gates behind him. The two tourists were enveloped in transparent plastic and only the guide book was getting wet. The woman thrust it under the Marshal's nose, reading aloud to him: ' "The eleventh-century church of San Miniato al Monte, open every day . . ." '

'There's a wedding going on,' explained the Marshal for the third time. 'The Chief Public Prosecutor's daughter. For reasons of security . . .' She didn't understand a word. The couple had already tried to dodge in along with the late arriving guest who was now climbing the flight of stairs towards the wet marble façade. Each time the Marshal began his explanations the woman interrupted him to say that not only had they come all the way from the United States but her husband used to teach architecture in High School. The husband was dolefully pointing his camera, sometimes up at the façade whose gilding glittered in the rain, sometimes down at the Arno valley where Florence lay invisible in a grey fog.

'Harry. *Harry*, do you have the phrase book?'

'You left it in the hotel.'

Bardi's black Alfetta came up the last curve of the drive, spraying up rainwater as it braked. Mastino jumped out before the car had quite stopped, slid his right hand inside his lapel and with his left snapped a negative at the tourist who had turned to point his camera at the new arrivals.

Before he reached the rear passenger door it had begun to open and Bardi stepped out on to the wet tarmac. The Marshal saluted and began opening the big gates as the guest came up the stone ramp, watched from behind by his bodyguard.

'Good morning, sir. A terrible day –'

'Listen, can we go in there with you? We won't disturb anyone, really –'

The small woman was blocking the Substitute's way.

Instantly Mastino hurled himself up the slope, his right hand sliding out from under his lapel. Bardi's own hand was moving automatically inside his mackintosh but the Marshal had already shifted the woman and got him through the gates and he was taking the steps in long strides when from behind he heard the woman saying, 'Harry! Did you see that? One of those men had a gun . . .'

Frightened for his life by a couple of harmless tourists! Lapo Bardi's normally pale face had reddened with annoyance. Blast that man and his warnings! *You don't know what it means to know you're under sentence of death for what you're doing even though you know it's right.*

Blast Gori, too!

He reached the top of the steps. The car with his escort was moving off round the side of the church, leaving a cloud of exhaust smoke hanging in the rain.

A stocky figure stood half hidden within the shadow of the bronze doors, waiting.

'Bardi, good morning. I saw your car arriving and thought we might make our late entrance together.'

'My dear Marchese, how are you? I'm afraid I'm always late for these affairs.' They shook hands briefly. 'I'm always under a great deal of pressure and in the middle of a working week . . .'

'I haven't such an impressive excuse, I'm sorry to say; nevertheless, my plane only got in from New York two hours ago, leaving me barely time to change. There's quite a crush, I don't know if we'll find a seat . . .' They fell silent on entering the inner doors. The ceremony had begun some time ago and every pew seemed crowded.

'Marchese Acciai.' With a stage whisper an officious young monk hurried forward and led the two of them up the right aisle where there was an empty bench below a gigantic fresco of St Christopher. They took off their raincoats and sat down in the semi-darkness. Seen together, they made an odd pair. If anything, Lapo Bardi, being tall, thin and hawk-nosed, looked more like a marchese than the shorter man beside him. Acciai's rather bulbous red face and stocky build gave him the air of a prosperous shopkeeper despite his well-cut English clothes.

Bardi's eyes were gradually adjusting themselves to the gloom and focusing on the scene unfolding in a space lit by a myriad of candles. He surveyed the pews immediately behind those of the family and caught sight of Laura's red hat as she turned to speak to the woman beside her. Bardi's lips pursed as he saw who it was: Giovanna. He'd hardly seen her, except briefly on occasions like this, for over two years. How long since it had ended? Seven years at least – no, ten!

'Carlo Luigi Raddi, do you take as your lawful wedded wife Sylvia Annamaria Corbi here present according to the rites of our Holy Mother the Church?'

'I do.'

Seven years. He couldn't even remember with any clarity exactly what her body looked like. Even so, once he had risked everything to have her, or so he still liked to tell himself, applying for a transfer to Bergamo where she had inherited some property so that they could escape the small circle they were both part of. What would his life be like now if that transfer had gone through before the thing had had time to peter out? He would have been out of Florence before the Carlo Rota abduction that had pushed him into the limelight. 'Substitute Prosecutor Lapo Bardi, terrorism's most predatory enemy' as the newspapers liked to describe him. Barely a day went by now without his name appearing in the papers even if it was only for his comment on some case of current interest that someone else with less charisma was handling. Bergamo, of all places!

'Do you, Sylvia Annamaria Corbi, take as your lawful wedded husband . . .'

The application for his transfer had been the death warrant for his affair with Giovanna. Before that they had never quarrelled. But, when it came down to it, a mistress was even more demanding than a wife and much more prone to hysterics when some case took you to the other end of the country instead of to her bed.

'Take each other by the right hand and say after me . . .'

'I must say I envy him,' whispered Acciai under cover of the next hymn.

'Who, the groom? She's a pretty enough little thing, I suppose, but a bit on the plump side.'

'No, no, I was talking about the Chief Public Prosecutor, Corbi. To have his only child well married and settled, it's something achieved.'

Bardi glanced sideways at him and murmured something noncommittal in reply.

'I pronounce you united in Holy Matrimony in the name of the Father and of the Son and of the Holy Ghost.'

'Amen.'

The bride and groom were all but hidden behind a mass of frothy white flowers. Only the priest was in full view, blessing them now with holy water. He was an old man, dry and thin, his movements economical, his pronouncements toneless and precise. Was *his* priest like that? The nameless one he'd been trying to hunt down for years, the one, it was said, who had confessed and given Extreme Unction to Carlo Rota before his kidnappers assassinated him? Unlikely. Whoever he was, he'd remained hidden and protected all these years. Whoever he was, he knew everything, everything that hadn't come out in court, and nothing much had come out, despite the number of arrests and the heavy sentences which satisfied the public.

'The husband is duty bound to protect his wife, to keep

her with him and provide for her in all the necessities of life according to his means.

'The wife is duty bound . . .'

As soon as the reading from the Civil Code had finished and organ music filled the church again, Lapo Bardi was on his feet and slipping his raincoat over his shoulders, impatient to have done with the best wishes to the couple and his chief and to get back to work. He made his way to the door and pausing here and there to greet friends among the congregation. It had stopped raining but everything still smelled damp and the grey light was hard on the eyes after the candlelit church. Laura came up behind her husband and took his arm without a word. Both of them smiled and nodded at friends. Children threw rice and the crowd surging out from the church behind them pushed them forward towards the young couple. Corbi, the Prosecutor, had spotted Bardi and was holding out a hand to him between the intervening guests.

'We'd given you up! Come and kiss the bride – what do you think of her, eh?'

'Brava, Sylvia!' Bardi gave her cheek a peck and her shoulder a pat. Laura was more effusive.

'Wouldn't have been late for the world,' Bardi apologized to his chief, 'but you know what a problem case I've got on my hands, and another coming into court tomorrow.'

'You work too hard!' The Chief blinked benignly behind his pebble glasses. It wasn't a fault he had himself, a peaceful life being his aim and steering clear of muddy political waters his method. People were pushing in to shake Corbi's hand.

'I have to get away,' murmured Bardi, trying to release his arm as gently as possible.

'Don't just go off like that, Lapo. At least stay for the toast.'

'Laura . . .' But the crowd was carrying them to the right to the low building where tourists usually bought their Benedictine, honey and souvenirs from the monks and which had been cleared to receive the wedding guests. Bardi found himself with a misted glass in his hand and drank the cold fizzling liquid off in one draught, grimacing as his stomach cringed on receiving it. If someone would only drag Laura away he could escape. But the Marchese Acciai was pushing towards him, his face redder than ever, a big cigar in his mouth, calling:

'Bardi, why don't you join us, too?'

'No, no, I'm afraid I can't be at the luncheon, I'm due back –'

'Not at the luncheon – I've invited Corbi and one or two others to come out for a day's shooting. What about it?'

Bardi was about to refuse. He really couldn't spare the time, but something made him hesitate and it wasn't his passion for hunting.

'You couldn't make it a Sunday?'

'Why not? Sunday it is. A good shot, plenty of good wine, and a hand of cards after dinner.'

'Perfect.' Bardi looked hard at him before smiling and touching his shoulder. 'I must leave, if you'll excuse me . . . I have my escort waiting.' Fortunately, a group of friends had swept Laura away.

'But you can't leave yet, you've only just arrived!' Acciai had taken his arm and was beaming up at him with insistent jollity. It took a further few minutes to shake him off. With only the briefest of nods at the dozens of other people who tried to detain him he managed to reach the open door. At least he had avoided Giovanna.

The car was waiting outside the Bastion gates at the side of the church and Bardi slid into the back seat with relief.

'Back to the Procura. I want to put in a couple of hours at the office and then you can take me home.'

Poma turned the ignition key and began revving up as if he were at the wheel of a Formula One.

'Pass my case over, Mastino, will you?'

He rummaged in one side of the case among his emergency night things and found the stomach pill he needed, then in the other side for Gori's file.

'Didn't expect to be so long.' He put on the tiny spectacles. 'Couldn't get away.'

'All the same to us, sir,' commented Mastino, his eyes swivelling constantly from right to left. His placid good looks might belie his nickname, but his right hand stayed under his lapel and his blue eyes missed nothing.

'What I was meaning,' said Poma, going on with their current argument with his other hand on the wheel, 'is that we Italians –'

'What Italians? Call yourself an Italian? You're practically from Africa.'

They reached the bottom of the drive and stopped before joining the stream of traffic going right on the broad winding avenue that led to the Piazzale Michelangelo and on down to the city. Luxury coaches and fleets of young people on mopeds were making for the Piazzale which overlooked the city and was a favourite spot for lovers and tourists. In the distance behind the black Alfetta a police siren was wailing.

'It's us they're looking for,' Poma interrupted himself unhappily, pulling at his big moustache with one hand and steering easily with the other.

'He's right,' Mastino turned to Bardi, 'we're going to be in big trouble for not waiting for that extra escort. Orders are orders, even if it means going against your wishes. All the worse for us that this time . . .' There was no need to finish the sentence. This time the Chief of Police was involved and it would be taken as a deliberate act of disrespect on the part of the carabinieri for the rival force, not just a breach of regulations. They would never hear the last of it.

'We'll never hear the last of it,' Poma worried.

'Don't worry,' murmured Bardi without looking up, 'I'll take full responsibility as usual. Put your foot down instead of grumbling. If those pests catch up with us we'll have to stop for explanations and I've already wasted the last hour. As it is it's going to take forty minutes to do a ten-minute journey in this traffic. Step on it!'

Poma pulled out and overtook a group of youths riding

their motorbikes four abreast, making the Alfetta roar, but immediately he was forced to swerve in again behind an enormous coach with a big orange sign on the back: 'World-wide Tours – air-conditioning – television – toilets.'

'Don't even have to stop for a pee,' muttered Poma, slowing reluctantly. 'We might have an armoured car and air-conditioning but we still have to stop for – Mastino! Behind!' Poma kept a constant eye on his rearview mirror. From a parallel, tree-lined drive, mostly used by joggers, a red Fiat 128 had shot out and scraped one of the trees in an unsuccessful attempt to get in right behind the Alfetta. There were two cars between them but the red one was pulling out ready to overtake.

'He's trying to get right on our tail, Mastino – watch him, watch him! Lie down, sir! If that warning turns out to be genuine, Christ Almighty . . .'

Mastino had drawn his pistol and sprung the first bullet into the barrel. Bardi had ducked sideways but he was reaching for his own Beretta. 'If there's going to be some shooting . . .'

'Keep down, sir! For God's sake, Poma, there's only one car between us!'

But traffic was streaming towards them on the left and it was impossible to overtake the coach. Poma began swearing steadily under his breath.

'Even so they can't do us any harm in this machine unless they stop us. Pull over, damn you, pull over!'

But by now they were in the Piazzale where Michelangelo's David loomed against the clouds and the coach suddenly stopped. Poma tried to edge round it but an avalanche of Japanese tourists poured out of both its doors and began milling about in the road, pointing at the David and looking neither left nor right. The red Fiat overtook the last car in its way and closed in. With a storm of hooting and shouting a gang of motorcyclists flowed around it and the Alfetta and came up against the tourists. One lost his balance and came off his bike and the Japanese group made a frightened dash for safety to the other side of the Piazzale. Poma had his foot down and was through the gap they left almost before it opened before him. Ahead, another Fiat shot out and tried to block him but Poma, still swearing, was too fast. With a rapid swerve and an angry roar of the engine he was out of the Piazzale and going at a hundred kilometres an hour down the winding road towards the city.

'Lost them,' said Mastino calmly.

Behind them the police siren was howling again, punctuated now by sharp blasts on the traffic policeman's whistle.

'Chief of Police been on the phone for you three times, sir!'

The switchboard operator's head popped out of a small window as soon as Bardi issued from the lift on the second floor of the Procura. 'The last time was only a couple of minutes ago.'

'Any other calls?'

'No, apart from journalists, only the Chief of Police – but he called three times. Do you want me to get him for you?'

'No.' And he moved off down the corridor, took a bunch of keys from his briefcase and unlocked the door marked DR LAPO BARDI, SUBSTITUTE PROSECUTOR OF THE REPUBLIC.

It wasn't a very grand office, most of the antique furniture being fake, but it was comfortable enough and there were two very good 18th-century oil paintings, left there because the Superintendent from the Ministry of Fine Arts had never come to any conclusion about which gallery they should be sent to. As always, they were the first thing Bardi looked at as he let himself in. His desk was placed so that he saw them each time he looked up from his work. The twin angels gazed down at the inhabitants of the room but pointed up to their varnished clouds with one finger. Once their exhortations had been for the benefit of the monks who had inhabited the building, but these days they looked down on the procession of terrorists who came and sat beneath them to be questioned.

Bardi dropped his briefcase on to a big leather armchair and took up the post and the day's newspapers which had been placed between the two telephones on his desk. He flipped through the post without opening any of it and then unfolded the first of the newspapers, fishing blindly for half a cigarette at the same time. Before he could read the first headline the telephone rang. He picked up the receiver distractedly, still reading.

'Yes.' *Head of terrorist gang captured . . .*

'Chief of Police speaking.'

'Yes . . . what can I do for you?' *. . . captured in Rome. Trapped by agents in his bunker-apartment.*

'This is the fourth time I've telephoned you, surely someone could have given you a message!'

'Yes, yes, they did, the minute I came in.'

'The minute you – so you've only just arrived! Do you mean to say you really went to the wedding?'

'To the wedding, yes, I'm sure I told you.' So they'd caught Li Causi. That meant somebody must have talked before Gori. Now who . . .

'My men said your car wasn't there. I sent you an escort and when they didn't find you at the Procura . . .'

Bardi dropped the newspaper reluctantly and turned his attention to the apoplectic Chief.

'Sorry about that,' he said blandly, 'I expect it was my fault, but I was in such a hurry I must have muddled things up.'

'Can I ask you to please listen to me for a moment!' The Chief of Police who knew that Bardi had never muddled anything up in his life was not going to be fobbed off so easily as that.

'We have every reason to believe that this warning of an attempt on your life was genuine and whatever you might think –'

'Yes, it was.'

'What?' The Chief paused, breathing heavily.

'Quite genuine. Thanks for getting on to it. Fortunately

the attempt was a failure. Perhaps my escort could send you a full report, given that the warning came to you . . .'

An eventuality so improbable that Bardi was grinning with the retrieved half cigarette between his lips at the thought of carabinieri writing a helpful report for the police. The Chief was nevertheless left speechless by this fatuous remark, which gave Bardi time to say thank-you and goodbye.

He spread the newspaper on the desk, lit his half cigarette and leaned forward, his eyes bright with interest.

> Rome. At dawn yesterday agents of Digos, the anti-terrorist department of the Ministry of the Interior, captured the last remaining historic leader of the Red Brigades, Antonio Li Causi age 40, professor of sociology, on the run for the last six years. The terrorist was trapped in his apartment which had bullet-proof windows. He was surprised while sleeping and had no time to react when he was woken up with a pistol levelled at his neck. According to official sources, Li Causi said nothing apart from making the usual statement: 'I am a militant of the Red Brigades. I declare myself a political prisoner.' In the apartment agents found three hand grenades, a machine-gun, a rocket ramp, a plan of the Regina Cœli prison and notes including the names, addresses and movements of a number of prominent magistrates, politicians and journalists. Little is known of the operation leading up to Li Causi's arrest but it is thought to be part of a large-scale anti-terrorist operation still in progress. What is known is that the same agents are now hoping to round up the entire Li Causi group and its supporters and that a press conference is expected to take place sometime today. According to unnamed sources, Digos agents were led to the discovery of Li Causi through revelations made by a repentant terrorist. One such terrorist, a Red Brigades supporter, was arrested near Rome central station a week ago and within a few days decided to collaborate with the police.
>
> Antonio Li Causi, of Neapolitan origin, known in

academic circles for his book on the social structure of the kibbutz, was living in Florence until his disappearance three years ago. As a lecturer in sociology he was in contact with magistrates involved in problems relating to prison organization. A man above suspicion until he went into hiding after being searched and interrogated by a Florentine magistrate, Substitute Prosecutor Lapo Bardi.

Bardi had found Li Causi's name in the diary of another terrorist but neither the search nor the interrogation produced any clear-cut evidence which would prove Li Causi to be a member of the Red Brigades.

There was a knock at the door.

'No!' snapped Bardi.

The two column headline read:

WILL THIS ROAD LEAD US TO
THE GRAND OLD MAN?

It is too early yet to say what might be the repercussions within the clandestine terrorist world. It is possible that a brain like Li Causi can be quickly replaced. However, the sociologist's arrest has had two certain consequences: it has brought nearer the possibility of a final defeat of terrorism and it has moved us a little further on the road leading to the 'Grand Old Man'.

The 'Grand Old Man' has been talked about for years, sometimes with scepticism, sometimes with conviction, but few political gatherings take place these days without some debate about the existence of this spider-like figure weaving the web that has brought this country to grief and to the brink of civil war. Nobody has ever claimed to have seen him and there is no certain proof of his existence, nevertheless a considerable number of experts are of the opinion that the Red Brigades could not have access to arms and large sums of money unless they were in some way in contact with a person or persons with an inside knowledge of international events, someone in close contact with Eastern bloc countries with a strong interest in the 'disarticulation' of the social and financial structure of Italy which is a bridge point between East and West. The 'Grand Old Man' has in some ways become a mythical figure, talked about by all but seen, if he exists, by very few. Among those few the sociologist Antonio Li Causi would have to be one, since there can be no doubt that this mysterious figure would have to have been involved in the case of the statesman Carlo Rota. Li Causi is already known to have been part of the small nucleus of high level terrorists who kidnapped and executed the leader of the majority party . . .

'Goddamn it!' Bardi got up and began pacing about his office, too angry to go on reading. The memory of Li Causi sitting in that very room and looking him calmly in the eye, knowing he was untouchable, had never left him. It had been a masterly piece of work, pouncing on him unawares with a warrant in the days when he was a respected academic and above suspicion. And then they hadn't found a thing, not a scrap of evidence though they had turned his flat inside out and questioned him for hours. Bardi had been clever but Li Causi had been cleverer; he had defeated him. That made him unique, the only blot on an otherwise perfect reputation. And now he had been arrested by somebody else. Well, it wasn't over yet. He might have lost a battle but not the war.

He paused by his desk and then sat down to light another cigarette. This journalist, Albanese, knew his stuff but he was mistaken if he thought that Li Causi would talk. He was a hardliner who would go to prison for the rest of his life before telling anything more than his own name. If they were going to arrive at the identity of the 'Grand Old Man' it would have to be by a much more tortuous route than by some helpful terrorist passing on his visiting card. That priest. He was the only weak link. If the story that had gone about at the time, of Rota's having been confessed and communicated before he was shot, was true, it was logical to assume that this was arranged by the 'Grand Old Man' because it was out of the question for left-wing terrorists to arrange such a risky encounter out of the kindness of their hard little left-wing hearts before loading up the rifles. Only the 'Old Man' would do it; he would do it because he knew Rota, must have done. Maybe they were old cronies and maybe that's why Rota was shot. It would have been more expedient to let him go once all possible mileage had been got out of the situation. They had everything to lose by killing him. The majority party was so manifestly corrupt that it was only to be expected that the populace would get some secret pleasure out of someone's taking so audacious and successful a swipe at it. It was true, as Gori had said, that in those days the Red Brigades had glamour, charisma. The mauled and bloody corpse dumped in a squalid side street finished that. Rota saw and recognized the 'Old Man' all right and so he was shot. That left the priest who confessed him. He was the only one. The 'Old Man' didn't call in the nearest parish priest, he called somebody he could trust, and that somebody . . .

The telephone rang.

'Good morning. Marco Nesti of the *Nazione* here.' A deep voice against the clatter of a dozen typewriters. 'What are your thoughts on Li Causi's arrest, sir? You've heard, of course? I've been trying to reach you all morning.'

'I'm an expert at avoiding pests, Nesti, an expert. What do you expect me to think? Of course I'm satisfied to hear he's been arrested. You could have worked that out for yourself without disturbing me.'

'Can you give me a personal statement, sir?'

Bardi drew on the last scrap of his cigarette and began feeling about for the other half.

'What sort of statement do you expect me to give you at this stage? Sooner or later I'll go to Rome and question him. You know I've already got a warrant out for him here. I'll have to go and question him, but not yet. Mine isn't the most important case against Li Causi.'

‘Do you think Li Causi’s arrest could lead to the identification of the “Grand Old Man”?’

‘No comment. And now leave me in peace, I’m trying to work.’

‘Fine. I’ll come round to the Procura tomorrow morning.’

Bardi dropped the receiver into place and pushed the phone away from him as if that would stop it ringing. He stared down at the newspaper for a few moments, drumming his fingers on the desk, then looked at his watch. Deciding how to approach the Li Causi problem was going to take time. Just now he had less than half an hour before a lunch appointment. Time enough for a smaller problem which had aroused his curiosity recently and which this morning’s ceremony had brought to the surface of his mind until the newspaper had distracted him. He got up abruptly and opened a glass-fronted cupboard that reached to the high ceiling and was thickly stacked with case notes. From these he selected a yellow cardboard folder which he placed on his desk, sitting down before it and pausing to regard the label thoughtfully before opening it and beginning to read. The first page carried the same information as the cover:

Criminal proceedings against Acciai, the Marchese Giancarlo Filippo.

CHAPTER THREE

At six o'clock on Sunday morning the shutters of all the big houses on the avenue were tightly closed in the darkness and the wide road was deserted. Nevertheless, once Bardi had stowed his shotgun in the boot and got into the old Lancia beside his chief, Corbi pulled out slowly; peering about him through his thick spectacles as though he were expecting a sudden onrush of traffic. At every junction when the orange lights blinked continuously he slowed almost to a stop before going through.

'I'm afraid we're going to be late,' murmured Bardi, doing what he could to suppress the slight irritation that was aggravated by an empty stomach.

'My fault,' said Corbi placidly, his gaze fixed on the empty road ahead. 'My wife's fault, I should say. Never lets me leave without giving me coffee and something to eat, though I told her we'd be breakfasting at the castle . . .' It didn't occur to him that Bardi's remark referred to his driving. He was thinking of his wife slipping back into the warm hollow they had left in the bed and almost envying her.

Signora Corbi was a big, plump woman almost a head taller than her husband, and the motherly way she treated his chief was a frequent source of amusement to Bardi. He himself had showered and dressed with even more than usual caution, taking extra care to close the front door quietly because although the house was very large every sound carried.

Despite the damp darkness of the November morning, it wasn't really cold. Nevertheless, the Chief had switched on the heater and the atmosphere in the car was becoming stifling. Bardi struggled out of his bulky hunting jacket and threw it on to the back seat. There were three folded newspapers lying there.

'Are these today's?'

'Yes. I stopped at the station kiosk on the way.'

No wonder he'd arrived late! And he was still driving at 25 miles an hour and peering over the steering-wheel as though he were fighting his way through the rush hour.

'Take a look at the *Nazione* – no, no, don't switch that light on while I'm driving, it distracts me. There's a torch in the back somewhere, try the left-hand pocket. You'll see there's an article on the famous "Bardi theorem".'

'You've read it? It might be an idea to put a spurt on. If we're really late they'll leave without us.'

'No, no, they won't do that. I haven't read it, just the headlines, you can read it to me. Acciai will be delighted to see you, delighted, made a point of saying so, telephoned the day after Sylvia's wedding and was asking about you . . . delighted, made a point of it. What does it say? The Bardi theorem, eh? Found it?'

'I didn't invent the law,' Bardi pointed out, opening the newspaper as best he could, 'It was already on the statute books. I just happened to be the first to apply it . . . here it is. They've given it a big enough spread, I must say.'

'Read it out.'

In the trial of members of the Florentine nucleus of the Red Brigades, including the notorious hardliner, Patrizia Rossini, the Substitute Prosecutor for the Republic, Lapo Bardi yesterday opened his case here for the prosecution. Though it will be some time before he arrives at his final summing up it is already evident that he will request a verdict of guilty for all the accused. In the Assize Court today the jury listened to his impassioned explication of article 306 which has become known as the Bardi Theorem.

The Bardi Theorem has been bitterly contested by the defence lawyers of left-wing groups. The Substitute Prosecutor's interpretation of the law is clear and simple:

anyone accused of the organization or leadership of an armed subversive organization must bear the responsibility for all crimes committed by that organization during the period in which he was a leading member. 'There is no question but that there is a moral complicity,' explained Substitute Bardi in his speech to the jury today, 'and it is inadmissible that the accused should claim to have no knowledge of offensive actions prepared and carried out by members of the same group. Are we to believe that they are left in total ignorance? And if we can manage to stretch out credulity that far, what difference, morally, does that make? Anyone organizing or accepting a leading position in an armed band which has already undertaken violent action, which has already imprisoned, maimed, killed, is accepting moral responsibility for such similar actions as may be carried out by the group in the future. He can ask us to believe that he doesn't know at what exact hour or in what precise place a particular attack will occur; he can ask us to believe that he doesn't even know the name of the victim and that he personally is not involved, but can he ask us to believe that there is no moral complicity when, in giving his organizational support to the group, he makes such an attack possible?'

According to the Substitute, then, if the accused X was a leading member of an armed group formed for terrorist purposes from for example, May 1st to 31st in a given year, and during that period the group carried out two assassinations and an armed robbery, then the accused X must be charged with those specific crimes, not just for membership of the group, and this even if he was out of the country when these crimes were committed. The law should also be enforced in the case of repentants for whom, at the same time, the usual reduction by half of the sentence would apply. But it is not to repentants that the application of this law presents a grave threat. The people most seriously affected are those charged with the organization or leadership of an armed band of terrorists against whom there is no proof of participation in specific actions, as in the case of many of the accused in this trial. Where once they risked a maximum 15 years' imprisonment, under article 306 of the Penal Code they could, if the Bardi Theorem prevails, find themselves facing a life sentence. It is on this front that the battle will be fought between Bardi and the defence lawyers, as the latter made clear yesterday morning immediately after the adjournment . . .

'It's getting difficult to read,' Bardi interrupted.

They had turned left and were taking an unmade road. The old car was being jolted this way and that by stones and potholes.

'I'm doing my best but really this road . . . Acciai ought to do something about it but, of course, the expense . . .'

'Of course,' said Bardi drily. 'Do you want me to try and go on?'

'Just read me what the lawyers had to say.'

'Hm . . . *immediately after the adjournment* . . . here it is, for what it's worth: *"With the Bardi Theorem,"* they said, *"the guilt spiral of terrorism becomes never-ending. We intend to fight the application of this law with every means at our disposal." When the hearing continues in ten days' time* . . . That's it, there's nothing else of interest.'

He switched the torch off. Daylight was beginning to glimmer faintly on the horizon as they bumped along between ranks of ghostly vines on one side and fruiting olives on the other.

'We might have a nice day yet,' said Corbi happily. The desire to go back to sleep in warmth and comfort left him when he saw the dark towers of the castle come into view against the lightening sky directly ahead. The ochre road began to climb steeply, straining the engine of the old Lancia. At the top of the slope they passed between high stone gateposts and entered the half-mile driveway lined with dark cypresses. Bardi reached over for his jacket.

'Let's hope we haven't been left behind.'

'No, no. They won't have left yet. Breakfast is always a long business here.'

Corbi was right. When they drove under the archway they found the flagged courtyard filled with cars and plenty of light and noise coming from a row of windows on the ground floor. The studded oak doors were open and their arrival aroused a muffled yapping of dogs in some outbuilding.

Acciai must have heard the dogs or the slamming of the car doors because they found him coming to meet them as they crossed the hall, his plump face flushed.

'Corbi! We'd given you up!' His eyes were fixed on Bardi. 'You'll be lucky if you get any breakfast.' He hustled them into a crowded room. 'I must see if they can bring more coffee.'

The long room was lit by wall lamps that gave out a yellowish light. At the far end of it a haze of blue cigar smoke hung in the air above a group of men who had gathered around the billiard table. A few people were still eating at the buffet under the glassy stare of a wild boar's head but most of them had finished and drifted away, talking noisily. At the centre of one of the conversations a thin, grey-haired man was recounting what must have been a hunting story to judge from the few words that were audible above the general noise. Acciai broke in on the group and interrupted him.

'Manni! I want to introduce these people to you. Alberto, the Count Manni, Alessandro Corbi, our Chief Public Prosecutor, and Substitute Prosecutor Lapo Bardi. The men who run our world these days. Always as well to keep on the right side of them. You never know, eh, Bardi?'

The Count acknowledged the two newcomers as briefly as was possible without being impolite, doubtless annoyed at having to break off his story. Nevertheless, Bardi noted that his hunting clothes looked very expensive and very new, making him look like a model from the pages of a fashionable sporting magazine rather than an experienced huntsman. Most of the men who now gathered round him again were similarly dressed and more likely to shoot themselves than shoot a boar. Odd that Acciai should be fool enough to invite them. The Marchese himself sported a much-battered sleeveless leather jerkin that all but reached his knees.

'A relic of the war, this,' he explained with some pride, leading them towards the buffet table, and introducing them to the people they passed on the way. 'We had German soldiers billeted here and then English ones – they left a good many bullet holes in the façade between them. It was one of the English boys who left me this, a fine young man, often wonder what became of him. Ideal for hunting, keeps you warm but leaves your arms free, never go out without it. Now, help yourselves!' He was obliged to shout to make himself heard and Bardi noticed that his breath smelled strongly of spirits. That, and the redness of his face, suggested that he had taken his coffee laced with grappa, perhaps more than once.

Corbi helped himself liberally, despite having already eaten, and he was beaming happily behind his thick spectacles, pleased with himself and the world in general. Bardi took some hot milk from a big silver jug and coloured it with the slightest touch of coffee, of which there was still plenty despite what Acciai had said when they arrived so late. He dipped some plain biscuits into the mixture in the hope of settling his stomach for the morning. Somebody had switched off the lights. It was bright daylight by now out in the courtyard. Some of the hunters had already moved outside and were comparing guns and strapping on ammunition belts. Acciai's gamekeeper had brought out the dogs and was cursing them as they yapped and strained at the leash in an effort to get under everyone's feet.

'I promise you there's no need to worry . . . yes, yes, quite possibly but nothing official . . .'

It was Corbi's voice, only just audible. He and the Marchese had moved away from the table and were talking in an undertone. It was only because of a sudden lull in the general conversation that Bardi had caught those few words. Why, when his first instinct was to turn and join them, did he remain standing where he was, staring out at the increasing bustle in the courtyard? He neither listened nor didn't listen, aware of the two voices murmuring below the level of all the other voices in the room. The only other phrases that reached him clearly was Corbi's again.

'I assure you, you're mistaken, and in any case he can't make a move without . . .'

Bardi had no reason to think that the 'he' referred to himself. Even so, he did think it, or rather, felt it, and it was because of that, not in response to some impatient shouts from outside the window, that he turned abruptly, saying: 'Isn't it time we were moving?'

He said it quickly, well before meeting their eyes which, as he had expected, were fixed on him. He was always careful to avoid embarrassment. He disliked embarrassment except when, created deliberately by himself, it formed a useful weapon. In this case he scooped it up and disposed of it with the sureness and delicacy of a surgeon, saying with an amused smile: 'You look for all the world like two conspirators. You must be exchanging state secrets at the very least!'

'Not at all, Bardi, my dear fellow.' The little Marchese came and took his arm. 'You're the one with all the secrets. Every time you go into court you astonish us with all your revelations.' And he looked up at Bardi with what appeared to be innocent admiration.

'Shall we go?' Corbi suggested. The room was emptying.

Out in the courtyard Corbi opened up the boot of the car and Bardi picked up their guns and ammunition belts. The cold morning air, already heavy with fermentation, was tainted by the smell of dogs and gungrease in the confined space of the yard. Most of the men were ready to leave, their loud voices echoing between the high stone walls.

'You stay close to me.' The Marchese murmured to Bardi. 'Some of these people couldn't hit a tree at ten paces but one has to invite them . . .'

Once he had his rifle securely under his arm, Bardi's tension dissolved and he prepared to enjoy himself. He was prepared, also, to accept Acciai's suggestion of staying close to him. If anything came out, well and good. In any case he would talk to Corbi this coming week because sooner or later the information he had collected on Acciai would have to become an official file which needed the Chief's blessing.

When the three of them followed the rest and left the cold shadows of the courtyard to pass under the archway, the brilliant red and gold of the wooded valley that opened below them caused them to blink and glance up with pleasure at the pure blue winter sky which they hadn't seen for weeks.

Although the sun was strong enough to penetrate the roof of almost bare branches and dapple the ground with warm patches, the dead leaves thickly covering the ground were still sodden and the tree-trunks were damp and black. The path they took was narrow and in part overgrown with brambles and juniper bushes which brushed and tore at their trousers until they reached a more thinly wooded area where they could begin to manœuvre.

Because of the inexperienced men among them, there was some confusion in getting everyone organized ready to dispose themselves in a large semi-circle. The gamekeeper stood watching, the dogs still on the leash, his green serge cap pushed far back on his head and his knobbly round face as red as the wine of which he had already drunk plenty.

'Now, Bardi, stay close to me,' Acciai repeated. Corbi had moved off with the overdressed Count and his friends and they soon disappeared from view beyond the trees.

'We're ready when you are,' the gamekeeper told Acciai, indicating the beaters who were all employees of the Marchese. The dogs must have understood because they began jostling each other in their mounting excitement, their tongues lolling, their breath steamy in the cold air.

Acciai lifted his head and made the call, his voice carrying for miles in the early morning silence. The gamekeeper loosed the dogs who vanished in seconds.

The beaters began moving forward in a line, smashing at the soft ground with their sticks, crushing small plants and whipping the scented berries off the juniper twigs, adding their voices to the uproar made by the now invisible dogs. Above them hundreds of tiny birds fluttered up in a cloud and filled the air with their frightened chatter. The commotion set up to start the boar disturbed dozens of smaller creatures and the wood which a moment before had seemed empty of life was now alive with discreet rustlings.

'This way,' Acciai directed Bardi. 'We don't want to find ourselves downwind – but I hardly need to tell you that. Corbi tells me you're an experienced hunter. Not just of boar either, eh? You've sneaked upwind on many a victim before now, I shouldn't wonder.'

'It's my job,' returned Bardi briefly, without looking at him.

'Ah, the professional attitude, of course. We have different ways of looking at things. For us, you see, family tradition is everything. The Acciai fought in the crusades, did you know that? We're not professionals but we fight, even so. Our name means steel, and with good reason. When we fight we fight to win, not because it's our job. We're fighting to defend a whole world. I don't know if you understand me.'

'I understand you.'

'Yes. But of course, whether you understand or not . . . we'll cross this brook lower down, there where there are stepping-stones . . . whether you understand or not, it doesn't change anything for you.'

'Understanding another's point of view? No, it doesn't change anything. I understand terrorists, for instance, their ideology, if it's worthy of the name. I still put them inside. Nevertheless, I see it as a tragedy; sending a young person to prison for the rest of his life is not something I enjoy. You who have a son should understand that as well as anyone.'

Acciai's only response to this was to fall silent. They were forced to walk in single file, working their way through a tangle of bare undergrowth. It suited Bardi to observe the

Marchese from behind. The fact that the going was difficult and the conversation necessarily broken helped to justify the fact that they were not going to look one another in the eye and admit what they were talking about. At the mention of his son Acciai's already flushed neck turned a deeper red, but he kept moving forward steadily, his breath heavy and audible, without turning or answering. If anything, his pace quickened imperceptibly as though he was beginning to feel himself pursued. Yet surely the son had nothing to do with the case? Or had he? Bardi's ability to follow any scent that turned up rather than trying to make the evidence fit his theories had often stood him in good stead.

'How is your son?' persisted Bardi when the silence continued, 'I don't think I even know his name.'

'Pierluigi Filippo, an only child, you know . . . he's named after me and after his grandfather, Pierluigi Guglielmo Acciai. As a child he used to call himself Gigi since he couldn't pronounce Pierluigi and the nickname more or less stuck. When his mother was alive . . . We haven't got ahead of the others, I hope. What do you think? No, I can hear the beaters over there . . . If his mother had lived . . .' He didn't finish what he had been about to say.

'He's not interested in hunting, I take it?'

'Oh, but he's abroad now. Here we can cross.'

The brook was shallow, its bubbling waters half choked with yellow leaves. After crossing they were able to walk side by side up a short slope.

'Now you mention it, I think Corbi might have said something about his being abroad,' lied Bardi, 'Australia, was it?'

'America. A course of study, you know . . .'

'University?'

'No, no . . . a course of study – what the devil?'

From somewhere in the distance, probably on the far side of the semi-circle of which the two of them formed the tip, came the sound of a rifle shot.

'Damned fools!' shouted Acciai. 'Can't even carry a gun

without having it go off. Granchi! Keep an eye on those men! Granchi!' But it was impossible to make the gamekeeper hear at such a distance and against the noise of the beaters. 'Granchi!'

It was no use. 'I'll have to leave you a moment or there's going to be an accident . . . Start moving to the left and I'll join you later if I can.' It seemed to Bardi that his companion had been glad enough to escape, but for his part he was happy to be left alone with his thoughts. He started moving left. The semi-circle would be starting to close in now but the rest of the hunters were still invisible to him because of the trees. He had to judge his position by the noise of the beaters, despite which he could hear his own footsteps as his heavy boots squelched through the leaves.

A hen pheasant appeared as if from nowhere and lumbered along before him for some yards before making a clumsy take-off. After a moment he paused to listen for information, leaning against a fungus-studded tree-trunk, his rifle tucked comfortably beneath his arm. Someone was calling above the general din but he couldn't make out the words. He began to regret having let Acciai keep him right at the tip of the semi-circle. He probably wouldn't see the boar until somebody had already shot it. He was getting warmer with all this walking. He unzipped his jacket and moved on. By his reckoning he should have had one or two of the others in sight by now, but a lot of them being so amateur they were probably sticking together in groups for fear of having to face a charging boar alone. Because of that, when he did charge, he might well find a gap and break through. Everything depended on the dogs holding him long enough for someone to get a shot, preferably someone who could shoot. Well, if Acciai were fool enough to invite Count Manni and his like, what could he expect?

The constant background noise of the beaters suddenly increased and quickened and someone was calling again, nearer this time.

'Bardi!'

The dogs were ululating hysterically. A shot was fired.

'Bardi! Bardi! Where are you?'

'Here!' He had barely time to ask himself if it was Acciai's voice and to wonder why he was calling when something whistled by his right ear. He heard the shot as the tree beside him seemed to explode and a sliver of bark sliced his cheek. For a matter of seconds he was too shocked to move. When he did raise his gun and start forward the feeling welling up inside him was not fear but anger. The wood vibrated with excited shouts and somewhere very near ahead the dogs had gathered. Their noise modulated to a concerted menacing growl punctuated by sharp yaps. Bardi continued his noiseless approach for a few yards and then parted two bushes carefully.

The boar was a big one. He stood in the centre of a small clearing surrounded by the dogs who leapt at him snapping every time he moved. His brown bristles were erect and his tiny eyes bright with fury and pain as he turned this way and that, seeking a gap through which to escape his tormentors. When the dogs attacked him from behind and he hurled himself round with a squeal of rage he would instantly be attacked from another quarter. Then he would stand stock still for a few seconds, tense and baffled. A rope of dark, viscous blood hung from a wound in his hindquarters. The stench of him filled the small space, maddening the dogs to renewed attacks. So intense was their deadly game that the beast didn't notice the erect figure and the gleaming rifle barrel immediately.

Bardi took aim. There was no one else in sight. If he made a mistake he was dead. But while his eyes were fixed on the tormented boar, waiting for the next time he was still, a series of words and images passed through his mind which remained quite detached from the scene before him.

Acciai waiting for him in the rain beneath the marble façade of San Miniato. Acciai, red-faced, waving a cigar and clutching at his arm.

You can't leave yet, it's much too soon.

And Corbi: *Telephoned the day after Sylvia's wedding and was asking about you.*

Bardi, stay close to me . . .

'I'll have to leave you . . . there's going to be an accident . . .

Was that what delayed him, made him wait a fraction of a second too long? At any rate the boar spotted him and understood and his rage was so great that it overcame his fear. For an instant he quivered in his whole body, then he lowered his tusks and charged through the dogs that a moment before had held him terrorized as though they no longer existed.

One moment the great brown-grey hulk was hurtling forward, then the head exploded spraying a pink mess and the beast lay silent and twitching, almost at Bardi's feet. Even when the eyes glazed over the legs continued their spasmodic movements as if he were still trying to run. Then the twitching stopped.

'Bardi!' Acciai was there with Corbi and Manni, all of them out of breath. The dogs who had backed off a little at the shot were whining and sniffing, drawn by the smell of fresh blood. Three of the beaters appeared and drove them back roughly.

'Bravo, Bardi! We were sure you'd get him!'

Bardi didn't answer Acciai. He was looking at their rifles, not at them. It looked as though two of them had fired, Manni and Acciai, though he only remembered hearing one shot. One of them had wounded the animal, the other had aimed high, very high. It was logical to assume that the inexperienced Manni had been the one to hit the tree and come within an inch of killing him. But the voice that had called out and established Bardi's position had almost certainly been Acciai's.

The rest of the beaters had arrived. One of them took a small sharp knife from his belt and began slicing off the boar's ears.

'Good shot, well done!' beamed Corbi as Bardi received the ears.

'Somebody else hit him, too.'

'I did,' Acciai said, 'or Manni did. We fired together so we can't be sure.'

'No,' Bardi repeated, 'we can't be sure.' He was wondering why no one had noticed he was wounded. Only when he looked down at the dark hairy ears he was holding did he realize that his clothes and hands and probably his face, too, were splattered with blood from the boar. He leaned his rifle against a tree and pulled out a handkerchief.

The beaters were working on the carcase. One of them made a deep slice in the abdomen and another, with his sleeves rolled up, plunged his hands inside and cut out the steaming entrails. The pancreas, liver and intestines were chopped up and tossed to the maddened dogs well in the distance to keep them out of the way of the carcase.

'A fine beast,' commented Acciai. 'If we want to try for another there's still time, just about. What do you say, Corbi?'

'Well, of course, if everyone else is agreeable I'll go along. What about you, Manni?'

The Count was bending forward, ostensibly to make a critical examination of the dead animal but being careful not to get a mark on his clothing. He even managed to avoid treading in the mess of blood and slime that surrounded the boar and the two beaters who were manhandling it.

'Whatever you like,' he said, straightening up and averting his face from the smell of the entrails, 'We could go on.'

Encouraged by the lack of enthusiasm in their voices, Acciai added, 'Of course, if you feel you've had enough we could start making our way back. Personally, I wouldn't say no to a good log fire and a glass or two of wine to warm up. We could take the walk back at a leisurely pace and I could send Granchi ahead to say we want lunch a little earlier.'

Corbi laughed. 'We're not as young as we were and that's a fact! I'm for the log fire and the early lunch. I don't know about Bardi here – what do you say? Another killing before lunch? You're just that bit younger than we are.'

'We'll go back.' It was almost an order and they took it as one, as though his victory over the boar had given him an unspoken ascendancy over them. Acciai went off to call in the rest of the men. The dogs were back on the leash, licking their bloody chops, and the beaters were tying the boar's trotters to a stout pole which they raised to their shoulders with some difficulty.

Bardi's face was very pale under the streaks of red. The double shock had left him physically exhausted but his brain was working clearly. Maybe he had waited just a little too long with Acciai as he had with the boar. Maybe the game he was playing in coming here had turned out more dangerous than he had bargained for. Nevertheless, he'd got the boar and he would get Acciai, too. Tomorrow he would make a start. What he needed immediately was a drink and a chance to clean up the cut on his cheek which he now realized was stinging badly.

'Something was certainly wrong with him. I've never known Acciai be like that in all the years I've known him.'

The old Lancia was following the line of cars slowly down the lane from the castle in the falling dusk of the November afternoon. When Bardi made no comment in return, Corbi went on:

'I noticed it as soon as we sat down to cards after lunch – of course, during the meal I was talking mostly to Manni. He's planning to open some sort of fashion house, what with the money they lose these days on wine – of course he's not a big producer, having had such a large part of his land confiscated, and he's always held out against joining the Chianti Classico syndicate – not that they're not losing money hand over fist these days like everybody else . . . ah well . . . Odd that Acciai should have behaved in that peculiar manner . . .'

'No doubt he was tired. We were all up very early.'

'No, no. We've been hunting together for years. Tired perhaps, well, we were all sleepy after such a splendid meal . . . But Acciai's the most hospitable fellow in the world, I've never seen him edgy like that. He was really almost rude to you during that last hand and I'll swear he was glad to see the back of us all. Many's the time we've ended up staying on for an evening apératif, just a few of us, his closest friends . . .'

Horns were sounding in salutes as the guests reached the end of the private road and went their different ways. Corbi turned right and took the road to Florence, going as slowly as he had at dawn though now there was traffic heavy enough to justify it as hundreds of people made their way back to the city after a Sunday afternoon drive out in the countryside, taking back glossy chestnuts, mushrooms or sprays of autumn leaves.

'You didn't upset him in some way?' suggested Corbi.

'How should I have done that? I barely know him.'

'Quite . . . of course not. On the other hand he was alone with you, apparently for a good part of the morning, so I just wondered . . . Damn this half-light, I can't see a thing!' It was getting foggy, too, which didn't help matters. Corbi's snub nose was almost on the windscreen.

'Would you prefer me to drive?'

'No, no . . . But if something did happen between you and Acciai I do wish you'd tell me. Filippo's an old friend of mine, you know, and a valued friend, too. Remember it was I who introduced you to him . . .'

Very fortuitously! Within ten days of Bardi's receiving a report from the Procura of Palermo containing the Marchese's name some three months ago. Not that there had been any further evidence. Bardi had been trying to collect that ever since, as discreetly as possible.

I assure you, you're mistaken, and in any case, he can't make a move without . . .

It was true that he couldn't open an official file without his chief's knowledge and consent.

'I hope you don't mean that you regret having introduced us?'

'Not at all. I didn't say that.'

'You feel he was rude to me. Do you imagine that I provoked that by having been rude to him in some way?'

'Not at all, not at all! You mustn't misunderstand me . . .'

But he didn't explain himself, only concentrated on the road ahead. Bardi knew him well enough to realize that he was torn between wanting to talk the problem over and wanting even more to deny that it existed. His attempt to treat the whole thing as a question of personalities having failed, they both lapsed into silence and remained silent for the rest of the journey which seemed inordinately long. Darkness fell and the few cars coming in the opposite direction dipped their headlights as they passed.

When they drew up outside his darkened house Bardi got out and collected his rifle from the boot with the aid of the cold blue light from a streetlamp before going round to the driver's door.

Sometime this week I'd like to talk to you about – some notes on a new proceeding I want officially opened.'

'Of course. I hope that cut's not going to give you any trouble. I'm sure you ought to have it looked at.'

Bardi had told them he'd grazed his cheek against a tree. Almost true.

'Acciai thought so, too,' Corbi persisted. 'He admires you a lot, you know. In spite of everything I still hope you'll become friends. He's a good man, whatever you may think . . .'

'I don't think anything. I'll see you tomorrow.'

'I'll say goodnight, then . . .'

Bardi watched the car move off and then paused under the streetlamp to fish for his keys.

CHAPTER FOUR

'I seem to be becoming accident prone,' said Bardi thoughtfully to the two angels on the wall facing his desk.

'Yes, sir,' said Poma from his habitual seat in the corner of the office.

'And I'd very much like to know why.'

'Yes, sir.' Poma glanced at the dressing on Bardi's cheek. Bardi drummed his fingers on the desk for a moment and then took a quick sip from his cup.

'This coffee's always too bitter.'

'Yes, sir. Do you want me to send for some sugar?'

'Doesn't matter.' He lit half a cigarette and then went on drumming and staring at the angels.

Poma settled back into his own thoughts, knowing that only the occasional grunt or 'yes, sir' was required of him, or of Mastino if he should happen to be the one who was there. Poma was wondering how they would manage if his wife was really pregnant. They only had one bedroom. What was worse, she was bound to use it to put pressure on him because she didn't like him doing escort duty. There was no hiding from her how dangerous it was, she saw the news every night the same as everybody else. But he liked his job, he liked driving about all over the country, he liked his mate Mastino and he liked Bardi. How long could a child sleep in its parents' room? He had no idea. It might turn out to be a false alarm anyway.

'Well, there's no point in wasting time speculating.'

'No, sir.'

'Do me a favour, Poma, fetch me the Li Causi file from the Archives. I can put in an hour on that before we're due at the prison.'

'Yes, sir.' Poma jumped to his feet and went out.

Li Causi was a hard case, Bardi knew that from the last time he'd questioned him. They'd known he was guilty and he'd known that they knew and he hadn't turned a hair. Nevertheless, it would all have to be gone through again now they'd arrested him.

Poma came in with the file and placed it carefully on the desk. He didn't sit down in his corner again but stood there twirling his big moustache, his brown eyes fixed on the boss, knowing that he would be dismissed now that the morning's ruminations were over and Bardi was about to start work.

'All right, thanks. You can go. I'll ring down when I'm ready to leave.'

It was a biggish file, a hundred and twelve numbered sheets with an index at the front. At some point he would go through every line of it again but for the moment he just wanted to browse through it and refresh his memory. There was nothing of much interest in it, anyway.

'Though there was one thing, if I remember . . .' he said aloud, forgetting that Poma was no longer there. He ran a finger down the index.

Search – report and statement p.2
Notice of proceedings p.4
Interrogation p.13
Sequestrated diary – photocopies pp.18–78
Report of proceedings against Tuscan
Revolutionary Committee, Red Brigades.
pp.79–112

Bardi turned to page 79 and skimmed it rapidly.

Ministry of the Interior, Digos, Florence, January 30th, 1982.

Search warrant requested in connection with investigation of Li Causi, Antonio Giorgio, b. Napoli 30.5.48, resident in Florence, Via delle Terme 18. Assistant Professor at the University of Florence Faculty of Sociology. Graduate

of the University of Trento. Author of *The Birth and Development of the Social Structure of the Kibbutz*. Research for the above carried out during a prolonged stay in Israel. As a student at Trento proved to have been in contact with Red Brigades leader CURCIO, Renato.
Proved to have been in contact with MARIANETTI, Giovanni, arrested in connection with Proceeding n. 144/81. MARIANETTI, Giovanni, found to be in possession of home and work telephone numbers of LI CAUSI, Antonio, who is consequently presumed to be connected with the Red Brigades.
Confidential sources affirm him to be a member of the above named subversive organization.

Bardi paused and turned back for a moment to page 2.

The search commenced at 16.30 in the presence of non-commissioned officers Cordi and Mannini and of the lawyer Chiari called in by Li Causi on presentation of the search warrant.

No material relating to the Red Brigades was discovered during the search. A Diary containing notes and telephone numbers which might prove to be pertinent to the present inquiry was sequestrated. Photocopies of the above appended.

They had had to give the diary back. Nothing could be proved against Li Causi and they had let him go. Shortly afterwards he had disappeared, which meant that he had become a clandestine member of the Red Brigades. Only now after all these years had they managed to find him again and that because some repentant had given him away. There was no doubt that he was clever. It wasn't often that a surprise search revealed no scrap of evidence, not so much as a telephone number. There had been a number listed in an odd way which had seemed as though it might lead somewhere but in the end it hadn't. That was what Bardi was looking for now, though unless some fresh information had come to light since Li Causi's arrest it was probably a waste of time.

'Abbiati, Luigi, 287989; Bianchi, G. 0575 345679; Burberi, C . . .'

No, it was much further on.

'Pignore, Franco, 02 645324 . . .'

He found it under R: 'R. sheqel 640 21 230'

What sort of name was that? It wasn't even written with a capital letter. And what sort of number? Not a Florentine telephone number, it was too long, and if it was some other city or even another country, there should have been a code before it. Li Causi had denied that it was a telephone number at all.

Bardi turned back to the index: Interrogation p. 13.

> Answered to questions: The number 640 21 230 is not a telephone number. It is not in code. It is not a secret annotation of any kind. It does not refer to a person. Sheqel is the Hebrew way of writing shekel. The letter R does stand for a person, one of my students, Roberto Altieri, if I remember rightly. I simply made a note of something I had to explain to him about the old Jewish monetary system. You already know what I teach and I think you have a copy of my book in front of you. I don't remember the exact context of the explanation I had to make but it probably had to do with the annual contributions made to the sanctuary of Jerusalem, an institution which the Zionists re-established at the end of the nineteenth century. I don't remember why I made the note against the list of telephone numbers. I don't remember what the number there refers to, it's too long ago. I don't think it was the number of the student concerned. It's true that if I don't remember, then it could be a phone number. I did say earlier that it wasn't because that's what I think. If you think differently, I imagine it would be easy enough to check.

They had checked. Not only did such a telephone number

not exist but Bardi had sent it to the Military Secret Service decoding people and they had tried every known method of decodifying the number with no results.

And Li Causi had been so confident he hadn't even bothered to try and sound convincing. He had invented no story, just shrugged his shoulders slightly and repeated, 'I don't remember.' And they had let him go.

Things were unlikely to go differently now that he was in prison. Bardi knew the formula well enough; the refusal to acknowledge the right of the court to try him, the refusal to defend himself as a consequence, the presentation of long-winded manifestoes to which judge and journalists half listened, not bothering to conceal their boredom. If Bardi wanted to know what that number meant he would have to find out for himself.

And meantime he had to face another two hours or so of Gori's being ostentatiously repentant. He copied the number 640 21 230 into his diary, closed the file and picked up the internal telephone.

'Alert my escort. I'm coming down.'

'I was put in a Logistics Brigade first, that's the lowest grade, and I soon moved up. Even so, the Logistics Brigades are important because they do all the basic work like getting false documents, finding houses and stealing cars and changing the number plates for the big jobs organized by the Columns.'

'How many were you?'

'Only three at first – there are never more than five to a Brigade and they're always irregulars. Later on –'

'Wait.' Bardi flipped open his case and withdrew a large sheet of paper folded in four which he spread on the table between himself and Gori. 'Logistics Brigades,' he repeated, finding them on the plan he had roughed out over the years and making a note, 'Documents, housing, cars. What about the Propaganda Brigades?'

'On the same level. There's one to each city. Never more

than five people to each again but they're usually fragmented, it's less risky than if they worked together. That way, if one gets caught the others carry on working.'

'What do they deal with?'

'It depends. Basically they're divided into three categories, the "Triplex", as it's called, deals with the forces of repression –'

'With?'

'The police and carabinieri . . . that's what we call them – what we called them.' Gori tugged at his moustache, his face reddening at this double slip. Clearing his throat nervously he went on: '. . . and the magistracy and prisons.'

'Go on.'

'The second category's a sort of political watchdog following the activities of the Parties. Then there's a third one for infiltrating the factories.'

'Wait.' He wrote again rapidly and then paused. 'They're not involved in any actions at that level?'

'Only woundings and small stuff. Assassinations are organized by the Columns.'

'That's the next grade up?'

'That's right. They're all full-time and there's a Column to each operation zone and each Column has a management group.'

'Consisting of?'

'A person responsible for the Logistics Brigades and another for the Propaganda Brigades in their area, and then other full-time members.'

'You mean these people are virtually full-time bureaucrats? Smoke if you wish.'

'I've no cigarettes left.'

Bardi took a pack from his case and pushed it across the table. 'Keep them. Well?'

'No, that's not how it works. There are no full-time bureaucrats. Everybody involved is expected to fight. The Head of a Column automatically becomes a member of one of the National Fronts, Logistics or Propaganda. They're the ones who evaluate proposals for actions coming from the Columns.'

'And the Executive?'

'That's top level. Two members from each of the National Fronts. They're the real bosses and they have to give final approval of all actions and superintend the bigger ones.'

'What about contact with other terrorist groups? I'm talking about on an international level, the ETA, IRA, PLF and so on. Who deals with that?'

'Only the Executive.'

'I see. Wait.'

Gori sat obediently silent like a schoolboy, as anxious to please his new master as he had been to please his old ones all those years ago in a bar filled with students among the warm smells of coffee and pizza.

Bardi made some brief notes on his diagram, then he sat back and screwed the top on to his tiny gold pen very slowly. Gori followed his every movement like a dog who isn't sure whether he is going to be beaten or fed.

'It seems to me,' Bardi remarked, observing the diagram before him, 'that this organization is somewhat undemocratic, for a group, that is, which claims to be fighting for the proletariat.'

'That's not true!' The remark was unexpected and Gori reacted automatically before remembering his new stance. 'All members of . . . what I mean is . . . I know now that everything they're doing is wrong and it's all been a mistake but even so, I told you, everyone's expected to fight, there's no distinction between the intellectuals, ideas people, and active soldiers – that is . . .'

'That is, when it comes down to it, between the better educated and the workers.'

'That's right. Exactly.'

'How many workers were there on the Executive when you were active?'

'On the Executive . . . none, but –'

'On the National Fronts?'

'None – but that doesn't mean – there was one, now I think of it, who was working class like me only he was arrested just after he'd been made Head of a Column, and I'd have made it, too, if I hadn't dropped out.'

'If you hadn't been arrested.'

'Anyway, with the best will in the world you're bound to get some people who are better at thinking than others but they had to fight as well.'

'Go back to your own case. Your Logistics Brigade. There were three of you, you said.'

'At first there were, but I worked mostly on my own. Then Acciai joined up and I had to work with him for a bit but he was crazy.'

'In what way was he crazy?' Bardi gave no sign of having recognized the name, but he was remembering Acciai's reaction to what, on his part, had been an innocent remark.

'Well, for one thing he was the son of some Count or Marquis or other – not that that – anyway, he didn't understand a thing about the problems of the working classes, that's one thing. I reckon he was just on some kick of his own. He was nuts, if you ask me. One thing he used to do was, when we had to steal a car – well, the first thing you learn is what sort of car to steal, an Alfa Sud, for instance, that's good because it has four doors and everybody can get out of it fast at once if necessary, and because it's fast and common enough not to be noticed on the road. But Acciai, he'd pinch anything he took a fancy to. "That's a superb car, let's take it," that was him. And the way he'd go about it! There are standard methods and you're supposed to stick to them because it's less dangerous, and what's dangerous to you is dangerous for the Organization. You don't do anybody any good by getting yourself arrested. If you want to steal cars you can steal them easily enough from a garage, even three or four cars at a time if there are enough of you. If you're on your own it's easy enough to spot some car parked with the keys left in it because the driver's nipped into a bar for a coffee or something, and it's even easier to watch out for a car that's always left parked in the same street, take down the make and serial number and then go to the dealers and say you've lost your keys. After that you nick the car during the night. No problem. But Acciai, he'd just pick any car he fancied and pinch it in broad daylight, breaking into it and maybe even starting it with jump wires. I've even seen him saw through one of those steering-wheel locks with half the population of Florence watching him and him grinning all over his stupid face and chatting to the crowd about how *frightfully silly* it was of him to have lost the key. Once he even went babbling on to everybody in English – God knows what story he was telling, but people just stood there gaping until somebody who spoke English turned up and bloody well *helped* him! How he got away with it I'll never know but he always did.'

'Then he was reckless, not necessarily crazy, given that his way of doing things worked.'

'No, I'm telling you, that bloke was crazy and I really mean that. The cars were just one thing but there was worse than that. Once we had to chuck a bomb into the Christian Democrat Party offices – and that was all we were meant to do, at night as well, we weren't supposed to injure anybody, just damage the building. Well, Acciai turns up with a pistol, pulls it out of his pocket just as we're about to get the hell out and starts shooting, right, left and centre out there in the street. If he didn't kill anybody it was only by luck because he was out of his head and screaming like a maniac. He shattered two shop windows before I managed to get him back in the car and away before the fire brigade turned up. I said to myself, that's the last time I work with this idiot. And it was, too, because they chucked him out of the Organization – not because of his crazy tricks, because I was the only one who really knew about them. They threw him out because word got around that he was taking dope and they won't stand for that. That's dangerous. Anybody who's hooked on dope will talk, for one thing, not just to anybody but to the police. You know as well as I do that they give out dope in exchange for information so that anybody who's desperate for his next fix . . . The Organization's really strict about it, like about sex with outsiders. They don't . . .'

'Yes?' When Gori didn't go on Bardi waited a moment and then asked, 'Is it yours, the child?' Patrizia Rossini, a leader of the Florentine nucleus now on trial, had appeared in court heavily pregnant. She was known to have been involved with both Gori and Li Causi.

'I don't know.'

'Or she doesn't know, is that more like it?'

Gori fumbled for a cigarette in silence.

'Very well. Leave it. We'll come to that later. So, you were part of this Logistics Brigade from, let's see . . . 1976 to 1978.'

'Yes.'

'That includes the time of the Rota abduction. What did you know about it?'

'Not much.'

'I find that hard to believe. It was planned in Florence.'

'I've told you, big jobs like that are organized by the Columns.'

'There were five stolen cars used.'

'And they had Roman number plates, you know that. They had to have or they'd have been too easy to spot.'

'Number plates can be changed, you said that was part of your job.'

'I didn't steal any of those cars. The number plates weren't changed, as far as I know, they were Roman cars.'

'Did you visit Rome at all during that period?'

'Just before it happened I went.'

'What was the purpose of your visit?'

'A message. I took a message.'

'Did it concern Rota?'

'It might have done but I don't know for sure.'

'I take it it wasn't a written message?'

'No. They never were.'

'You memorized it?'

'Yes.'

'Do you still remember it?'

'More or less. It was just three addresses. They were houses we were thinking of renting in Florence. I can't remember them exactly but two were near Santa Croce and the other was a cottage out in the hills, in the Mugello region.'

'Is it possible that Rota was to be transferred to Florence once the road blocks were removed?'

'I don't know. I'd tell you if I did, but I don't know. In any case it makes no difference because once Rota was kidnapped they passed that new anti-terrorist law saying that landlords had to report the names of all their tenants to the police. After that we had to buy a house each time we needed a new base. It was a bad time for us.'

'Did you bring any message back from Rome?'

'No.'

'Who did you talk to when you were there? Who did you give this message to?'

'To Li Causi. He was Head of the Rome Column by then and on the National Front for Logistics.'

'And you know so little about the kidnapping?' snapped Bardi. 'You talked to Li Causi, Head of the Rome Column, immediately before the biggest job they've ever pulled off and he told you nothing? Come on, Gori, you'll have to do better than that!'

'I was only an irregular then.'

'But you became a regular immediately afterwards. They must have trusted you. In any case you can't tell me that you didn't hear talk.'

'Everybody heard talk. I knew something big was going on.'

'Did you know it was a kidnapping?'

'I might have had an idea . . . but I didn't know who it was going to be.'

It was probably true. Nevertheless, there was more that he wasn't telling, that was obvious from the way his eyes avoided Bardi's, flickering between the cigarette he was holding between his knees and the door where the two guards stood silent and bored. But if it was true that he wasn't in Rome when it happened . . .

'What about afterwards, did you hear talk afterwards too?'

'What do you mean?'

'Talk. About what went on while Rota was a prisoner.'

'Some . . .' A bead of sweat broke on his forehead. The room, though small and airless, was cold.

'Did you, for instant, hear that Rota was given the Last Sacrament before he was killed?'

'No. That is . . .'

'That is?'

'I heard the rumour generally, not inside the Organization.'

'Did you believe it?'

Gori only shrugged.

'You weren't interested enough to believe or disbelieve, is that it?'

'Why should it matter to me? I mean then . . . now, I suppose . . . well, if it was what he wanted I hope it's true.'

'Kind of you. Did you go to Rome afterwards? After Rota was killed and dumped?'

'Yes . . .'

'And?'

'It was the time when I was going to become a regular. I went to talk to Li Causi.'

'How long were you there?'

'About two weeks, I suppose.'

'Doing what?'

'I've told you, I went to talk –'

'You spent two weeks talking? I'm sure it's already been made clear to you what the terms are in the case of repentants and if I think you're not telling me what you know, then your status is at risk. You'll find that being considered only dissociated rather than repentant will make a very big difference indeed when it comes to sentencing you. Is that understood?'

'Yes, but . . .'

'But what, Gori, but what?'

'I'm not thinking about my trial, that's what! I'm thinking about the danger I'm in from *them* – you promised to get me transferred to a special prison!'

'I promised no such thing.'

'Listen, you've got to help me, I've signed my death warrant talking to you and you know it!'

'Did I ask you to talk to me?'

'That's not the point.'

'But it is, Gori, it is. You've chosen to avoid a life sentence –'

'And risk a death sentence.'

'But the choice was yours. I'm not responsible for the homicidal tendencies of your old friends.' Bardi snapped his case shut and pushed his chair back.

'Where are you going? I haven't finished, I –'

'You're wasting my time. Guard!'

'No, wait . . . You can't blame me for being scared, so would you be scared, wait!'

Bardi was already at the door when Gori jumped to his feet in a panic and the two guards moved in on him in an instant with the handcuffs.

'Wait! I'll tell you what I know! For what good it'll do you I'll tell you!'

'Let him go.' Bardi sat down again, expressionless, staring at the whitewashed wall above Gori's head while the other lit himself a cigarette with hands that were shaking badly. There was a sour smell of sweat mixed with smoke in the small room. The smell of prison and fear.

'I was telling the truth when I said I wasn't involved, not during the kidnapping. But after . . . If I tell you . . .'

Whatever he had been about to demand in return he thought better of it and went on.

'Afterwards I went back to Rome. There were four of us,

me and Li Causi and two others. We went to dismantle the base where they'd kept Rota. It was a rented flat and we got rid of it because it had become too risky to keep it after the new law. You know where it is . . .'

'I know.'

'The police found it about a month after we were there. We had to clean it up. It wasn't easy, we spent hours . . .'

Even so, police technicians had found traces of Rota's blood dried in cracks in the walls and between the floor tiles.

'You can't imagine what it was like. Two weeks had already gone by since the . . . since it happened, because it would have been dangerous to go back straight away when it was still on the news every night and somebody might notice something and start putting two and two together. Besides that, there was a lot of argument about who should go. The ones who'd taken the flat and had been there all the time on guard had told neighbours they were going on holiday to account for their sudden disappearance. They were the ones who really should have gone back but they were shit scared. You couldn't put your nose out the door at that time without being stopped and searched. In the end the Executive decided that they should stay under cover and we went. The worst thing was that the weather was so warm . . . When we got there the woman from the flat next door came out on the landing. We'd got a story ready about collecting some extra clothes for our mates before joining them on holiday – we had a suitcase with us – in case we should meet any neighbours, but she didn't give us time to open our mouths.

' *"If you're friends of that lot who live there you want to tell them it's about time they cleaned that place up. I don't know what sort of state they've left it in but there's a stink on this landing and it's coming from in there."*

'Li Causi laughed in her face. It's incredible how naïve people are. They see it all in the papers and on TV but they never think of it happening right under their noses. That woman, all she cared about was keeping her landing clean.

It's people like that who make a revolution impossible, I can tell you, that's one thing I've learned.

' "*I'm not having the neighbours think it's my house that smells! I polish this landing floor and wash these stairs every two weeks and they're supposed to do it every other week. I told them that when they moved in. If they want to pay somebody else to do it, they can, we can't afford to, but we've always been clean in this building. If you ask me they've left their rubbish bags in there stinking, it's disgusting!*"

'Stupid cow!' He was shaking even more now. Li Causi might have laughed in the woman's face but the incident had evidently shot Gori's nerves to pieces. 'She was right about the smell, though. I was sick and so was one of the others. If it had just been blood I could have stuck it, but there was all stuff . . . and there'd been flies. It was disgusting, much worse than anything I'd seen in the hospital because in hospital you expect it and anyway it's all provided for and you never really have to touch it. In a house . . . it was all over everything. If you want to know, I was sick twice, and Li Causi laughing and cracking jokes about mopping up Christian Democrat shit. There were even two of his teeth . . . I'm not a coward, I can tell you that, once when I had to do a kneecap job on a journalist I was dead calm, waiting and watching him coming towards me along that corridor for what seemed like hours. A lot of people would have fired as soon as they saw him and messed the thing up, you can kill somebody by mistake doing that, but I never flinched. I waited till he was right up close and I could even see the expression on his face, not scared, just surprised, he couldn't believe it. I've never been as calm in my life. But in a case like that you just do the job and you're off, there's no mess. I've always been sensitive, that's the trouble, and the way Li Causi behaved was disgusting to me.'

'Come to the point. What did you take away from there?'

'Everything, mostly clothes belonging to the lads who'd been on guard.'

'None that belonged to Rota?'

'No, he had his clothes on him when they found him, you know that.'

'He was a prisoner in that room for two months. Do you mean to say he was never given a change of clothing in all that time?' Bardi had had no great liking for Carlo Rota but he remembered him now as always discreetly, austerely well-dressed.

'He was a prisoner,' Gori said. 'When I was first arrested I was kept in a cell for over two weeks without a change of clothes.'

'Go on.'

'As well as clothes we took the documents.'

'What documents?'

'The ones of his trial.'

'The police found those documents still in the flat.'

'I don't know what they found. We took the documents away.'

'The ones that were found were planted then, they were false? Who went back there after you?'

'I don't know. I only know we took all the documents away.'

'Anything else?'

'Just bits and pieces, like the newspaper they made him hold to be photographed to prove he was alive, cigarettes, matches, everything that was lying around, even a tube cigar, and that caused a row when we delivered it all to the Executive and Li Causi tipped all this junk out of a plastic bag on to the table and rolled this fancy cigar tube across to them saying, "Somebody's got some expensive tastes." '

'Why should that cause a row?'

'Because there was always trouble about money. Regulars were only paid about a hundred and fifty a month and it was never enough to live on. You got people sometimes who'd give in false accounts like saying they'd spent twice the amount they really had on ammunition or false documents, stuff like that, and they'd use the money for a blow-out in a restaurant. We were always hungry . . . That crack of Li

Causi's about somebody spending money, probably the Organization's money, on expensive cigars, was a serious criticism. There was a real nasty row about it. You'd have thought it was our fault, one of the Executive even said to me –'

'Can we get back to the question of the flat.' It was typical of Gori that he only remembered his own nausea and the squabbling they'd done among themselves. 'I want to know if you noticed anything to indicate that Rota was given the Sacrament, a white cloth, a jug of water, anything.'

'I don't remember anything like that.'

'Nothing at all, you're sure?'

'Nothing.'

It had been a faint hope anyway. Anything that could really be called evidence, such as the cotton wool stained with oil, would have been taken away by the priest and burnt as a matter of course, according to the rites.

'There's nothing else you can tell me?'

'About Rota? No, that's all.'

'All right. That will do for today.'

'What about . . . I'm in danger now, now I've told you that. Li Causi's been arrested and now I've given evidence against him that nobody else could have given. They've got at people in prison before.'

'I'll do what I can.'

And he wasn't the only one who appeared to be in danger. Li Causi would be tried and condemned for the Rota case and a good many others, probably without ever opening his mouth except to hurl insults at the judge. This morning's interrogation would have precious little effect on him. But it would have a great deal of effect, sooner or later, on the Marchese Giancarlo Filippo Acciai.

' 'Evening, sir.' The carabiniere on guard at the main entrance saluted. It was almost seven when Bardi entered the carabinieri barracks in Borgo Ognissanti, and lamps were lit along the one-time cloister when he passed through the electronic gates and took the stairs on the right two at a time. The first floor housed the judicial police, the second the CID. What had once been monks' cells had been converted into offices. Bardi continued up to the third floor where, in the Military Secret Service Department, few people were in uniform. There the guard looked at him in silent inquiry.

'Colonel Tempesta is expecting me. I telephoned half an hour ago.'

The guard knocked on an unmarked door, waited for an answer and then opened it for the Substitute.

The Colonel stood up slowly behind a cluttered, 16th-century reproduction desk and held out his hand. The window behind him was half open despite the cold and darkness outside.

'Lapo! I can't imagine what brings you here but it's good to see you again. Sit down, sit down.'

Tempesta was a stocky, bald man who wore his not very good government issue suit with the air of a humble town hall clerk. His mild blue eyes added to this impression, but Bardi, who had known him since they had been at University together, knew that his was a formidable intelligence and that his tranquillity lay in the amount of power he wielded with ease. He settled himself into a comfortable chair opposite the Colonel and smiled.

'For God's sake, Tempesta, can't you close that window? It's freezing in here.'

'You think so? Well, all right.' He turned in his swivel chair and pulled the window to. 'You're not getting soft in your old age, I hope.'

'Let's say I'd rather not get 'flu in November if I can put it off until February, but I suppose that means nothing to you.'

'I'm never ill,' said the Colonel complacently. 'How's Laura?'

'Fine.'

'It's a long time since we got together. Why not come to supper? Nicoletta would be pleased to see you.'

'We'd be glad to. The problem is arranging it, you know how much time I spend on the move.'

'Always the same excuse. I don't believe you do anything with your life except work. It's a mistake, you know, and a thankless business in the end. Relax a little before it's too late.'

'There'll be time to relax when I retire.'

'Maybe. I suppose I was thinking more of Laura.'

'Laura's not the sort to cause trouble over that sort of thing. We have our problems but that's not one of them.'

'If you say so. You'd do well to give it a moment's thought, nevertheless. A day off now and then would do no harm.'

'I went hunting yesterday, if that's any consolation to you.'

'And shot a boar. So I heard.'

'You did?'

'A colleague of mine was there. Nobody you know. Said it was a fine beast.'

'It was.' So Acciai had friends here, too. Bardi noted the warning bell and dropped the subject. He wasn't there to talk about Acciai. He took out a cigarette and broke it.

'What's this?' smiled the Colonel. 'An economy measure?'

'I'm supposed to be trying to give it up.'

'Not trying over-hard, I see. You'll never do it that way.'

'After six months I've come to that conclusion, too, but by this time the method's become a habit in itself.'

The internal telephone rang. All the Colonel said into the receiver after listening briefly was: 'No, no. I'm busy.'

After hanging up he leaned back heavily in his chair and observed his friend.

'How's Corbi?'

'Edgy.'

'He is always edgy, more or less. I suppose you're not contributing to his edginess, his blue-eyed boy? With this trial and the famous Bardi Theorem?'

'No, not that. If anything, he enjoys the polemic in the papers. He knows I'll win. It's not really a problem case, though it's a pity Li Causi wasn't arrested earlier. It would have tied up a lot of loose ends for me if I could have put him on trial with the rest of them.'

'Ah, Li Causi. Well, he has bigger things coming to him than the stuff you have on him.'

'For what good it will do.'

The Colonel shrugged and opened his big hands. 'One does what one can.'

'I'd be right in assuming that the signal on his whereabouts came through your people?'

The Colonel's face assented but he only said, 'You'd also be right in assuming that I wouldn't dream of telling you where the information came from.'

Bardi grinned. 'And naturally I wouldn't dream of asking. Obviously a repentant, not that I'm interested anyway, but I am interested in Li Causi himself. I've been looking through my file on him since he was arrested.'

'Ah! It still rankles, does it? That you got him first and had to let him go. So that's why you're here – it really still bothers you after all these years?'

'You could put it that way. Or you could say that his case still interests me.'

'Oh, surely not. He won't open his mouth. Having him behind bars was as much as we could hope for.'

'Maybe. He won't talk, I agree. But I imagine his rooms were searched and so on. I'd be glad of any information you could give me.'

'Me? I know nothing about it, Lapo. All I've had is the usual official message to suspend any current inquiries, given that he's been arrested. I can't think that there would be anything in it that would be useful to you, but . . .'

He pushed a button on his desk and a uniformed carabiniere knocked lightly and came in.

'Colonel?'

'Bring me the Li Causi file, will you?'

'Yessir.'

When he had gone Tempesta looked hard at Bardi.

'When you get your teeth into something you don't let go, do you?'

'It sometimes pays.'

'I suppose so. But I doubt if I can be of much help, as I said . . .'

There was another knock at the door.

'Come in.'

'The file, sir.'

'Thank you. That's all, you can go.'

The carabiniere closed the door quietly behind him.

'Here you are.' The printout was the topmost paper in the thick file. Tempesta pushed it across to Bardi who scanned it without comment.

'As you can see, there's nothing you haven't already read in the papers. All it says is where and when he was arrested and to suspend all inquiries.'

'So I see. I was hoping, nevertheless that you might know something more.'

'I know where we got the tip-off and, as I said, I'm not telling you that. Trade secret.'

'You remember that first search we made? In his apartment here in Florence?'

'Perfectly. My men didn't find a thing. Clean as a whistle. I don't know when we've come across anything so efficient. They're all careful nowadays, of course, but at that time when the Red Brigades had it all their own way because we weren't ready for them they were quite careless about the stuff they carried on them or left lying around at home. A surprise raid like that usually produced enough evidence to put a dozen of them away. A bright lad, our friend Li Causi, not so much as a sniff of any evidence.'

'Except for that number.' Bardi lit the other half of his cigarette.

'What number's that? I don't remember any number.'

'Surely you do? A number in his address book with some sort of Hebrew word beside it. He was questioned at length about it but with no results.'

'Possibly. I can't say I remember, even so.'

'How can you not remember? You assured me at the time that your people had tried every possible method of decoding it.'

'I did? Well, if I told you that, it was true. Now you mention it I have a vague recollection of some decoding work being done. If I'd forgotten it's obviously because, as you say, nothing came of it.'

'I'm convinced it was important, even so, and if nothing came of it that doesn't mean the matter was cleared up, only that we were unable to clear it up. Let me refresh your memory: the unexplained number was listed under the letter R and followed the initial R and a word in Hebrew. During questioning Li Causi said the word referred to some sort of Jewish coin and that the note was to remind him about something he had to explain to one or other of his students, probably one named Roberto as the note had been made under the letter R. He made no attempt to explain the number, only said it wasn't a telephone number as far as he knew. But I'm convinced that it was something of the sort and that it could give us a lead.'

'A lead to what?'

'I can't say, obviously, without knowing what the number meant, but Li Causi was an important leader of the Red Brigades, very important, especially at that time when he was a respected professor and could move freely in any circle. For all we know, that number could lead us to the Grand Old Man.'

'Bardi! I wouldn't have believed it of you. Don't tell me you still believe in all that stuff? Fairy tales made up by the press! There's no such person as the Grand Old Man, you know that as well as I do.'

'I don't know anything of the sort,' replied Bardi calmly, 'and if we've heard less about him since the Rota case that could just be because he was involved in it. More involved than he wanted to be, possibly, so that afterwards he disappeared, or seemed to, from the scene.'

'No, no. There have been some plausible stories, of course, but it's all theory.'

'I know there's no proof, if that's what you mean –'

'Not only is there no proof. What's more to the point is that the whole idea of there being some mysterious figure manipulating left-wing terrorists on behalf of some interested State –'

'Or of more than one State.'

'Or of more than one State, if you like, it comes to the same thing. The point is that it's what a great many people would like to believe. It's more convenient, more comforting, if you like, for a lot of people to believe in some sort of diabolical plot than to accept that terrorism is a phenomenon produced by our post-war society. There are those who prefer the international conspiracy theory and those who like to imagine – or used to when it was still possible because the Red Brigades were still faceless, anonymous – that they weren't Italian at all but sent here by some foreign power. What nobody wanted to believe was that they were the product of our too rapid post-war economic boom and all the false expectations that resulted from it. Remember Maurice Duverger's observation? That it's no coincidence that terrorism is present in three industrially advanced countries, Italy, Germany and Japan, all of them at one time fascist, all of them having undergone precipitate development after their defeat.

'By this time, now that we've got these once-mythical characters behind bars and so many of them have talked, stories about foreign infiltration had faded out in the face of the infantile ideology and the squalor that lay behind the one-time glamour of the Red Brigades. People have been forced to see them as they really are, and I can't seriously believe that a man in your position, Lapo, could want to go on deceiving himself. You more than anybody –'

'I, more than anybody, know all about the infantile ideology and the squalor. But I go one step further. I see all that and I find it impossible to believe that somebody wasn't all too ready to take advantage of their existence. Look at the historic parallels: there was secret service infiltration in all the Russian terrorist movements – it was the German secret service that helped Lenin to get back to Russia, there were police informers in the first Central Committee of the Bolshevik party. There have been infiltrators and informers of the various kings and presidents in every terrorist and revolutionary movement in the world. So why should Italy be any different?'

'I take your point – looking at the thing historically, it seems plausible. But we have no evidence of it.'

'No evidence? One Red Brigades leader who made frequent trips to Czechoslovakia, the known relationship between one of the Columns and the communists of Radio Prague. Li Causi himself and the time he spent in the Middle East – not to mention the statement of the Egyptian police about contact between the Red Brigades and the PLO.'

'Those are indications, certainly, but they can't be called evidence.'

'Call them what you like. Personally I'm not even convinced that it was necessarily the Eastern Bloc that was most likely to offer them help. The risk of violent left-wing action discrediting Communism in this country was too obvious. An infiltrator from a Western power interested in creating an anti-communist climate and obstructing a Christian Democrat-Communist coalition – which the Brigades also wanted to obstruct – would be much more plausible.'

'All theory, nevertheless, Lapo, all theory.' The Colonel leaned back in his chair with a smile.

'All theory, yes. But you know as well as I do the advantages gained by the Right out of all this. Laws passed in the name of anti-terrorism that nobody would have even dared propose before, for instance.'

'Come now, taking advantage of a given situation – pushing a law through, for example – is a far cry from manipulating the situation itself. No government is that well organized for action or that far-sighted. The facts are much simpler.

Terrorism had its day up till ten years ago when it was a new phenomenon and nobody was ready for it. People reacted as they were bound to react, according to their own interests, and things changed. Can you imagine anyone trying a job like the Rota abduction today? They wouldn't have a chance and they know it. In the last ten years the Brigades have only kept going by allying themselves with common criminals.'

'Common criminals who can occasionally let them have a consignment of arms originally meant for the PLO?'

'As far as we know, that's no longer happening.'

'If you say so. But when it was happening it wasn't through the good offices of the common criminal.'

'The Red Brigades have always been in contact with the PLO, you pointed that out yourself.'

'And the PLO kindly suggested that they waylay a consignment of arms on its way to Palestine now and then?'

'All right, all right, you want to cling to your Grand Old Man theory. What can I say?' The Colonel was laughing, his pale blue eyes narrowed and twinkling. 'You remind me of a bulldog once you get your teeth into something . . . Even so, coming back to Li Causi – you don't seriously think that someone careful enough not to keep a single scrap of evidence in his flat that would indicate his membership of the Red Brigades would go around with the telephone number of your Grand Old Man in his address book?'

'No, I don't think so. But that number was the only thing he did have that he couldn't or wouldn't explain. All I'm saying is that it could lead us in the right direction.'

'You're not making sense. Either the Grand Old Man exists or he doesn't. For my money he doesn't, you think he does. Even if you should be right, the Red Brigades would have to have trusted him on a personal level. There could hardly have been intermediaries.'

'There could have been one. Not an intermediary, a third party, a witness, someone who knows.'

'I don't follow you.'

'Then I'll be more exact. A priest.'

'A priest! That's all we need to complete the cast of characters in this fairy tale. Bardi, you're having me on!'

'You saw the autopsy report on Rota. There were smears of oil on the palms of his hands, or traces of recent smears, as though he'd been anointed.'

'Or had a snack before he died.'

'He didn't. Same autopsy report. Those traces of oil were ignored – I could say hushed up but I'll say ignored. The rumour of his having been given the Last Sacrament got out anyway.'

'And that's all it was, a rumour. If a couple of smears of oil were ignored it was because they had no importance as far as the investigation was concerned. Besides which, I still don't see what you're trying to get at.'

'I'm trying to get at why Rota was killed. Alive in captivity he was valuable, released he might well have been even more valuable, given his anger at the colleagues who abandoned him to his fate, refusing to negotiate his release, and given the sort of questions that would have had to be asked if he hadn't died and become a hero instead. The Red Brigade damaged themselves badly by killing him.'

'So they made a mistake, out of pride, out of rage because of the refusal to negotiate, or even out of sheer stupidity.'

'Or they had no choice.'

'You mean your mythical manipulator intervened? Why should he want Rota killed?'

'I don't think he wanted Rota kidnapped. Manipulator is your word, not mine. The way I see it, he could only have been an infiltrator, manipulating when and where he could. I doubt if he expected to be faced with anything on the scale of the Rota kidnapping. Nobody did. Rota's death would be the logical outcome if he saw the infiltrator and recognized him. If he knew him well, if he was the one who would in the end when Rota's death became inevitable, bring in a priest he could trust.'

'So many ifs!'

'Take another if, then, nearer to your own views. If Rota

was given the Last Sacrament without the intervention of any infiltrator who knew and presumably respected him, that leaves us with the men who imprisoned him, who shot down his escort in cold blood, who wrote a series of bloodthirsty communications against his party which included a condemnation of the Church as their collaborators. These people suddenly have a change of heart and call in a priest – what priest, for God's sake – before shooting him to pieces?'

'So he wasn't given the Sacrament. This idea of yours has become an obsession, Bardi. You haven't a scrap of real evidence. You're wasting your time, and I don't see why you come to me, of all people, with your story.'

'You mean I'm wasting your time too.'

'I didn't say that. I'm always glad to see you. I don't see what I can do for you, given that you have, I repeat, no evidence.'

'I have that number. And now we have Li Causi. I'm not asking you to stick out your neck for me. All I'm asking is that if your people didn't do every possible check on that number, they do it now. And that if anything comes out of Li Causi's arrest, anything at all that suggests I may be right, you'll inform me. Information has been known to be channelled into places where it disappears.'

The Colonel stood up slowly and turned to open the window again, forgetful of his friend's earlier protest. He stayed with his back to the desk looking out at the night for a moment in silence. Then he turned and asked: 'Why me?'

'You're the only person I know well enough to trust. If I'm asking too much you can say so and we'll leave it at that.'

'You're not asking too much. I'd rather you hadn't asked at all.'

'Does that mean you'll help me or you won't? You're too clever a diplomat for me.'

'I'm glad to hear it. You're no diplomat at all.'

'The last thing I want to do is put you in a difficult position.'

'I'm always in a difficult position. It's my job.'

'Then you'll help me?'

'I don't know yet whether there's any way I can help you.'

Something about the way he continued standing there rather than sitting down again suggested that their talk was at an end.

Bardi got up.

'You'll be in touch?'

'I'll be in touch. Give my best to Laura, and don't forget that invitation. I mean that.' He pressed the bell for the guard. 'Alert the Substitute Prosecutor's escort.'

'Immediately, sir.'

The two shook hands and the Colonel put a friendly arm over Bardi's shoulders as he saw him through the door.

CHAPTER FIVE

'Hello? Can you hear me? The line's bad at this end.'

'I can hear you.'

'You recognize my voice?'

'Yes, indeed. Also your paranoia. How are you?'

'Not paranoid, careful. In my job it becomes a habit. You sound as though you've got a cold.'

'I have. A very bad cold. But you didn't ring to inquire after my health, I'm afraid.'

'You're quite right. We have a problem.'

'I'm listening.'

'I can't tell you much over the telephone – yes, forgive my paranoia as you call it, once again. Unfortunately it's serious. All I can say at the moment is that one of our magistrates, a certain Substitute Prosecutor, is asking some uncomfortable questions.'

'About?'

'About that affair of ten years ago.'

'I see. Though I don't see what I, of all people, can do . . .'

'I'm not asking for help. Not yet. I think we can cope with it here. This call is more by way of being a warning. Some of the questions he's asking are about a priest. The priest who gave the Last Sacrament to our friend.'

'I see. What sort of man is he?'

'A good man. A good magistrate. He's also an old friend of mine.'

'An old friend . . . There's no chance that if he goes too far you could take him into your confidence?'

'It's too late for that. He would take it badly. He's one of the magistrates that we, shall we say, helped along a little.'

'Ah . . . What a tangled web we weave . . .'

'I'm sorry?'

'Nothing, nothing . . . How far has he got, this good man?'

'Not far. In fact nowhere, in concrete terms. But he could, he's no fool.'

'And he trusts you, you're his friend. That is, since you know what he's doing and he is, as you say, no fool, then he must have confided in you.'

'He was in my office an hour ago.'

'I'm sorry. Very sorry indeed.'

'No sorrier than I am. This could be a bad business for all concerned.'

'You misunderstand me. I'm sorry for you. The man is your friend. You're in a very unhappy position.'

'Your own position, if you'll forgive my bluntness, could be a great deal unhappier than mine if he isn't stopped quickly.'

'Ah, my position . . . My dear friend, I'm an old man and I've never cared overmuch about what you call my position.'

'You care about very shortly being made a cardinal, unless I'm very much mistaken.'

'Well, well, I have my faults and no doubt that is one of them. But I'm an old man, even so. And the Church would not lose much in losing me as a cardinal, I think.'

'Forgive me. I had no right to say that. I'm being blunt in the hope of making you understand, of putting you on your guard. You're only the secondary target, you understand that, of course.'

'I understand.'

'We're going to have to do some rapid thinking and, if possible, get together to talk the situation over. In the meantime I'm sending one of my men down to Rome to see you – he's already on his way – and give you the details in person.'

'He's already on his way . . . But it's quite late already. I'm afraid your man's going to arrive at midnight.'

'More or less. Is that a problem?'

'Only because, as I told you, I have a very bad cold and had hoped to be in bed early.'

'I'm afraid you're not taking me very seriously.'

'You're always afraid I'm not taking you seriously. I've told you that I'm very sorry indeed for the situation in which you find yourself and I meant it most sincerely. I'll pray for you.'

'It might be better . . .'

'Yes, yes, you would prefer me to react in more concrete terms, or in what to you are concrete terms. Be patient with me, good man that you are. My praying is like your paranoia; in my job it becomes a habit.'

'There's Father McManus to see you, Monsignor.'

The tiny, bespectacled nun shuffled briskly across the marble floor and stopped at the edge of the carpet to glare at the figure slumped in an armchair before the blazing log fire. When there was no response she shuffled back to the door and whispered, 'Go in, Father.'

'Is he resting?'

'He always has forty winks after supper. Will you take something, Father? A drop of vinsanto?'

'Gladly, if it's no trouble.'

'No trouble at all. I'll bring it to you. Go in, now, go in.'

The young man strode across to the fireplace and stood observing the sleeper who made an odd contrast with the polished orderliness of the room. His head had fallen to one side and a few strands of grey hair, a little too long, had stuck to his moist forehead that was reddened by the heat from the fire. Beneath the double chin a broad expanse of cassock showed that the Monsignor had recently eaten.

'Not a pretty sight,' admitted the sleeper, without opening his eyes.

The young man flushed, but remained where he was, watching.

'Instead of mentally criticizing the stains on my cassock

you could make yourself useful by putting another log on the fire. That's better, that's better . . .'

The young man gave the log a kick that sent a shower of sparks up the broad chimney. When he turned round the watery, expressionless eyes were open.

'I sleep . . .' observed the Monsignor softly, 'and I don't sleep . . . A cold night, or at least I imagine so from the look of your hands. I haven't been out myself.' He heaved himself into a more upright position and removed a dog-eared breviary from the folds of his lap. 'Sit down and warm yourself.'

The young man settled into the red velvet armchair opposite and held out his big hands to the blaze in silence.

'Well, John? I imagine you didn't come here just to have your own thoughts repeated to you?'

'I thought I'd come and see how you were. I heard you weren't well.'

'I have a cold.' The Monsignor stared into the fire for a moment before adding, 'You were an honester man when you first came here, I think. Ah, but you still blush. We can be thankful for that at least. Now what did you come to see me for?'

'To ask your advice – no, to ask for your help.'

'That's better. And how can I help you?'

'My two years at the college are up. I've had a letter from my Bishop recalling me to Chicago.'

'Good, good.'

'I'd like to stay here.'

'I see.' The Monsignor heaved himself sideways to fish out a handkerchief from his pocket, mopped his brow, blew his nose loudly and protractedly and buried the handkerchief again among the crumpled folds of his cassock. 'Two years . . . How old are you?'

'Twenty-eight.'

'Twenty-eight. Go home, John, go home.'

'But I've been happy here in Rome. It's been a wonderful experience.'

'I've no doubt of it, but if I may say so, you weren't sent here to be happy.'

'I know that.'

'You've been a secretary at the American College, and a very good secretary, too, from what I've heard. But you knew when you came here that it was for two years only. I imagine your successor will already have been appointed.'

'He has.'

'Well, then. I can't see what help I can be.'

'I don't want to stay on at the College – not that I haven't been . . . not that it hasn't been worthwhile, but it's been very much like being in America itself, a sort of outpost. Not that that isn't as it should be, but I want . . . I feel I'd like to work in the *real* Vatican.'

'By which you mean?'

'I'd like to work with you.'

'At the Secretariat of State? No, no, John, you don't want to become a politician. You're too good a priest for that.'

'You said I was a good secretary. I think I could be useful. I want to learn. I'm only asking for six months, a trial period. If you wrote to my Bishop –'

'But I won't. What in the world made you think I'd be the one to help you with a scheme like that? There must be half a dozen other people who'd care little enough about your immortal soul to help you.'

'I honestly thought you'd be pleased. You've always . . . and I suppose, to tell the truth, because you're from Chicago, too . . . I thought my Bishop . . . well, that you'd be the best person to convince him.'

'Then you were mistaken. I am not, as you put it, from Chicago. I'm not from anywhere. I was born in Czeckoslovakia and I was fifteen when the war started and my mother took us to America.' He fixed his pale eyes on the young man. 'She worked in a laundry and died, worn out with the struggle of trying to feed five boys, without ever managing to learn the language. I did manage, and at nineteen I came over here to study at the College and I've been here on and off ever since. I don't know your Bishop but I very much doubt whether we would have enough in common to understand each other. Even supposing that I wished to help you, which I don't.'

'You've often helped me before.'

'Not on the road to damnation.'

'How can you say that when you . . .'

'When I stayed on myself, when I am what I am? Precisely because of that. You're different. Besides which, I doubt if I've helped you much. I seem to remember once recommending that you dress, at least occasionally, as a priest, and look at you. That check shirt. You might be a football player.'

The younger man laughed. 'Well, I am a football player. I've played for the College. Besides, we all dress like this and I'm sure you did, too, in your days there.'

'When I was a student, in the days when Martin John O'Connor was Rector, things were very different. Ah well, I'm no paragon of sartorial elegance – What is it now, Sister?'

The little nun had tapped and entered, carrying a silver tray.

'A drop of something for your guest.' She set the tray on a small mahogany table between their two chairs. 'Will I light the other lamp?'

'Do.' He opened the bottle and sniffed the cork. 'Good . . . Now . . .' The Monsignor filled their glasses to the brim as the Sister closed the door silently behind her. 'Your very good health, John.'

'And yours.'

'Try the biscuits, one of Sister Agatha's specialities. I can't remember now whether they're left over from All Souls or a foretaste of Advent but they're excellent. Sister Agatha may be as waspish an Irishwoman as ever took the veil but she's an exceptionally good cook.'

'She doesn't seem waspish to me.'

'That's because you get special treatment. You've got a good Irish name. Hence the biscuits. The good Sister doesn't care for me.'

'You don't care for her. But then . . .'

'But then I don't care for women in general? One thing you've learned to do in two years here is to gossip. However, my antipathy to the opposite sex does not imply a predilection for my own, in case the gossips say so.'

'They don't.'

'Really. What do they say?'

'That your chief predilection is for food.'

'Perfectly correct. Hence my tolerance of the waspish Sister. You're being honest again, which I like. Have you ever been hungry?'

'Hungry . . .? Of course.'

'Of course, then you haven't. So that's a point on which we can't understand each other. Odd that the imagination functions only in the regions of the mind and heart. One can empathize with grief, for example, but not with a toothache. You might put on another log . . . not that one, it looks a little damp. That one, good. So what news of you people up on the Janiculum? What's happening at the College? You must always bring me news, you know I never go out.'

'But you hear everything, even so.'

'When kind people like you come and tell me things.'

'There's talk of a visit from His Holiness.'

'That I had heard, though not the reason why.'

'No reason, I think, except the usual courtesy visit each Pontiff pays us, though in this case perhaps precipitated by the Presidential visit to him.'

The Monsignor chuckled softly. 'And a fine mess you all got into over that.'

'It was hardly our fault. It's ridiculous our trying to organize these things if then the CIA moves in and reorganizes everything without even knowing their way around the Vatican. It's no wonder he ended up in the wrong building. It might have been even worse.'

'I don't see how. With His Holiness waiting like Patience on a monument, if ever anyone waited like Patience on a monument. And not a word of reproach from him afterwards, I gather.'

'No. But it'll be a long time before it's forgotten at the College.'

'True. Embarrassing moments have a way of staying vividly alive in the memory, much more so than great joys or tragedies. I remember when the new college was dedicated in '53, I was doing post-graduate work then, and a group of us heard a broadcast in English on Radio Prague – one of those propaganda news bulletins that always begin "The Capitalist forces of the West . . .' I imagine they still do them.'

'They do.'

'Well, this one began with "This so-called college" – I remember a lot of it word for word – "This so-called college has its counterparts in espionage centres in Western Germany and elsewhere. The same tasks – espionage, fraud and subversion – have been allotted to the American College in Rome." According to them, our purpose was to train "new heavyweight champions in the American cold war . . . to prepare, in exchange for American dollars, new agents of United States imperialism." Apparently "new Spellmans" were to be trained for the task.'

The old man chuckled, shifting himself a little to fish once more for his handkerchief. 'Well, I was young and no doubt a little stupid, and I was deeply embarrassed in front of my fellow students.'

'I don't see why.'

'And it wouldn't be easy to explain why, except that although an American citizen, in those days I still felt myself to be a Czech.'

'Even so, you could hardly have felt yourself to be part of a propagandist attitude like that.'

'No, no . . . But you see . . . the automatic response of my fellow students – I didn't feel myself to be a part of that either. So I was embarrassed. No doubt it's an embarrassment that all expatriates feel at one time or another.'

'Surely the Church unites us all.'

'Oh, surely, surely. But we all have our weaker moments, such as would make us ask a favour of a "fellow Chicagoan" rather than someone else.'

'I apologize. Doubly.' The young man accepted the rebuke humbly.

'Oh, you needn't apologize quite so solemnly. I've said I was young and a little stupid and we can allow you the same excuse. At least you have humility.'

'And so have you.'

'I need to have. It's my only virtue apart from a sense of humour. Now, cheer up a little and fill our glasses.'

'Espionage, fraud and subversion,' the young man laughed, taking up the bottle, 'I'd take it as a compliment. Any school ought to be proud of being branded as an anti-Communist centre because of its sound Americanism and sound Catholicism. It's a sort of tribute.'

The Monsignor stared at the soft red ash falling in the grate, contemplating this echo from the past.

'Go home, John,' he said at last, 'go home to Chicago and look after your flock, or your Bishop, whichever it is he wants.'

'My flock, I think. He wants to give me a parish soon. I've never had one.'

'Your flock, then. Play football with them. Listen to their troubles. Be the good priest you are. And now go away. I'm an old man with a cold and I'm going to bed.'

But when the young priest had gone he sat on by the fireside and took up his breviary again, his head nodding every so often. An hour or so later he roused himself sufficiently to look at his watch and heard the doorbell ringing in the distance. With some difficulty he heaved himself from the deep armchair and went out to meet his second visitor. Sister Agatha was crossing the hall with a tall, dark-suited man in her wake.

'You've another visitor, Monsignor.'

The good sister glowered disapprovingly through her

glasses, her thick eyebrows knit, as she handed over the visiting card that was closed inside a small envelope.

'Thank you, Sister Agatha, thank you.' He didn't remove the card to look at it but opened the door of a small study and stood back to allow the man to pass through.

'I apologize for arriving at this late hour but Florence Central feels the matter's urgent. I came straight here from the station.'

'Monsignor,' interrupted Sister Agatha, 'you'll see your visitor out? I must get back to St Mary's.'

'That's all right, Sister, I'll see him out. Good night.'

He closed the study door behind them.

When the Monsignor's visitor left it was midnight. Even then he didn't go to bed immediately but, feeling the need to breathe clean cold air, climbed the stairs to the roof, catching his breath as he inhaled the icy night wind.

'I suppose that this is where I belong,' he said quietly to himself, looking out over the carpet of glittering city lights beyond the pale, floodlit dome of St Peter's. 'Which isn't saying much. So does everyone in what we call the civilized world.'

The freezing wind was delicious on his feverish brow. Delicious but dangerous. Here he was, an old man with a cold out at midnight in November without even a coat. He turned back and started down the stairs. A foolish old man with a cold that would certainly be worse in the morning.

CHAPTER SIX

The glass doors of the Café Rivoire swung open to admit a group of noisy young men and a blast of cold morning air. Mastino looked the newcomers over rapidly and then took a turn about the room beneath the high glass globes of the chandeliers, affecting to look at the piles of little cakes and stacks of freshly cut sandwiches under a glass counter and the boxes of chocolates displayed on the walls. Having checked the rear entrance, he moved back to where Bardi was leaning on the green marble central counter engrossed in the newspaper and took up his habitual stance behind his chief. Poma stayed glued to Bardi's side, his brown eyes watchful. A waiter was rapidly rearranging tables for the big group, flapping and swirling the pale orange linen with rapid efficiency.

' "Government declines Deputy's resignation as inopportune," ' read Bardi aloud, flicking at the newspaper, 'So another scandal fizzes out.'

'Good morning, sir. The usual?' The stout barman in a bow tie presented himself to take their order.

'For me, yes. Boys?'

'Usual for me,' Mastino said without taking his eyes from the surrounding people.

'I'll have a hot chocolate,' Poma said.

Bardi raised an eyebrow at this unexpected pronouncement.

'I've given up coffee,' added Poma in explanation. Usually he drank five or six strong coffees a day. 'It's bad for my nerves.'

'First I've heard of your having any nerves,' said Bardi, amused.

'Me, too.' Poma looked uncomfortable.

In contrast to the rest of the customers who were making the most of the elegant surroundings by savouring their Saturday morning drinks and snacks at leisure Bardi and his two guards downed their drinks in one and made for the exit as though they were in a station bar and had a train to catch. With a movement that had become synchronized over the years the two guards reached the door a fraction of a second before their chief, swung it open, glanced over the piazza and let him through.

The grey stone flags of the Piazza della Signoria were still wet from the cleaning wagon, for the sun had not yet reached them. The loggia with its statuary and the façade of the medieval palace were also still in shadow but a watery sun lit the topmost crenellations of Arnolfo's tower. The three men crossed the square with rapid strides and cut through Via de' Gondi.

'Wait for me down here,' said Bardi as they approached the baroque façade of the Palace of Justice, 'I'll be going home within the hour.' And he took the steps two at a time.

In the gloom of the entrance hall a group of journalists stood gossiping and comparing notes. A few lone tourists wandered about, their cameras lighting up the scene with occasional flashes. Bardi strode through without looking at anyone except for a quick glance at a lawyer he knew well and who was explaining something to his client in a dark corner and supplementing his *sotto voce* instructions with discreet but insistent gesticulations.

'Excuse me . . . Excuse me, sir . . .' A small shabby man was trotting beside Bardi trying to get his attention by waving some sort of summons at him. 'They told me I had to be here at eleven but I don't know where to go . . . which room . . . Excuse me . . .'

'Ask the guard on the main door,' said Bardi without slowing or looking at him. He went to the lift and stabbed at the button. The doors opened instantly, as if in response, to reveal two pompous lawyers clutching their briefcases and both talking at once. They deflated slightly as they stepped out and saw Bardi, murmuring in unison, 'Good morning, sir' as they made way for him.

By the time he got out on his own floor and set off down the corridor, his mind was already working fast. Slamming the door of his office behind him, he threw off his raincoat and took the Acciai file from the glass-fronted cupboard. With a glance at his watch he mentally gave himself a quarter of an hour to prepare for his interview with Corbi and then sat down at his desk and began to read.

Procura of the Republic, Palermo.
Extracts from documentation of the Fietta case.
Transcript of calls intercepted on 73567 registered in the name of FIETTA, Antonio, during November 1986.

The above telephone number was subject to control by order of the Procura of the Republic, Palermo, because the above named Fietta, Antonio, was suspected of illicit trafficking in drugs. This trafficking was carried on under cover of normal agricultural commerce.
Extracts from relevant transcripts as follows:
20.11.86. Telephone call from a person addressed by the accused as Marchese, later identified as the Marchese Filippo Acciai. The latter made inquiries as to the arrival of a consignment of oranges for which he was waiting. The inquiry was repeated a number of times.
22.11.86. A further call was intercepted from the said Marchese Acciai during which the latter made complaints about the poor quality of the consignment of oranges received.
24.11.86. The Marchese asked for a discount on the price as yet to be paid for the consignment, claiming that he had been charged for the cost of the containers.
The above transaction would appear to be a cover for traffic in heroin. Complete texts of transcripts are attached.

Bardi looked through the transcripts. He rather wished he had the tapes themselves; perhaps that would have more effect on Corbi. Or perhaps not. What he needed was to search the castle and tap Acciai's telephone, but even that, now that Corbi must have warned his friend off, might turn out to be useless.

'In any case he can't make a move without . . .'

Without Corbi's consent on the opening of an official file. Well, they would see.

Bardi took up the file, locked his office and went off down the corridor.

Corbi, wreathed in pipe smoke, looked up and peered over his newspaper as Bardi knocked and walked in.

'Ah, Bardi, sit down, sit down . . . It looks as though we might have a fine day after all if it doesn't cloud over again.'

The big room with its wood panelled ceiling gave on to the noisy piazza and rays of pale sunshine were coming in through two tall windows.

'They've refused the resignation, did you see? A good thing, too. That sort of thing should be kept out of the papers in my opinion. All these scandals can only make people restless . . . never used to happen in my day . . .'

Bardi wondered what exactly he meant by 'my day'. The ostrich-like behaviour of his chief had once been a source of mild amusement to him but of late he had begun to find it irritating. He sat down and placed the file on the desk without comment.

'Now, you wanted to see me, of course, I hadn't forgotten . . .' Corbi folded his newspaper with exaggerated care and placed it neatly on top of a pile of folders. Nevertheless, his eye had caught the name on the file lying in front of Bardi and his face was already showing signs of embarrassment and annoyance.

'I seem to think you've already let me see that,' he began defensively, peering at the offending file through his thick glasses.

'The day it arrived,' said Bardi shortly, 'but no decision was reached as to what we should do about it.'

'Well now, if I remember rightly that was because we felt nothing concrete was indicated . . .'

'You felt so. I've since talked to the Drug Squad and it seems they have some suspicions of their own.'

Corbi had taken the file and was fiddling through it nervously.

'This is all a long time ago, of course, a good two years . . .'

'They were also able to tell me that Acciai's son was a known addict, though never caught pushing.'

'Yes, yes; I know all that, but by this time it's all water under the bridge.' He had taken up a pen and was twirling it round between his fingers as though tempted to cancel out the words he was staring at without reading them.

'Did you also know all about this same son being part of a Logistics Brigade along with Gori in 1976? Gori had plenty to tell me about him.'

Corbi hesitated. If he had intended to say he knew all about that, too, he thought better of it and only said: 'I don't think that's relevant here, is it?'

'For all I know, it's not.'

'Well, then . . .'

'Though it does seem to me relevant in the sense that the Goris of this world are expected to pay for their sins and the Acciais, apparently, not.'

'Acciai's son is in the United States, and has been for some time.'

'Very convenient for him since we could hardly extradite him. Acciai himself, on the other hand, is still here.'

'And you seriously expect me to open an official inquiry on the strength of a couple of telephone calls about oranges?'

'Unless you can convince me that the Marchese Acciai is a wholesale greengrocer, yes. We've opened inquiries for less.'

'Not when they concerned one of the oldest and most important families in Florence!'

'The Code of Penal Procedure makes no such distinction as far as I'm aware.'

'For God's sake, Bardi! There is a distinction and you know it, in common humanity. Start proceedings against an ordinary criminal and if they come to nothing he's hardly suffered anything more than minor inconvenience; do the same to a man in Acciai's position and you ruin him.'

'I agree with you that he's not an ordinary criminal but that's as far as I'll go.'

'Bardi, this anarchistic stance of yours might stand you in good stead with the press but it seems to me you're taking it too far. I cannot see what reason you have for persecuting Filippo. What in heaven's name do you have against him?'

'A couple of telephone calls about oranges, if you remember. I'm not persecuting him, and as to what I've got against him – if you mean on a personal level – nothing whatsoever. He's a very charming man and I'm not unimpressed by his being a friend of yours. But I'm not unimpressed either by the fact that since I've had this file on my hands he has been good enough to want to be a friend of mine, too. And to give me the opportunity of meeting some of his many other influential friends. If I could be said to have anything personal against him at all, which I don't admit, it would perhaps be the change he's brought about in me.'

'I don't follow you.'

'Then I'll explain. I've never considered myself to be a superstitious person but I must confess myself shaken by the coincidence that on each of the two last occasions that I've come into contact with Acciai I've come within an inch of losing my life.'

'Of . . .? You're surely not referring to that scratch on your cheek? That sort of thing happens every day during the hunting season! That's ridiculous! You can't be serious.'

'Of course not. It's ridiculous, as you say. And as to the previous incident after your daughter's wedding where Acciai was so anxious to make me stay the expected amount of time, well, it's not the first time such an attempt has been made on me and I don't suppose it will be the last. It can only be coincidence. But I'm growing quite superstitious. I'm in danger of believing that Acciai has the evil eye, a thing I wouldn't have thought possible before you were kind enough to introduce me to him.'

'Well, really, I've never heard anything so far-fetched! What reason could Acciai have?'

'What reason could he have for suddenly wanting to be a friend of mine? Well, if you'll authorize the opening of the official inquiry we can bring him in for questioning and clear the whole thing up.'

'We'll do no such thing! Listen, Bardi, I'll go so far as to take your point about his seeking you out. But, for heaven's sake, if he feels threatened he has every right to defend himself as best he can. But as to his trying to remove you from the scene altogether, that's utterly absurd and you know it . . .'

Corbi's pipe had gone out but he kept it between his teeth with no attempt to re-light it.

'Quite apart from his being quite incapable of such a thing, there's nothing in this business, even supposing there's any truth in it, that could possibly make it worthwhile.'

'You think not? His friends in Palermo who were so fond of sending him oranges got quite a stiff sentence between them.'

'That's beside the point. Acciai wasn't . . .'

'Wasn't in that deep? I think you're probably right. I suspect, and the Drug Squad people likewise suspect, that the Castello Acciai was a stopping-off place, a sort of warehouse, if you like, and that Acciai didn't soil his hands with the stuff to any great extent. Nevertheless, they must have paid him handsomely for such an elegant and eminently safe warehouse. So safe, indeed, that even with the entire Palermo gang in prison and written evidence in our hands we made no move against him. You realize that there had to be a Florentine end to the set-up, Acciai apart, and that the Palermo authorities expect us to do something about rounding them up on the basis of this report?'

'Then they expect too much. Acciai has nothing to do with these people.'

It was a flat and confident statement. Bardi accepted it.

'I've no doubt you're right. But can we say with equal conviction that he has *had* nothing to do with them?'

'I can only repeat what I've already said. I don't consider that there are sufficient indications to warrant our trying to make a case against Acciai.'

'And I'm to communicate this to the authorities in Palermo?'

'Certainly, certainly, if you see fit. I fail to see what else you can do.'

'I can inform the Drug Squad that you feel further evidence is required before being willing to open an inquiry. No doubt they'll come up with some sooner or later. I can also send a judicial communication to Acciai to that effect.'

Corbi slowly removed his pipe and stared at Bardi. His round face which had been flushed with annoyance was now pale.

'Bardi, I must ask you not to do that.'

'I'm sorry. If you won't or can't take any action, then I can only, as you say, proceed as I think fit.'

'Lapo . . .' It was the first time he had ever used Bardi's Christian name. It sounded odd and very out of place. Bardi found it both annoying and embarrassing.

'I've said I'm sorry. I appreciate your feeling for your friend and I do realize that there is real friendship involved, that it's not the way it was when he tried to become friendly with me.'

He had meant that to be an honest statement but though he had intended no irony he saw from his chief's face that some irony had been understood. Then he realized that he had been lightly touching the scar on his cheek as he spoke. He withdrew his hand and held it out for the file.

'We had better talk this over . . .' Corbi kept his plump

fist on the file. The beams of pale sunlight from the windows vanished and reappeared. There was nothing more that Bardi could say, either to force matters or to ease them. His gaze followed the sunbeam to the photographs on Corbi's desk. One of them was of the recent wedding.

'We seem to have talked it over already,' he said, 'and to very little effect.'

'All I'm asking is that you take no hasty action.'

'Hasty? We've had this communication from Palermo for almost three months now.'

'Then a few more days can hardly make any difference.'

Except that it would give him time to talk to Acciai again.

'Perhaps your friend is thinking of following his son.'

'His son . . . Listen, Bardi, Acciai's son –'

'Is comfortably settled in an American college. He told me. I can't prevent your talking to Acciai about this and I can't prevent his leaving the country as long as you withold your signature but that judicial communication goes off first thing on Monday morning. He may leave but he'll leave with the knowledge that he has failed to intimidate me. For a man like that, self-imposed exile will be worse than anything I could do to him.'

'You're making a mistake, Bardi. You've got this all wrong.

'Only an official inquiry would prove that, so I shall probably never know whether I've got it wrong or not.'

'I hope that's true.'

'By which you mean?'

'Nothing. We'll see. One thing I can promise you, however. Acciai won't leave.'

'As you say, we'll see.' And he retrieved the file from under Corbi's fist.

All the way home Bardi was silent in the back of the car and the two guards, always sensitive to his prevailing mood, carried on their usual exchanges in an undertone.

'There's no doubt, then?'

'The doctor confirmed it yesterday and she started in on me last night in a big way.'

'Take no notice, it's bound to wear off.'

'Anybody can tell you're not married.'

'Got more sense. Look at the state you're in – at least try and keep both hands on the wheel, if you keep yanking at your famous moustache like that it'll come off. Mind you, I always suspected it was false.'

'Fuck off, Mastino.'

Bardi, aware only of the comforting familiarity of their voices, heard nothing of what they said. When he got out in front of the big wrought-iron gates of his house he hardly answered when Mastino called after him: 'Usual time Monday, sir?'

He hung up his raincoat in the hall and went to see if there were any messages by the telephone. There was nothing.

'Lapo?' Laura's voice came from the dining-room. He hadn't noticed her as he passed the open doorway though he had automatically glanced in at his father's portrait as was his habit. He turned back and went in.

'I'll be here for lunch.'

'You will . . .? I wasn't expecting you.'

There were porcelain plates stacked on the big dining table. The room smelt strongly of furniture polish. Laura held a duster in her hand and her hair was tied up in a brightly coloured cotton scarf which for some reason reminded him of when they used to go to the seaside together in August years ago. A reminder of burning sand and the smell of suntan lotion, and of the days when he'd been able to leave the city for a month's holiday like most of his colleagues still did. Nowadays, Laura went without him and he joined her occasionally for a weekend.

'Is something the matter?' She didn't go on with her work. She looked as if she were faintly embarrassed and waiting for him to leave the room. He realized at once why.

'Why are you doing that, where's the girl?'

'She's off sick.'

'Again?'

'It doesn't happen as often as all that and besides it's not her fault.'

'No, but it's your fault that you employ her when she isn't fit to do the job.'

'She works very well.' She turned away from him and began stacking more plates. 'And I get on with her, she's company for me. Do you want to eat now? It's early.'

'In half an hour. I'm going to have a shower.'

The dining-room was still in disorder so they ate at the white marble table in the kitchen with the television news on. They spoke very little and then only of what they were eating or what they were watching. For Bardi it was soothing and familiar and his ill-temper with Corbi began to cool off. The news was followed by a special report on the ski championships.

'Lapo . . .'

'Mm.'

'This case you've got in court . . .'

'What about it?' He frowned, still watching the skiing. Laura never tried to talk to him about his work and he preferred it that way.

'I was wondering if, when it was finished, we could get away, at least for a long weekend.'

'Away? Where to?'

'I don't know . . . anywhere. To the mountains.' One of the skiers had taken a spectacular spill and a rescue helicopter was flying over the heads of the multi-coloured crowd strung up the mountainside.

'I can't leave Florence at the moment.'

'I didn't mean immediately, I said when the trial is over.'

'I can't leave Florence. You go, by all means, if you need a break . . .'

The incident was over and the next competitor was adjusting his goggles at the top of the run.

'You're not still annoyed about the girl?'

He shrugged, his eyes following the swerving figure, 'It's really your concern.'

'She'll be back tomorrow.'

'Well, it's something, I suppose, that she only ever seems to get sick for a day at a time. The Austrian's going to win, by the look of it.'

'Do you want coffee?'

'Please.'

She brought it to the table.

'By the way, Colonel Tempesta telephoned this morning.'

'What?' Bardi jumped to his feet and switched off the television. 'What time did he call? Why was there no message on the pad?'

'There was no need. I suppose it was about eleven . . .'

'I'll try and get him at home –'

'But there's no need. He only wanted to speak to me to say they want us to go to supper on Friday.'

Bardi had been making for the door. He stopped.

'That was all? He didn't want me to call him back?'

'No. He said he'd already mentioned it to you.'

'He had.' So this was Tempesta's answer. An invitation to supper. If he'd thrown Bardi out on the spot that day the refusal to cooperate couldn't have been clearer. His silence and then this. Before he could turn to leave, the suspicion, the certainty, of something worse took hold of him.

'It wasn't, by any chance, Tempesta who put the idea into your head about going away?'

'We did talk about it . . . I was saying I thought you were over-tired.'

'Then you were mistaken, I've never been fitter. And I'll thank you not to discuss me with my colleagues!'

'But surely he's a friend –'

'A colleague! And one who's not above using my wife to get me conveniently out of the way! If he tries telephoning you again you refer him to me, is that understood?'

'No it isn't! What's going on? They just want us to go to supper –'

'We're not going to any supper.'

'But I've accepted, at least provisionally –'

'So now you can refuse, definitively. If you need an excuse you can tell him I'm leaving for Rome.'

'Rome? But . . . is it true?'

'I've no idea. It might be. I have to go down and interrogate Li Causi and you can tell him that. You can also tell him that in no circumstances will I be leaving for any holiday!'

Upstairs he slammed the study door behind him and began pacing the room in an attempt to calm himself sufficiently to start thinking. He had half expected it anyway, but the invitation added insult to injury, not to mention the feeble attempt at getting him away.

He continued striding to and fro for a few minutes and then paused as he reached the window, fishing for a cigarette. Could it be he was exaggerating? It could hardly do Tempesta any good to have him out of the way for a matter of days. He stared out at the dark leaves of the magnolia tree. Corbi, too, had tried to gain a few days' grace, but why should Tempesta be playing for time?

'For the same reason.' Bardi spoke the answer to his question softly. If Tempesta wouldn't cooperate he had a good reason, a much stronger reason than his claim that it was all a wild goose chase, because in that case he would have had nothing to lose by it. So, there was indeed a priest involved in the Rota case but whoever he was and however involved he had been with the Red Brigades, he had enough friends in the right places to save his neck and cover up for him. Another Acciai. What was it Corbi had said about the latest scandal? 'In my opinion that sort of thing shouldn't get into the papers, it can only unsettle people.' No doubt Tempesta and his friends were of the same opinion. A priest on the side of the Red Brigades wouldn't look at all well in the papers. Well, they would see. Tempesta and Corbi both. He went over to his desk and sat down. The photocopies of

Li Causi's diary with the elusive number lay before him. He had the rest of Saturday and all of Sunday. They would see.

Three minutes into the second half now and still no score. All the initiative coming from the Florentine side but nevertheless it's going to take more than a nil-nil draw at home to keep them in the First Division. Back to the studio for the latest from Turin . . .

Bardi reached a hand out to the dashboard to turn the radio off but was unable to find the switch, which confirmed his suspicion that the car wasn't his. The insistent yammering of the commentary irritated and tired him and he risked taking his eyes off the road for a few seconds in the hope of locating the radio but found it so difficult to focus his eyes that it might as well have been pitch dark, though he was aware of a rectangle of pale light to his right. There was nothing for it but to leave the radio on and tolerate the noise. He had enough to cope with already. Twice the engine had died for no apparent reason and that wasn't the worst of it. What was much worse was that a lot of the time the car raced along as though he had his foot down to the floor and it was becoming increasingly difficult to control it. The road to the castle was not the sort of road you could race along in comfort, quite apart from the danger of taking the bends too quickly. Thank God that at least the steering was efficient. Even so, his inability to slow the car down was causing him to sweat so much that the wheel kept slipping through his ever-tightening grip.

Passakella to Massaro . . . to Pecci. Back to Massaro, Massaro going well in this first game since his injury . . .

Surely he should have been there by now? But the castle was nowhere in sight and he didn't recognize the landscape around him. If only he could slow down! But the car went racing on and he didn't dare stop altogether in case the engine gave out again. The road went on and on, the landscape shifting and changing, his wet hands straining to get a grip on the wheel. Then, quite unexpectedly he found himself climbing the cypress-lined drive he'd been trying to find for what seemed like hours. But at the top of the hill there was nothing. The countryside rolled down before him to the valley on the other side. The castle was no longer there.

'Haven't you heard?' said a small voice, and he turned to see Acciai seated beside him, smiling, 'He's gone to America.'

'Then this is your car . . .'

And it's in the net! The goalkeeper hadn't a chance. One-nil and seven minutes into the second half . . .

Bardi opened his eyes. The rectangle of pale light was the study window on his right. That was all he understood immediately. It was some moments before he managed to work out why he should be lying on his bed fully clothed or even what day it was. The clock on the bedside table showed almost half past four. He must have fallen asleep while listening to the news bulletin after Sunday lunch, a thing he rarely did because he always woke badly feeling disorientated. What surprised him most was that he had slept so long. He had no real reason for feeling especially tired, yet the dream he had just had was one of many, most of them involving attempts to do simple everyday tasks that became fraught with unsurmountable difficulties, a sure sign of exhaustion. He often had dreams like that towards the end of some particularly difficult court case or when he had been working for too long without a holiday. If it wasn't exhaustion now it must be plain frustration. Thanks to Corbi. He had always known his chief to be pusillanimous as regards keeping out of trouble with those in power, but even so, he had believed him to be basically honest. This Acciai business was something else again.

Oblivious of the radio still giving out its low volume commentary, Bardi got up and went over to the window. The sky was colourless, the big leaves of the magnolia tree dark and still. He felt tired and jaded. Not only was Corbi frustrating him, there was Tempesta, too.

He sat down at his desk and regarded the slip of paper that lay there, his irritation rising. That morning, in his impatience, he had made an attempt at deciphering the number from Li Causi's diary himself but with no results. He knew a few of the basic tricks but to try all the permutations would take him days. He had neither the skill nor the time. He lit a half-cigarette and almost immediately put it out again. His mouth was furred and unpleasant-tasting after his sleep. Unable to decide whether he could be bothered making himself a coffee, he eventually got up and poured himself a small cognac, drinking it off in one draught to clean his mouth. There was little point in going on with his futile efforts at deciphering. He lay down on the bed again and began flicking through a weekly news magazine. The noise of the radio remained a vague irritation like a fly buzzing in the room, not making itself felt sufficiently to provoke action. The rest of the big house was silent so Laura had presumably gone out somewhere, unless she, too, was sleeping.

A header very neatly stopped on the line there . . .

Gaudy-coloured photographs of the famous and the powerful stared back at him as he listlessly turned the shiny pages and glanced at the headlines. A Summit meeting. A cabinet minister decides not to resign. Civil war in India. The law computerized.

Bardi sat up and switched off the radio.

'The Law Computerized: Giorgio Galli, the Florentine lawyer with a passion for electronics has revolutionized his work by computerizing a major part of it. Interviewed in the office he shares with his brother, Galli explained: "It's not just a question of simplifying routine office tasks. Our computer is programmed to do all the research necessary for any given case, saving us many hours of work." Galli built the computer himself as well as designing the software for which he has taken out a patent.'

Giorgio! Bardi flung the magazine aside and got up. He took his address book from the pocket of his jacket which hung behind the door, found the number he wanted and sat down on the bed by the telephone to dial.

'I want to speak to Giorgio Galli.'

'Speaking.'

'Giorgio, it's Lapo Bardi.'

'Lapo! How are you? Haven't seen you for years – except in the paper, of course.'

'That's where I've just seen you – or rather, in a magazine.'

'Oh, you saw it? What did you think of the photograph? My brother says I look like an owl!'

'You always do look like an owl. Listen, there's a small favour I want to ask you.'

'Ask away.'

'Not on the telephone, I have to talk to you. Are you doing anything now?'

'Watching the match. Why? Do you want me to come round to you?'

'No . . . no. I'll come to you if that's all right. Are you alone?'

'All alone. Why the mystery?'

'I'd just rather no one knew about my visit. For one thing I'm coming in my own car without an escort which I oughtn't to do.'

'Is that wise?'

'No, but it's necessary. Expect me in a few minutes.'

CHAPTER SEVEN

The grey Sunday streets were quiet. The few bars which were open were packed with men grouped around the television for the match in a fog of cigarette smoke. Bardi skirted the city, taking the wide avenues that surrounded it, and took the road that led up to Michelangelo's fort. The Via San Leonardo where Galli lived ran just below the fort, a narrow, winding street with the city wall running along one side and stuccoed villas with walled gardens on the other. Giorgio's garden was somewhat neglected except for the fruit trees and olives which a neighbouring peasant farmer came and pruned every year. A persimmon tree overhung the wall near the iron gates, dropping its squashy, brilliant orange fruit into the leafy road. A dog began barking when Bardi pulled at the old-fashioned bell. The gate clicked open. Giorgio was waiting at the front door, peering short-sightedly through his owlish spectacles, the fingers of one hand burrowing in his reddish beard.

'I should have asked you on the phone,' Bardi said as they shook hands and went in. 'Have you got a computer here?'

'There's a terminal for the one in the office for when I want to work at home. But I've got two word processors here as well if that's all you need.'

'I've no idea what I need. You know I don't understand these things.'

'Well, come and sit down and tell me all. Excuse the mess, I had a few friends in last night and the cleaner doesn't come until Monday . . .'

There were glasses and half-empty bottles parked on every surface in the big, comfortable sitting-room that gave on to the garden. The television was still on with the sound turned down.

'Make yourself at home. What can I give you? A whisky?'

'I'd better not, thanks.'

'Don't tell me you've given up drinking! Last time I saw you you were giving up smoking.'

Bardi had already taken out his cigarette case. 'All right, then, but a small one.'

Galli poured him a large one and the same for himself.

'Right.' He settled down in an armchair opposite Bardi. 'Tell me all.'

'I can't do that. But what I do tell you must remain between these four walls.'

'You're not in some trouble?'

'No, no trouble. I just need your help with something I'm working on and it's classified information. The less I tell you the better.'

'Tell me what you think fit, then. If you really think I can help . . .'

'I'm sure you can.' Bardi took the slip of paper with the number on it and passed it to Galli.

'What is it?'

'That's what I want to find out. I suspect it's a telephone number in code. I've had a go at deciphering it and so have . . . other people but with no results.'

'Hmm . . . .' Galli got up with the paper in his hand and paced about the room staring at it, fingering his beard agitatedly as always. 'Do you mind a bit of music?' He switched on a large and complicated stereo set and the silent football match was accompanied by Bach. Having two gadgets switched on appeared to soothe him, though he continued to pace about the room as he talked. 'Hm. Hm. Well, there are plenty of ways of codifying a number, some of them extremely simple, others more complicated. The simplest way is to multiply or divide by a given number, or to add or subtract a given number to or from each figure of the original. That way you only have to memorize one number and in most cases you could decodify the thing in your head and avoid the danger of leaving any incriminating calculations lying about. Multiply each figure by five, for example and you keep the resulting number in your notebook or whatever and you only need remember the figure five. Of course, if you multiply by a much bigger number, a four figure number, for instance, then you'd need a pocket calculator to decodify. That would mean carrying it with you permanently in case you needed it.'

'Then we can probably exclude that. This person didn't have a calculator on him or in his home. In any case even I know that method so I'm sure that when checks were run on the number those possibilities were exhausted.'

'We'll leave that for the moment then – another drop?'

'Not for me, thanks.'

'Right. Now, another way – simple enough again, is to insert a sequence of numbers alternating with those of the number you want to disguise. Taking shall we say a rising series of numbers: one, three, six, ten . . . do you follow me?'

'No.'

'Starting with one I add two, then to the resulting number I add three, then I add four and so on. With me?'

'I think so.'

'Right, those numbers I insert between the figures of the number I want to disguise. If we take my phone number, 52174, and codify it in this way it would become 5123167104. I could make it even longer, of course – or, I could insert that same series of numbers or even the same number each time after the first digit, the third, the sixth, the tenth, etcetera. Mind you, if I were to choose, I'd choose multiplying by a hefty number and use a pocket calculator, much safer because anyone not having the code would be faced with an endless number of permutations to check and no way of knowing which was correct. Still, if you say your man doesn't use a calculator.'

'Not only that, he's not a mathematical genius like you. I

doubt if he'd be any better informed than me. It's just not his field – and in any case I'm sure all the obvious methods have been checked.'

'In that case there's not much I can do. If you were to give me more information – if your man's not likely to have used a mathematical key, for instance, knowing something about him I might be able to hit on the key by guesswork.'

'No . . . Giorgio, the less I tell you the better.'

'Well, that's up to you to decide, but given that you've already run the risk of coming here . . .' He went to turn the record over, crouching to make adjustments of half a millimetre to the battery of knobs and buttons. 'How do you manage to get rid of your escort, anyway? It can't be easy.'

'It's perfectly easy. They have to have time off, like today. If I need to go out I'm supposed to call the Questura for a police escort.'

'And you don't.'

'Not if I can help it, and certainly not today. When I talk about running risks it's you I'm thinking of. There's no way I can avoid running risks but I've no right to ask you to run them.'

'You could let me decide that. I admit I'm curious, but apart from that I'd be glad to help you if I could – and the way I look at it, either nobody knows you're here, in which case it can't make any difference what you tell me, or else somebody does know you're here – or will find out – and will assume the worst, that you might have told me.'

'You're right. I suppose I'm kidding myself, trying to avoid having a guilty conscience. I had no business coming here at all.

'But you *are* here.' Giorgio scratched happily at his beard. 'So let's hear it. Wait – I'll pour us another whisky, and don't say "not for me". You ought to relax now and then, you're a candidate for a stomach ulcer, if anyone is – they've scored!' He turned up the volume of the television for a few seconds and then turned it down again. 'Have to leave it on, I'm recording it. I usually have a few friends round on Sunday evenings and we watch the match over a drink. I'll just put a cassette on instead of this record, then I won't have to interrupt you . . .'

When he eventually settled in his armchair again, Bardi repeated, 'I've told you this is classified . . .'

'That's understood. Professional secrecy's nothing new to me, Lapo.'

'Of course not. Otherwise I wouldn't . . . All right. That number was found in the diary of a terrorist.'

'The one they've just arrested? Li Causi?'

Bardi took a sip of his whisky before answering, 'Li Causi, yes.'

'I see. One of the big boys. Well, if that's all that's worrying you –'

'It's not, but never mind that. The number wasn't found on him when he was arrested. I found it years ago when I first got on to Li Causi but there wasn't any evidence to arrest him then. That was when an attempt was made to decipher the number in the usual ways – and, of course, he was questioned about it – but with no results.'

'Hm. Isn't he some sort of professor?'

'He was before he went underground. He lectured in sociology at the University here. He's supposed to have been one of the best young men they've ever had. He would have had a brilliant academic career.'

'I see. Instead of which he became a terrorist.'

'As far as we have been able to reconstruct his life, he was already deeply involved in terrorism when he was a student at Trento. He became the classic mole, infiltrating the academic world, recruiting promising students, etcetera. It was in 1982 that his name was first brought to our notice. Both the Digos and the Military Secret Service received signals – I can't tell you where from because I don't know myself. I issued a search warrant and then had Li Causi brought in for questioning.'

'1982. That's six years ago – will he talk, do you think, now he's been arrested?'

'No.'

'So what are you after with this number business?'

'That I can't tell you. I can only say it may turn out to be important. We'll get nothing out of Li Causi now just as we got nothing out of him six years ago. But six years ago I was convinced that this number could lead somewhere and I still am.'

'If you say so. But you haven't given me anything that suggests a key for deciphering it. Tell me more about him, family, hobbies and so on.'

'He was born in Naples. Middle-class family – I think his father worked in the Curia. Li Causi himself is well known for his book on the social structure of the Kibbutz. He lived for quite some time in Israel, which is probably what gave rise to rumours of his having been trained in the use of arms and so on over there, but I doubt it myself. He knows Hebrew – in fact when I found that number I also found a Hebrew word which I questioned him about.'

'What sort of word?'

'If I remember rightly it was the name of a coin or some such. He said it was a note for one of his students, but the number, which was near it, he couldn't or wouldn't explain. The obvious explanation would have been that it was the telephone number of the student concerned but he said it wasn't and I assume that's true. If he'd claimed untruthfully that it was we'd have checked, naturally. He was clever enough not to invent anything, just said he couldn't remember.'

'You mean the Hebrew word was right next to the number?'

'On the same line, yes, if not right next to it.'

'Right. Think back. When the number was sent for decodification was the diary itself sent, or a photocopy at least, or just the number?'

'I don't know.'

'You don't know? But you could find out, I imagine?'

'I could . . .'

'You could but you'd rather not, is that it?'

'More or less.'

The two looked at each other in silence for a moment. Bardi offered no further explanation and it was Giorgio in the end who spoke quietly.

'You're working on your own, Lapo, is that it?'

'Something like that.'

'That's what's bothering you. Not the terrorist side, your own side. Trouble?'

'There could be. If you want, we can stop this conversation now and I'll leave.'

Outside the evening was growing dark. The only light in the big room came from the television screen. Giorgio got up and paced about the room for a while, then paused, staring absently at the coloured figures running on a bright green field.

'You're crazy, Lapo.'

'I've said I'll leave if you want me to.'

'I said you're crazy. That's just my opinion, take it or leave it. For ten years you've been everybody's blue-eyed boy. You're one of the best-known magistrates in the country if not *the* best-known. You're never out of the papers. But don't let it go to your head. This is something different. You could be eaten alive.'

Bardi got to his feet.

'I'll leave you to your football.'

'What was the word?'

'The word?'

'The Hebrew word. What was it?'

'Shequel. But if you don't –'

'Sit down.' Giorgio turned. His eyes behind the owlish spectacles were gleaming. 'Sit down – or pour yourself another drink. I'm going to get the encyclopedia.'

Bardi sat down.

When Giorgio returned he already had the volume open at the right page. He switched on a reading lamp.

'This will probably give us all we need, but if not we can

continue our researches elsewhere.' He pushed his glasses further up with one finger and began to read. *'Shequel: Ancient unit of weight used in the Babylonian sexagesimal system and diffused throughout civilizations which came under the influence of that of Babylon, in particular that of the Hebrews, hence its frequent mention in the Old Testament* – of course, the Book of Numbers! We'll need a Bible – I think we're there, I'll go on: *The Babylonian shequel had two different values, the heavier being 16.83 grams, the lighter 8.41 grams, but these values varied at different times and in different places* – well, that gives us two numbers to check out for a start. But there's more, listen to this: *The variation was partly the result of the fact that the silver shequel soon became the unit of value used in trading and it became convenient to establish its value in relation to the gold shequel. Half a silver shequel was the annual contribution exacted from each Israelite for the upkeep of the sanctuary at Jerusalem.'*

Bardi stubbed out a cigarette nervously. 'I can't see what you're getting at.'

'Nor can I yet, but we'll get there all right, don't worry. Pass me that pocket calculator from the table beside you. We'll check each possibility as we come to it. Right. No, wait, I'll give you pen and paper and you can take down the numbers as I give you them . . . Here, use the back of this and we can burn it afterwards. Now, we'll start with the two weights we've been given, removing the decimal points, of course.' He dabbed at the calculator: '64021230, that's your number, and we'll start by dividing by 1683. Start writing. We get 38039.946. That's not it – we could cancel the numbers after the decimal point but then it's short for a phone number. In any case I think we'll get an exact answer when we hit the right code. Write down 38039, anyway, for the moment.'

Bardi wrote while Giorgio tried the second number.

'This one comes out as 76125.124. Same problem, but make a note of 76125 and we'll see.'

'Look, Giorgio,' Bardi interrupted. 'Not that I haven't

faith in you, but this all sounds a bit far-fetched. Don't you think –'

'Talking of faith, we'll need a Bible. I'll be right back.'

Bardi sighed and lit himself another half-cigarette. There was no stopping Giorgio now, and at least he had the illusion of trying to do something concrete instead of wearing out his nerves and the carpet in his own study.

'Here we are! Not a fancy edition but it will serve. Book of Numbers is where we start, if I'm not mistaken. What do you think?'

'I suppose so. What can I say? I've really no idea.'

But Giorgio was not to be quashed. 'Book of Numbers it is, then.' He flipped rapidly through the first pages of the Bible and found what he wanted. 'There are endless possibilities here. Listen to an example picked at random: "Clan and household that came down from Reuben, Israel's first-born, could muster warriors of twenty years and more, forty-six thousand five hundred. Of Simeon, fifty-nine thousand and three hundred, of Gad –" '

'But aren't we looking for a reference to shequels?'

'Of course, of course, I'm just showing you that we've got plenty of numbers to play with here. Don't lose your patience. I'm going to have to read the whole thing through to find what we want. I hope you're not in a hurry?'

'No, no. That is, if you really think it's worth –'

'Right. Amuse yourself as best you can.' He pulled a squashed newspaper out from under himself and tossed it over. Then he buried his beard deep in the book and was silent except for the occasional grunt, whether of satisfaction or not Bardi was unable to judge.

Three-quarters of an hour passed. Bardi had glanced through the paper without much interest, watched the end of the match, watched Giorgio, taken up the paper again.

VIOLENT CONFRONTATION BETWEEN POLICE AND ECOLOGISTS. THREE DEAD. Three people died and ten others were injured in yesterday's clash between riot police and demonstrating ecologists attempting to prevent the construction of a new nuclear power station, the eighth of its kind, near Reggio Calabria. A spokesman for the protesting ecologists claimed that their group had been infiltrated by armed politically motivated elements who had begun firing as soon as the police closed in, probably in an attempt to discredit the movement. Whether this is true or not, the result was a battle between police and demonstrators in which two young men died instantly and a third on the way to hospital. All three were civilians. Seven other civilians were wounded and three riot policemen. The condition of one of the latter is reported as being grave. A police spokesman claimed that every effort had been made to –

'Lapo.'

'Have you read this? Ecologists demonstrating –'

'Lapo, listen! I've found what we're looking for.'

Bardi raised a sceptical eyebrow.

'Put that paper down and listen to this. I'll read you the chapter that concerns us. Follow me carefully, it's complicated:

And now the Lord said to Moses, count up all the male first-born in Israel who are more than a month old, and find their number. I must have a Levite for every male in Israel; it is the Lord's due. And they must have cattle to match in number all the first-born cattle the Israelites possess. So Moses counted the first-born of Israel as the Lord bade him, and found that there were twenty-two thousand two hundred and seventy-three such persons. And the Lord said to Moses, Set apart the Levites to be my own, instead of the first-born Israelites, and the cattle of the Levites to be mine, instead of the first-born cattle; it is the Lord's due. Meanwhile, here are two hundred and seventy-three first-born who have no Levites to match their number; for these, ransom must be paid. Claim five silver pieces, by sanctuary reckoning, for each of them, (the silver piece is worth twenty pence), and pay the money to Aaron and his sons, as the ransom for the first-born who are left over. So Moses took ransom for those who were left out of the count when the Levites stood as ransom for the first-born sons of Israel, a thousand three hundred and sixty five silver pieces by sanctuary reckoning; and these he paid over to Aaron and his sons as the Lord had bidden him.

Giorgio sat back contentedly, the Bible open in his lap.

'Well?' asked Bardi, 'what does it tell us? All this stuff about Levites?'

'Not the Levites, the silver pieces, the shequels, the key we're looking for. The number you've got is a certain number of shequels, that's what was written in the diary, right?'

'All right, but where do we go from there?'

'That depends. We have to experiment with the possibilities we've got. It's my guess that whoever sent that number of yours to be decoded made the same mistake you made, they sent the number only, otherwise, with the bit of research that I've just done your people would have had no problem. Now then, pencil and paper: there are twenty pence to a shequel but we can eliminate the idea of multiplying your shequels by twenty because we want the number to be smaller than the one we start with – that's if it's a telephone number as you think. That leaves us with dividing the number of shequels by five because the ransom given was five shequels per head, or in some way using the number 1365, the amount of ransom.'

He took up the calculator again and paused for a moment.

'I'm not going to ignore the twenty, I'm going to divide instead of multiply.'

'Why?'

'Because you said there was a space between the word and the number.'

'So?'

'So it might be a number that has to become shequels, a number of Levites to be ransomed, that is multiplied by five – or in this case a number of pence to become shequels, that is to be divided by twenty. Here we go . . . Hm . . . no. 3201061.5. We don't want a decimal point and even if we ignore it that's too long to be a telephone number. I'll divide by five . . . 12804246.'

'There are no telephone numbers beginning with 1,' said Bardi, having written it down. 'In any case you said before you'd have to multiply by five.'

'If I took your number as Levites to be ransomed, yes, but I won't because your number's already too long. I want to divide to get something the right length for a phone number so I'm working from shequels to Levites instead of Levites to shequels.'

'You're making my head spin.'

'Don't worry about it – in any case, it's no go as you pointed out, because it begins with a 1. Right: 64021230 divided by 1365 . . .'

'We could try applying Pythagoras . . .'

'Just write down what I tell you . . . 46902. That's taking the code number as being the amount of shequels actually paid as ransom according to this chapter. And there you are. You've got a telephone number. A possible one, anyway. But you don't know in what city unless we assume it's Florence.'

'Maybe it begins with R . . .'

'Why R?'

'It was listed under R, that's all. In fact the initial R preceded the word shequel. Li Causi claimed the note was for a student called Roberto . . .'

'Now he tells me. Blood out of a stone. Well, there you are. Probably Rome but you'd better try all the other cities beginning with R.' Giorgio closed the Bible on his knee. 'Well? I don't suppose my telephone's tapped if you want to make a start right away.'

'No, no. No, I'll go home . . .' He folded the sheet of

paper he had been writing on and tucked it in his inside pocket. 'I'll go home . . .'

'Have one for the road, then.'

But Bardi was already making for the door.

Only when he found himself trapped in a solid mass of football traffic did he remember that he hadn't said a word of thanks to Giorgio. He didn't remember, even then, that he hadn't said goodbye to him either.

The next morning was as grey and motionless as the previous day had been and Bardi awoke at six after having half woken at four-thirty, five and five-thirty, his brain still churning as it had been when he had finally given up telephoning and gone to bed supperless. There had only been three possible numbers to try: 38039, 76125 and the more probable 46902. But there had turned out to be four hundred and one area codes beginning with the letter R. He'd tried Rome first, as being the most likely, but the first had been an electricity station, the second a restaurant with a riot of noise in the background and a very harassed waiter on the other end of the line. The third number hadn't answered at all and he had started on the other area codes. When he gave up and went to bed it wasn't out of tiredness. He had simply lost all his enthusiasm, which had probably been exaggerated in the first place. What point was there in calling over a thousand numbers? He could write down the name of the subscriber – at least when it didn't turn out to be an electricity station – but what then? Well, it was too early to start again now. He got up, showered, and prepared some milky coffee and biscuits to settle his neglected stomach. At ten he had to be in court and a stack of notes lay waiting for him on his desk.

It took him about three-quarters of an hour to really begin concentrating. After that, habit took over and it was past nine o'clock when he looked up from his work and began to think, reluctantly now, about telephoning. He began by trying the Rome number which hadn't answered yesterday.

A woman's voice answered: 'Attilio Tailoring, can I help you?'

'Excuse me . . . I must have the wrong number . . .'

A tailor's shop. Which explained why no one had answered on a Sunday evening. That was Rome discounted, then. There was nothing for it but to go on with the list of other area codes. One thing he had got done last night was to make himself a separate list of places beginning with R, the cities and bigger towns. He had tried some of them before giving up. Now he went on with Reggio Calabria and the second number. What must have been a very tiny child picked up the receiver at the other end and gurgled into it. A radio was playing in the background.

'Is your mother there?'

The child went on gurgling, making an imitation conversation.

'What's your name?'

There was a piercing squeak and more gurgles. He hung up and then lifted the receiver to try Reggio Calabria and the third number. He could still hear the radio playing. The child must have gone off leaving the receiver dangling. His phone was blocked.

He tried again three times with the same result. The fourth time the receiver had been replaced but no one answered. They must have gone out.

Reggio Calabria 46902. A woman's voice answered abruptly.

'It's already sold.'

'Excuse me . . .?'

'The Honda 125. If you're ringing about the advert in the paper, it's already sold. Somebody came yesterday morning. The phone hasn't stopped since the paper came out, I'm thinking of taking it off the hook.'

'It wasn't about the 125. Perhaps I have the wrong number. Is that Signora Bianchi?' His standard question to elicit the subscriber's name. But the woman wasn't listening.

'My son should have sold it himself – he's gone to do his

military service and I said to him, get yourself organized and sell it before you leave, but young ones these days. He wants a Cagiva once he's out but I'd rather he got himself a little car, these motorbikes are lethal but his father always takes his side – you don't know anybody who has a Cagiva for sale? Of course he should see to these things himself, I can't be expected –'

'Signora Bianchi . . .'

'Bianchi? You've got the wrong number!' She hung up.

After looking at his watch he decided against trying that one again. He dialled the next number on his list, realizing only as somebody picked it up that it was Rome, the tailor's shop that he'd tried already a moment ago. It wasn't the same woman's voice that answered, and perhaps it was the peculiar high-pitched male voice which made him listen rather than hang up immediately.

'Ecclesiastical Tailoring. Attilio himself speaking, can I help you?'

CHAPTER EIGHT

The car wound its way up the Janiculum in the darkness. Colonel Tempesta, seated in the back in the opposite corner to the General, looked down at the city lights they were leaving behind, thankful that the presence of the driver prevented any further discussion. Nevertheless, the silence was not a comfortable one. Tempesta had spent almost two hours in the large office from which the General controlled the workings of the Military Secret Service, taking the brunt of the irascible old man's anger for no other reason than that he was there and knew enough about the business to allow the General to express himself freely. Tempesta neither liked nor respected the General who had an oblique way of giving orders which ensured that responsibility fell on others when things went wrong and credit went to himself when they went well. 'If you would like to do that . . .' he would often say on winding up a briefing, 'I can promise you my full support.' Or: 'If you feel you can handle that – and I have every confidence in you . . .'

The young or relatively inexperienced would be flattered by his every confidence and eager to believe that the plan he had outlined, the import of which they only vaguely understood, had originated, at least in part, with themselves. If things went well their mythical contribution was naturally forgotten. If trouble ensued they sometimes found themselves transferred. Tempesta was neither young nor inexperienced but he knew that though his own position was solid enough, there was no moral defence against the General's behaviour. Normally he would let him have his say, maintaining a stolid silence, but this time there was Bardi . . .

The General shifted slightly in his corner and spoke to the driver: 'You know where to turn right?'

'Yessir.'

Tempesta continued to stare out at the dark night.

The General hadn't come out with it openly but it had been evident that the real cause of his anger was the foiling of the attempt on Bardi's life. If matters had been left to take their course the problem would have solved itself nicely, but the signal had come to Tempesta through their agent and Tempesta had made the usual anonymous call to the police.

'It would have helped if you'd found out why they intended to attack him.'

'Our agent gives us what information he can. I'm sure you are aware of just how much he is risking in calling us like that at all. Naturally I thought it concerned the current trial –'

'Well, you thought wrong! In my opinion you didn't think at all!'

Which was true. But if he had thought, should he have let Bardi be butchered? He tried to say something of the kind as tactfully as possible but the General rolled over him like a tank.

'Just how much real danger is there of this man Gori talking? Or haven't you thought of that even now?'

'Considerable danger, apparently. It seems he was a rabid militant and pulled off some pretty nasty jobs in his time, but he's a weak character and liable to take orders from anyone in whose hands he finds himself.'

'In this case Bardi.'

'They say Bardi's good with repentants . . .'

'Good! What do you mean by good?'

'That he knows how to get what he wants, especially out of the ones who are hoping to save their own skins without risking their necks by telling anything too dangerous.'

'Then we can thank God that in this case he doesn't really know what he's looking for.'

Tempesta hadn't contradicted him but he knew what a

nose Bardi had for finding things he didn't know he was looking for. All he said was: 'The chief point in our favour' – in Bardi's favour was what he was really thinking – 'is that Gori himself doesn't know all that much.'

'He knows he removed those documents, not to mention that business of the cigar! Our agent was there when they brought that stuff in and there was a scene about that damned cigar tube – a bunch of damned idiots! A gang of cretinous schoolboys!'

The General never made moral distinctions, he simply expected everyone, including the Red Brigades, to come up to his standards of discipline and efficiency. He got up from his desk and began striding about the room, one hand behind his back, the other passing repeatedly over his fine grey hair.

'I'd like to know what you intend to do!' Another favourite phrase of his when things went badly. 'It would have helped if you'd found out the reason for the attack – well, it's not too late, even so –'

'You mean they might try again?' asked Tempesta calmly. His back was to the General as he spoke. If the General wished to stride about the room in that manner it was his privilege to do so, but Tempesta had no intention of shuffling his chair about like a schoolboy.

'Certainly not, certainly not!' The General was put out because that was just what he had meant. 'I mean this man Bardi must be dealt with, at which point –' He stopped and turned suddenly. 'Has there been a lawyer present at these interrogations?'

'No. I made some discreet inquiries. He had no lawyer of his own and so was offered legal assistance but apparently refused to have a lawyer present when he saw Bardi.'

'Hmph. Then it will only be necessary to edit the transcription.'

After Bardi had been 'dealt with'. Tempesta was pinning his hopes on this evening's dealings as Bardi's only hope of getting out of this mess alive. He was well aware of the General's part in strangling with red tape Carlo Rota's last desperate request for an armoured car during his attempt at setting up a coalition government with the Communists. Bardi was already well protected but the General, odious as he might be, was a very clever man. If things went badly tonight . . .

The General's car turned in at a driveway on the right and stopped at the doors of the American College, a massive modern structure with many of the large windows of its six storeys brightly lit.

They left their coats on a stand in a long, silent corridor and followed the porter past a glass case of football trophies and a series of photographs taken on papal visits.

Monsignor Lazurek was waiting for them, a tiny, dark figure standing by the fireplace at the far end of a large reception room. The only movement was a slight stirring of the yellow velvet curtains that hung from the high ceiling to the floor, a reminder of the cold windy night outside though the room was overheated. As the two men crossed the room the little priest did not move to greet them but only waited, observing them with his tiny, sleepy eyes.

'I hope you didn't mind my receiving you here,' he said when they reached him, 'I had people to see here all afternoon so there seemed little point in my going back home. General, how are you? Colonel . . .'

There was nothing in his words or manner to suggest it and yet Tempesta felt that he hadn't wanted to receive them in his own house and felt uneasy. If the General, too, was uneasy it was for quite another reason. Lazurek, observing his rapid glance around the room, said: 'We won't be disturbed. They keep American hours here. They dined some hours ago and have all gone off to their rooms long since.'

A tray of emptied sherry glasses stood at one end of the long mahogany table.

'Can I offer you something to drink?'

'A whisky, if you have it,' the General said with a dubious glance at the sherry glasses.

'And for you, Colonel?'

'The same. Thank you.'

The General was not one to waste more than the minimum time necessary on courtesies. Even as they were settling around the fire with their glasses he began, with a trace of irritation already discernible in his voice:

'I'm disturbed to hear that, according to Tempesta, at least, you're not taking your situation as seriously as it deserves.'

'No, no . . .' Lazurek said softly, though whether to contradict or agree with him was not clear. 'Though it may be that I simply don't see what I can do about it or whether, indeed, I should do anything.' He blinked mildly at the heavy and imposing figure before him. 'It's natural, of course, that my attitude should irritate you. I'm such an amateur in these matters and the amateur always irritates the professional.'

'Not at all, not at all!' The General was doubly annoyed at having his own thoughts repeated to him. 'You've often been a great help to us in the past and we're more than sensible of that.'

'In the past, yes. Though I'm afraid I may not be able to be of much help to you in the future. Probably I'm getting old . . .'

The General, though not over-sensitive, could not help but understand him. With a glance at the silent Colonel at his side he cleared his throat loudly.

'Naturally, I understand your feelings. Even so –'

'My feelings? Do you imagine it to be a matter of, shall we say, some sort of squeamishness on my part?'

'Come, come, Monsignor, the Church was as much against the historic compromise between Christian Democrats and Communists as we were.'

'Oh yes . . .' murmured the Monsignor, staring thoughtfully into the fire, 'the Rota case was a great success for all concerned . . . except of course for the Red Brigades and the unfortunate Rota himself. The Church did, as you say, wish to avoid the historic compromise, but not at the cost of human lives.' The General lifted a hand to interrupt him but Lazurek's thoughts were elsewhere and he didn't even notice. 'When this man, the one they call the Grand Old Man, first got in touch with me I had no reason to believe he was acting in any other capacity than as a high official of the Foreign Office. And yet I did suspect him, for no reason I could explain to myself. I did suspect him and I informed you of what was happening even before the call came from Li Causi. In ten years I've asked myself the same questions so many times without finding satisfactory answers. I've often wondered, for instance, if things would have gone better had I not suspected anything – not that I went so far as to imagine he was working for Moscow . . . it was merely an instinct. I have always believed, you see, General, that our instincts are the most positive source of good in us. Nevertheless, by instinctive suspicions of this man and my consequent action of informing you, you might well have signed Carlo Rota's death warrant.'

'Well, you did inform us, which is what you thought you should do and for which we were rightly grateful.' The General was anxious to cut short the philosophizing and get down to more urgent problems. 'At any rate your conscience is clear – which is no doubt why you face the present threat to your life with equanimity.'

'With equanimity . . . Well, we must all die and our lives are threatened from the day we draw our first breath. The thing that most distressed me about Rota was that even from the first I felt, or even knew, that it wasn't the Sacrament he wanted from me.'

Tempesta spoke for the first time: 'You know, not all of us have your strength of mind in the face of death. You were his last hope.'

'Then why –' the Monsignor turned his gaze from the flames to meet the Colonel's – 'why did they allow it? They must have known what he was trying to do.'

'They knew. You see, you were their last hope, too. The government had refused point blank to negotiate for Rota's life. An attempt at negotiations with the Socialist Party had failed . . .'

'But what could I, or even His Holiness, have done?'

'Nothing at all,' interrupted the General. 'They were desperate. They'd pulled off the biggest job in history and achieved nothing, that's all there is to it, they were desperate.'

'I see. At the time they seemed to be in such a strong position but I suppose what you say is true. Rota was certainly desperate. He was not a man I liked and I confess to my shame that in that moment of his desperation I liked him even less, although I pitied him. We are frail creatures indeed but that I should have been frailer than he at that terrible moment . . . No, General, my conscience is not as clear as you seem to think. I couldn't find it in my heart to love a man I had mildly disliked in the hour of his greatest suffering because he was trying to cling to life through me on the pretext of my helping him to face death. And by what right did I judge him? Even Christ himself asked that the cup should pass from him and yet He had made His choice in the name of all humanity. In whose name did Carlo Rota die? It certainly wasn't his choice. They say he'd asked repeatedly for protection, that he had requested an armoured car which might well have saved his life that day . . .' Lazurek's tiny eyes were fixed on the fire again. He looked at neither of them but left his remark hanging in the air. Tempesta watched the General's face. It was never possible to guess how much Lazurek knew and how much was his unerring intuition. The General evidently wasn't even trying but had begun running a hand repeatedly over his hair, which meant his irritation was rising. When he spoke it was brusquely.

'Well, you did give him the Sacrament, which is all you could do in the circumstances.'

'I did. And he watched me. It isn't often we are called upon to give the Sacrament to someone not already in the last stages of illness to whom the end will be a release and the Sacrament itself a comfort. A man fully conscious and in perfect health . . . He was weakened of course by what he had gone through; his body was cold and limp but his eyes burned as if he had a fever, which I suppose he may have had . . . but all the time he watched me –'

'Monsignor Lazurek, I'm trying to clarify matters in the hope of making you understand just how dangerous the present situation is. Up till now, chiefly because of your refusal in the past to even discuss the case with us, you've known only your own part in all this –'

'And a little of yours, I think, General, a little of yours. I told you where he was and you made no move. They blindfolded me in the car and, no doubt, drove me all over Rome before taking me there, but they couldn't take me inside blindfolded with the risk of meeting someone at that hour of the night, and I knew that building or at least that group of buildings. With the information I gave you you could have found him.'

'We had our reasons for acting in the way we did, and in the last analysis what happened was to the Church's advantage, as I've already pointed out. What's more important to understand now –'

'I'm trying to understand. Tell me whatever you wish to tell me, but tell me first if Rota knew about my contacts with you.'

'It would seem so.'

'And he told his captors.'

'He would certainly have told them. They would hardly have allowed you to go there if they hadn't known that you might prove useful to them, given that all attempts at overt bargaining had failed.'

'I see . . .'

'And so –'

But the Monsignor had turned to the Colonel.

'Perhaps you would like to refill our glasses. Forgive me my laziness but I don't seem to have recovered too well after my cold.'

For a moment the only sounds in the large room were the faint clinking of glasses and the shifting of logs in the grate. The General managed a surreptitious glance at his watch as he accepted the second drink.

'I'm not making us late, I hope?' The Monsignor spilled a drop of whisky on his cassock and dabbed at it absently with a crumpled handkerchief.

'We ought to be leaving within twenty minutes.'

'Then go on telling me about your Grand Old Man. Odd that they should have given him a title like that . . . the newspapers. I suppose. He could only have been in his mid-forties and slight in his build. A small man with a very big cigar, that's almost all I remember of him. His chief characteristic was his insignificance – and it was he who planned the whole thing?'

'We don't know. According to our Red Brigades agent, the job was planned at Executive level but was presented by Li Causi who was their contact with the Grand Old Man, which means the idea might well have come from him. We know for sure that he interrogated Rota during his so-called trial.'

'A fact,' commented the Monsignor, sipping his drink slowly, 'that did not appear when the transcripts of the trial were published in the papers.'

'Quite.' The General glanced across at Tempesta. 'The actual documents were removed well before the police arrived at the apartment. We assume that our Grand Old Man has them in his possession and that's one of the reasons why we can't touch him. Those documents are dynamite. Rota told enough to virtually destroy the Christian Democrat Party. The documents which were published were planted in the apartment by us before the police moved in. Given that the Red Brigades had publicized the trial and its documentation, it was thought best to give the newspapers, and for that matter the police, what they were expecting to find to avoid any danger of a search for the real thing.'

Lazurek absorbed this in silence. Then he turned and fixed

his little eyes on the General: 'He must have planned other kidnappings, then, other murders.'

'He did.'

'And you always knew.' They weren't questions but the General chose to treat them as such.

'Very often, through our agent. What was important was that we always knew about him without his suspecting it.'

'But you never moved against him.'

'We occasionally blocked an action by informing the police anonymously, if that's what you mean.'

Tempesta watched the General's hand move over his smooth hair and knew he was thinking with displeasure of Bardi. 'But we preferred, especially in the case of kidnappings, to move after the event, not only because it was safer for our agent but because it made the police work look highly impressive.'

'No . . .' said the Monsignor slowly, 'that isn't what I mean . . .'

'Then I can only repeat what I have already pointed out to you. This man is holding some highly sensitive documents – apart from which, and I'm sure you are as aware of this as I am, without the fear of Communism inspired by the Red Brigades all hope of maintaining a democratic government would almost certainly have been lost in those years. With the danger of the historic compromise it so happened that our interests and those of the Eastern bloc temporarily coincided, particularly given that the leader of the Communist Party at that time was both a charismatic figure in his own right and one who was quite prepared to go against Moscow and to cooperate with the Christian Democrats.'

'And now?'

'And now that danger is past. The Party is once more under the thumb of Moscow and terrorism no longer serves us or the East. The so-called Grand Old Man has long ceased to concern himself with left-wing terrorism. We have good reason to believe that he is now one of the chief instigators of the scandal war. It is probably owing to his machinations that a large number of right-wing politicians have been arrested or at least forced to resign over the last few years.'

'And would I be right in thinking,' asked Lazurek, regarding them each in turn, 'that you have not gone entirely unscathed yourselves?'

'We've been obliged to shed a few more than dispensible people,' concurred the General, taking a satisfied sip at his drink, 'but nothing of any relevance.'

'So you intend to let him carry on his work, because of these documents.'

'We can hardly make a move at this stage without its coming out that we always knew about him and his involvement with the Red Brigades. And, needless to say, he sold a fair amount of information to the Americans over the years, some of which we felt ourselves obligated to buy back from them. They would hardly appreciate that coming out, knowing that we'd let it go on. I'm afraid they wouldn't find it amusing.'

'They would not,' Lazurek agreed. 'Evidently you are not dealing with an idealist.'

'Those days are long past, if they ever really existed. We're dealing with a man who likes power and who likes to make a profit out of it.'

'You couldn't . . .' Lazurek looked at the Colonel, 'You couldn't pack him quietly off to Moscow?'

'No,' replied the Colonel with a faint smile, 'we couldn't. They certainly know, and for all we know, approve, of his selling to the Americans but he's made too good a thing out of it for them to trust him completely.'

The Monsignor sighed and fished out his handkerchief to dab at his brow. 'Between you, you've created a monster.'

'The times created him,' said the General brusquely, 'or he created himself. At any rate he's no longer involved in terrorism. Our immediate problem is that we can't afford the scandal that would ensue if the truth about the Rota business comes out. We've been under pressure for some years now from the US to clean up our political scene as much as possible, especially after that banking scandal. Nobody could be expected to enjoy a trick like that being pulled in their own country and, practically speaking, by the very people they're supporting to stay in power here.'

'No, but it's hardly disinterested support. If a scandal of these dimensions breaks with the risk of the Communists filling the ensuing vacuum, they will surely only be obliged to do even more to prop up the Christian Democrats.'

'If a scandal of these dimensions breaks nothing and nobody will be capable of propping them up! The country will be in chaos!'

'This country,' observed the Monsignor tranquilly, 'has been in chaos for the last two thousand years.'

The General was not amused.

'A controlled chaos that serves a purpose is another matter. This time it would be out of our control!'

'There is another aspect of the problem,' put in Tempesta, afraid that the General himself was getting out of control when it was essential to be on good terms with Lazurek. 'There has been an upsurge of recruiting among what's left of the Red Brigades, an almost inevitable result of keeping so many of their number in prison for so long.'

'But so many of them were released.'

'We released as many as we could in the hope of avoiding just this situation, but there were over five thousand known or suspected terrorists inside at one point and there are still far too many for safety, all of them with relatives and companions on the outside. That's a lot of people smouldering with resentment. Sooner or later the present resurgence was bound to happen and by this time there are a lot of dissatisfied youngsters around who are too young to remember the squalid defeat that followed the big campaigns of the 'seventies. These kids are ripe for recruitment, as you know from our decisions to pack in as many upper schools as possible for the Rota memorial service. Apropos of which, and I'm sure the General is of the same opinion, we very much appreciated your sermon. It struck exactly the right note.'

'Quite, quite,' said the General. His voice was gruff but he had collected himself considerably.

'Well now,' said the Monsignor softly, 'the problem of these young people is one that concerns me – a good deal more than this supposed threat to my safety. Oddly enough, though, when I was reading through Rota's last letters in order to prepare that sermon the one phrase that remained in my mind, though I didn't use it, was: "Do not imagine that my liquidation will resolve the Party's problems. I shall always be there . . ." Of course, as you said before, he was desperate, and he made worse threats than than before the end. Even so, it was true. "I shall always be there . . ." You still have your agent in the Red Brigades?'

'We do,' said the General, 'but that isn't enough. What we need more than anything at this crucial stage is a calm situation which will allow us to take the appropriate action where and when we need to. What we don't need is a scandal which would force us into precipitate and makeshift measures. And that means that this whole Rota–Grand Old Man business must be kept secret at all cost. Which brings us to this magistrate and the reason for this evening's talk.'

'Ah, the good magistrate.' Lazurek's tiny eyes flickered from the fire to Tempesta and back again, but Tempesta, at this point, did not trust himself to speak.

'Yes, a magistrate,' the General went on, 'who has taken it upon himself to seek out the Grand Old Man and who hopes to find him by first of all finding you. We can't afford to underestimate him –'

The General stopped and whipped his head round, his face darkening with annoyance. The door had opened and Father John McManus stood hesitating on the threshold. Lazurek, too, had looked round but he showed no discomposure.

'Good evening, John.'

'I was looking for Father Honan . . .'

'As you see, he isn't here.'

The young man still hesitated, as though he would have liked to join them, but the group of dark figures around the fire showed him closed faces.

'Monsignor . . .' But across the large room the Monsignor's eyes, though they confronted him, might have been the windows of a roofless house for all they communicated. 'Excuse me . . .' The young man vanished, closing the door silently after him.

Lazurek turned his gaze from the door. 'Ah, General . . . if you can't spirit your Grand Old Man away to Moscow I wish you could at least help me to dispatch that young priest to Chicago . . .'

'Chicago? I don't understand you.'

'No, you wouldn't understand me . . . you were saying about the good magistrate – might I ask his name?'

'Bardi, Lapo Bardi.'

'Lapo Bardi. A Florentine name, I think.'

'Quite correct.'

'And you say he's looking for me. Is he going to find me?'

'Tempesta here is a better judge of that than I am. He knows the man and has the situation in hand at present.'

Tempesta did not fail to notice that 'at present', but his placid face did not register it.

'Some years ago,' he began, 'Bardi arrested the terrorist leader Li Causi at a time when he was above suspicion, a respected young professor. It was a brilliant piece of detection on Bardi's part but it ended in nothing. There was no concrete evidence against him. Shortly afterwards, however, Li Causi went underground, confirming Bardi's suspicions, and the police lost sight of him.'

'But you, of course, didn't.'

'Our agent was always in contact with him.'

'And now he's been arrested, has he not?'

'Yes. You have to understand that he was the only charismatic Red Brigades leader still at large and that it was useful to have him at large because, through him, our agent could keep a finger on the pulse of terrorism. But with the recent upsurge of recruitment we began to worry about the situation getting out of control. Consequently, we informed the police of his whereabouts, giving the source as a repentant, and he was arrested. At which point Bardi began to take an interest in him again, most probably for personal reasons because the only piece of evidence – or what he thinks may be evidence – that he has in hand is something he found on Li Causi when he brought him in for questioning that first time.'

'What sort of evidence?' Lazurek bent to put another log on the fire.

'A coded number he found in Li Causi's address book.'

'I see.' For the first time the Monsignor looked seriously interested. 'And since on your advice I gave the number we use to my visitor from the Foreign Office, after which Li Causi contacted me there, I imagine it's that number that the code refers to.'

Tempesta felt the General's cold eyes staring at him.

'I . . . it may be. The fact is –'

'The fact is,' put in the General, 'that we don't know.'

'Having suggested you give them that number so that we could record what passed between you, we naturally guessed that the number found on Li Causi might be that one. To avoid any risk of it getting out, we simply told Bardi at the time that we were unable to decode it. In fact, we didn't try.'

'And Bardi accepted that?'

'He had no reason not to. In any case he was obliged to let Li Causi go and the matter was dropped.'

'Until now.'

'Until now. As I told you, he came to my office recently and asked me to make a second attempt at decoding.' Tempesta was taking care to avoid the General's eyes, addressing himself to Lazurek whose attitude was steadily becoming graver.

'Did you refuse?'

'I neither refused nor agreed. Nevertheless, I immediately sent the number for decoding. At this point we urgently need to know whether it is or isn't the number we think it is, in case of the possibility, however remote, of Bardi's managing to decode it by some means of his own. Unfortunately . . . unfortunately our people have up to now been unsuccessful.'

'Then surely Bardi will be equally unsuccessful. Your men are experts . . .'

'I said the possibility was remote.' Knowing Bardi, it wasn't nearly remote enough for comfort but Tempesta had no intention of saying so in front of the General. He found himself wishing that he'd managed to talk to Lazurek alone on arriving in Rome but the General had taken good care to monopolize all his time. 'It may well be that it's some other number and there is no real cause for alarm . . .'

'And failing that,' said the General in placid tones that were loaded with cold menace, 'the number is, as always, under our surveillance. If Bardi calls it, we shall know.'

Lazurek looked at him.

'In that case, the situation is, indeed, much graver than I thought.'

'I'm so glad we've been able to convince you.' The General drained his glass and placed it carefully on a small round table beside him. 'Your position –'

'You misunderstand me. If the telephone number concerned were my own I should be a good deal less concerned. As it is, there's an entirely innocent person involved.'

'Fortunately for you,' snapped the General, 'since, with any luck Bardi's researches will come to a dead end there.'

But the Monsignor looked anxiously to Tempesta.

'What do you want me to do?'

'In the first place, be on your guard. You were temporarily deceived once by an innocuous-looking person from the Foreign Office. Needless to say, if anyone tries to contact you now on any pretext whatsoever, you'll inform us immediately. Frankly, we'd prefer it if you could find an adequate excuse to leave the country for the time being.'

'An adequate excuse . . . If you mean one that wouldn't arouse anyone's suspicions . . . It's impossible. I haven't left

Rome for decades and my work at the Secretariat of State hardly permits me to take random holidays. No, it's impossible, unless you want to put His Holiness in the deeply embarrassing, not to say compromising, situation of hearing all that you've just told me . . . not that he couldn't work it all out for himself but I imagine he would prefer not to try.'

'I imagine so, too,' said the General drily. 'Well, we've asked you to be careful. And now I think we should go on to the restaurant. Binetti's a stickler for punctuality – he knows nothing, incidentally, and will want to know nothing.'

'I see.' The Monsignor got slowly out of his armchair, shaking out the creases in his cassock like a plump, dishevelled bird. 'But you feel my presence is indicated.'

'I do. He particularly wanted to meet you. He's well aware that you have His Holiness's ear and that of a good many others.'

'Then surely the Cardinal . . .'

'Binetti doesn't get along with the Cardinal. Besides, you'll soon be a Cardinal yourself, provided that we succeed in stopping Bardi, and Binetti is one of the ways in which we can try and stop him. He was at the memorial service, incidentally, and appreciated your sermon as much as we did.'

'Ah yes,' sighed Lazurek as the other two stood up, and he repeated softly, ' "I shall always be there . . ." '

'And as long as he is there your life is in danger,' insisted the General as they walked towards the door.

'Oh yes, but you're wrong in thinking that I haven't understood that, General. I know I'm in danger, but, you see, I'm not sure from whom. Now I must excuse myself for a moment and go and wrap up warmly. I rarely go out at night and I'm not in the best of health.'

And he switched off the lights in the large empty room.

The restaurant, which had once been Garibaldi's house, stood high up on the Janiculum. With its warm lighting and soft green and pink linen the long dining-room, humming with the contented chatter of the well-fed and well-served, had a welcoming air of calm to which Carlo Binetti, vice-president of the Upper Council of Magistrates, provided a sharp contrast. His black hair was very short and very smooth, his black suit severe, his regimental tie garish. He was seated at a secluded table for four and he glanced at his watch as he rose to greet them without a smile.

'I'm afraid we've kept you waiting,' the General said after making introductions. 'The traffic in this city never lets up, even at night.'

Binetti was taking in the shabby appearance of the little Monsignor, who was muffled up to the ears in a black woollen scarf topped by an ancient black beret from which his untidy grey hair sprouted in tufts around his ears.

'I've only just arrived,' he lied politely.

A waiter came to take their coats and the Monsignor unwound his muffler slowly, his eyes fixed on the menu which had been placed beside Binetti's plate.

Once they were seated Tempesta began discreetly sizing up Binetti. He had seen him before only at conferences and official dinners, and they had never spoken. Nevertheless, he knew the type well enough. The ostentatious concern with punctuality, for example, he took to be a sign of Binetti's wanting to appear busier and more important than he was. Tempesta himself, though he carried an enormous workload, always gave the impression of having acres of time to spare and anyone who came to see him felt that he had been doing nothing in particular until his arrival which was consequently a welcome and important event. Binetti, Tempesta thought, would keep you waiting around in his ante-room while he fiddled with papers already signed and settled or kept some puzzled underling talking about trivialities.

'Menu, sir?'

'Thank you.' Tempesta went on with his observations from behind the folder. They each had a menu but Binetti made it his business to consult with the Monsignor over every item, bombarding him with comments, advice and flattery, an attention to which Lazurek remained quietly impervious. The General studied his in silence, looking up to grunt or cough every now and then. Binetti, Tempesta decided, was a small-minded man of limited talent who had got where he was through cultivating the right people at the right time. The right person was now Lazurek but he might find the going difficult there.

A plate of mixed hors d'œuvre had arrived to encourage their appetites and the Monsignor was immediately distracted from his reading. He looked for all the world like a shabby little mole, vaguely surprised but pleased to find himself out amongst light and people. Yes, Binetti would find it hard going all right. Having decided that he thoroughly despised him, Tempesta set out to aid and abet him with every means at his disposal. He found it helpful to address his remarks to Binetti's thick purplish lips, avoiding both his eyes and the regimental tie.

'Perhaps you would choose the wine for us,' he suggested. 'If I'm not mistaken I seem to have heard it said that you're something of a connoisseur.' He had heard nothing of the sort and Binetti knew it but the purplish lips widened to show a row of small even teeth and the mistake was allowed to pass uncontradicted.

'I'll certainly do my best – but we must hear what the Monsignor would like to eat before we can decide.'

'You're waiting for me . . .' Lazurek looked up, having caught, it seemed, only the tail-end of this exchange. 'I think fish. The seafood risotto to begin with.'

'The same for me,' said the General, snapping the menu shut and lighting a cigarette.

'Risotto for everyone, then . . .' And the Colonel, in his turn, let that one pass. 'In that case, I think a Pinot Bianco . . .'

'Good evening, Monsignor.' A different waiter appeared, smiling. 'I've only just heard you were here. It's not often we see you apart from Sunday lunch. If you'll permit me, I think the risotto . . .'

'We're all having it.'

'Excellent. Then you'll want your usual Tocai di Lison. I'll see to it right away.' And with a brief bow to the rest of the company he hurried away.

By the time they began eating the steaming piquant risotto the General had steered the conversation firmly back to the safe waters of the Roman traffic problem where Binetti could be let loose again and he himself could eat in peace.

'Nobody appreciates more than I do,' Binetti was saying now, leaning back expansively, glass in hand, 'that protective measures are necessary if the city's monuments are to be preserved. But to think of closing what is one of the main arterial roads through the city with things already in the drastic state they are in . . .'

Which reminded Tempesta of those racially prejudiced people who always begin 'No one could be less racially prejudiced than I am, nevertheless . . .'

Aloud he said: 'Someone suggested a couple of years ago that the only way of unblocking the streets of Rome was to persuade either Parliament or the Pope to move out. Let me fill your glass.'

But Binetti redirected the bottle towards the Monsignor's glass, almost bowing, seated as he was, as he said gallantly: 'Then it must, of course, be Parliament. After all, the Pope was here first.'

Lazurek watched the misted glass as it was filled to the brim with chilly golden liquid, his sleepy little eyes expressionless. He took a long draught, half emptying it before remarking solemnly:

'Well, the Pope has moved out of Rome before but I wouldn't say the results were altogether positive. I'm glad to know that you consider His Holiness as one of the monuments to be protected.'

Binetti checked the faces of the other two listeners before allowing his teeth to show again.

At a nearby table a prosperous-looking family of four, including two teenage children, burst into sudden laughter and raised their wine glasses to each other. They were obviously celebrating some special event. Beyond them a very elderly cardinal looked up from his solitary meal as though annoyed by their gaiety.

When the waiter returned the Monsignor ordered fillets of sole. Binetti, of course, followed suit.

'Naturally, what else? After all, it's Friday and old traditions die hard, isn't that so, Monsignor?'

The General expressed a desire for half a roast duckling and Tempesta resigned himself to eating the other half and forgoing the succulent roast of veal he had seen being served to the family of four. Binetti was still paying Lazurek compliments on his excellent taste.

'There are so few restaurants one can rely on when it comes to fish, but I must say you're absolutely right in this case, absolutely spot on . . .'

Tempesta knew that Lazurek always ate fish when dining out because of the chronic difficulties he had with his teeth, a result of severe malnutrition during his childhood exacerbated in recent, more opulent years by a weakness for Sister Agatha's sweetmeats.

Binetti was certainly working hard, but Lazurek, concentrating on the sole, his sleepy eyes shining and his chin greasy, was giving him little encouragement. The General, too, was concentrating on his meal. Diplomacy wasn't his strong point, which was why Tempesta was present. He also had other alternatives up his sleeve if nothing came of this evening's business. Tempesta, afraid of what those alternatives might be, was growing tense, and the more tense he became the less he felt able to control the situation. Every now and then he glanced across at the celebrating family who seemed enclosed in their small private world. There was something unreal about it. The two groups of four were enjoying the same sort of meal in the same bright tranquil room and yet while they raised their glasses in yet another intimate toast, at his own table a man's life was being fought for.

Again Tempesta was wishing he'd had a chance to talk to Lazurek alone.

The solitary Cardinal was examining his bill item by item, frowning.

'I know, of course, that a great deal has been done internally to remedy the situation but there comes a point, and I'm sure you of all people understand that that point has been reached, when this isolationist policy must necessarily be abandoned if the sort of boost that is required . . .'

Tempesta caught the General's warning glance. He didn't want Binetti making off with the bait before they had hooked him for their own purposes. The reappearance of the waiter bearing the menu provided a useful interruption. When they had chosen a sweet and Lazurek, undecided, had chosen two, Tempesta moved in quickly and smoothly.

'Do tell me, if I'm not being indiscreet, these rumours about the President of the Council retiring early . . . is there anything in it or is it just gossip?'

'I hadn't heard anything,' Binetti said cautiously. He hadn't, any more than Tempesta had, but he wasn't one to make pronouncements before he was sure which way the wind was blowing. He knew there would be a price to pay for his meeting with Lazurek and was willing to pay if it was within his power.

'Just gossip, then, I suppose.' There was just the right touch of regret in Tempesta's voice. 'Hard on you, I would have thought, if he goes his full term.'

'Oh, I wouldn't say that.' Binetti leaned back a little and smoothed his garish tie complacently. 'Life is difficult enough as it is. The vice-presidency being an executive position entails some heavy responsibilities.'

'Ah yes, indeed. In fact, the General and I were saying only today that we must have rather added to your already heavy responsibilities in what must seem to you an unpardonable way.'

Binetti, not knowing the correct response to this kept silent, his thick lips making hesitant preparatory movements in case he should be required to smile.

'I can see you don't want to say so,' insisted Tempesta, 'but we must have left you with quite a problem on your hands. You mustn't think, however, that we have forgotten your indispensible cooperation in our fight against terrorism.'

The smile now appeared, a deprecating smile.

'I did what little I could, of course . . .'

'You did a great deal in ensuring that we had the right magistrates in the right place at the right time. Those go-ahead young Substitute Prosecutors with personality, charisma, with whom the newspapers could make a splash . . .' He didn't add 'and who were sufficiently provincial not to be uncomfortably well-informed in tricky areas', which had been the unspoken basis for choosing them. 'It meant a great deal in the fight to shift public opinion on to the side of the law in the days when the Red Brigades were unduly popular. We haven't by any means forgotten your invaluable help and we'd hate to think that there should be any backlash as a result of your efforts.'

'Nothing I can't cope with,' hazarded Binetti, filling their glasses in the hope of gaining time to understand where this was leading. 'On the contrary, it does no harm to have a large number of talented magistrates scattered throughout our larger cities who feel that they owe their brilliant careers to my help.' He smiled again, a smile that said, 'you see how disarmingly candid I can be, you can drop the mask, too.' For he was still struggling in the dark and becoming increasingly uneasy about it.

Tempesta had regained all his stolid composure. Binetti's stupidity surpassed even his expectations.

'That,' he said with heavy accents of friendly concern, 'is exactly what we were thinking. Thanks to you, they made brilliant careers, a good many of them are famous throughout the country . . . and by now they're ten years older. They must by now be expecting promotion.'

'Promotion . . .? Well, in fact two of them have recently been appointed Chief Public Prosecutor. Not all of them, of course . . .'

'Quite.' Tempesta allowed himself a gentle smile. He took a sip from his glass and glanced at Lazurek. The Monsignor, as he might have expected, was happily forking little mounds of fluffy cake into his mouth. There was a light sprinkling of icing sugar down his black-shirted chest and a faraway look in his eyes. Binetti followed the Colonel's glance and then waited for him to go on.

But all Tempesta said was: 'I think we might order some coffee.'

'Not for me, please,' said the Monsignor, without looking up from his cake, 'Not in the evening, it keeps me awake. Doesn't it keep you awake?' he added, suddenly fixing his little eyes on Binetti.

'I . . . no. No, I'll take coffee . . .'

'Not for me either.' The General pushed his plate aside and lit a cigarette.

Tempesta lifted a finger and ordered two coffees.

'He's quite right, you know, Binetti,' said the General gruffly, 'quite right. I'm glad he brought it to my notice, very glad indeed. I feel we should have thought of it before but we haven't been altogether neglectful. Naturally, in our field we're constantly in touch with the work these magistrates are doing and we haven't forgotten the fine job they and you have done for us. Your problem now, as I see it, is that of finding positions for those who have made brilliant careers, as you say, at your instigation. Some of them are young, of course, and can wait, but others are not so young. Tempesta mentioned a man by the name of Bardi, for instance, who would be a case in point. One of the most successful of your chosen men, if not the most successful, and he must be over fifty.'

'Bardi, yes. Florence. Well, as far as I know he intends staying there, being a Florentine, and his chief, Corbi if I remember rightly, won't be coming up for retirement for a few years yet. He's the most brilliant man they have there, so when Corbi does go . . .' He was talking too quickly, exhibiting his relief at its being only a simple question of pushing somebody's promotion.

'As it happens,' put in Tempesta, reassuring Binetti still further by now returning his 'here I am letting the mask down' smile, 'Lapo Bardi's an old friend of mine.'

'I see.' Binetti was now totally relaxed and speaking with slow assurance. 'And he feels he's been overlooked?'

'He hasn't said so in so many words . . .'

'I do assure you he hasn't – oh dear, we could hardly forget his existence, given that we see his name in the papers every day!' A hearty laugh in which Tempesta and the General joined cordially. Lazurek reached for the wine bottle which turned out to be empty.

'Perhaps a little cognac for everyone,' he suggested meekly.

'Of course! Waiter!' called Binetti. His face was flushed with goodwill and self-satisfaction.

'No, no,' he went on when their glasses were filled and the waiter had, as if accidentally, left the bottle at the little Monsignor's elbow, 'Bardi's a good man, an excellent man, and would have been promoted before now if we hadn't assumed he would want to take over from Corbi. If, as you say, he prefers not to wait, then I'm sure there will be no difficulty – in fact, if he has any preference for a particular region . . .'

'He hasn't said so . . .' Tempesta looked at the General.

'You were thinking, were you not,' said the General, 'that somewhere a little quieter than Florence . . . You can imagine,' looking now at Binetti, 'that the last ten years, between the amount of work involved and the pressure of publicity . . .'

'Undoubtedly, undoubtedly. Well, he's now prosecuting in court against the Florentine nucleus of the Red Brigades. I think if he concludes that successfully *and* gets the famous Bardi Theorem approved he'll be quite entitled to rest on his laurels. I quite appreciate that he must have been under considerable strain.'

'More than anything,' said Tempesta quietly, 'his marriage has been under considerable strain.'

'Then leave the matter entirely in my hands. Monsignor, a little more cognac?'

'Thank you very much. You're very kind.'

'I wonder,' said the General, pushing back his chair, 'if the Colonel and I might beg to be excused for a moment – just a brief telephone call. I'm afraid we're never off duty entirely . . .'

The Colonel rose and followed him without a word. As they left a huge birthday cake was carried to the family at the next table. The other remaining diners in the room turned to smile and join in the applause that greeted it.

They stayed away as long as they decently could. When they re-entered the dining-room it was almost empty. A waiter had begun to collect the jumble of glasses and crumpled ribbons and wrapping paper that remained from the birthday party. At their own table Lazurek was sitting silently, his hands folded in his lap. Binetti, his face still rather flushed was leaning towards him, gesticulating discreetly with both hands to emphasize his words.

'A Catholic of unimpeachable reputation. Even the Cardinal himself, despite his very understandable diffidence, would not deny that.'

'Indeed, no.'

'Then I can leave the matter in your hands?'

'I can only say I'll think it over.'

'And at this stage I ask no more than that – ah, General, I've taken the liberty of settling the bill in your absence . . .'

Which accounted for the look on Lazurek's face, Tempesta thought. The General could have spared him that.

When the General's car reached the Monsignor's residence the Colonel risked the disapproval of his superior by getting out and seeing the little priest to his door. It was only a question of a few yards, a few seconds, and no time to choose words, but the Monsignor himself spoke immediately.

'I can't do it.'

'I know. All I ask is that you don't tell him so yet.'

'Of course, it's true that this man he says is to direct the bank is a prominent Catholic, I know that, but I also know that Binetti is a Mason who got out of the big scandal unscathed, as did so many others. I know, too, that neither Binetti's family nor his present post could permit him to live as he does – nor for that matter to be involved in this financial enterprise he wants to involve the Church in. It's not impossible that he'll succeed, do you know that? We're still in difficulties, serious difficulties, as he well knows, but I don't want to be the one –'

'Please! I'm only asking for time, time for this promotion to go through. I'm not asking you to compromise yourself.'

'Not compromise myself? I have dined publicly – in that restaurant of all restaurants – and at his expense, which I think I might have been spared.'

'I'm sorry, I, too . . . it's a man's life . . .'

'You're convinced of that?'

'I am.'

'Then God help us all,' sighed the Monsignor. 'God help us all.'

CHAPTER NINE

'Ho scel-to un no-me ecc-en-tri-co Ni-ni Ti-ra-bu-sciò . . .' sang Poma under his breath in time with the rapid clack of the windscreen wipers.

'Shut up.'

'Helps me to concentrate. I can't see a damned thing.'

'Get the wipers going faster,' suggested Mastino.

'Oh, sure, get them going faster! They don't go any faster than this and for all the good they're doing I might as well turn them off. If it gets any worse . . .'

And Poma went back to singing under his breath, or rather, humming this time. After a while he tailed off, craning forward over the steering-wheel in an effort to see better through the downpour.

They had set out very early in the morning. It was barely light and unlikely to get any lighter unless the rain let up. It was swilling in sheets down the windscreen and the wipers could do little more than swish it about uselessly. A blurred line of lights passed overhead, the service station restaurant bridging the motorway.

'Maybe we should have stopped there . . .'

'Boh . . .'

The steady hum of the engine. The rapid clicking of the wipers. Every now and then a swishing roar as some sports car overtook them, its tail lights swallowed up almost immediately by the dark rain. They took a long time to pass an autotrain, its giant wheels churning up dirty water. When they drew level with the cab which was decked out with multi-coloured lights Mastino caught a glimpse of the white blur of the driver's face looking down at him.

'Must think it's Christmas.'

'It soon will be.' Poma was still straining forward. 'God, it makes you wonder where it all comes from, it's been pouring like this since two o'clock this morning . . .'

'Two o'clock? You been up all night, or what?'

'Awake all night, or most of it.'

'What's the matter with you?'

'You know what's the matter with me.'

'Where you went wrong,' observed Mastino smugly, 'was in getting married in the first place.'

'So you keep saying and a fat lot of good – for Christ's sake, it's coming on even worse . . .!'

The water seemed to be coming at them in waves and the drumming on the roof had become a steady roar. Poma expected no sympathy from his mate. If he left, Mastino would be transferred and a new pair assigned to Bardi. That was the rule.

'You want to put your foot down.'

'Are you crazy?' Poma was crawling along at less than twenty kilometres an hour.

'I mean with your wife. You're supposed to be the head of the family. What happened to all that southern *machismo* you used to be so full of?'

'I'm going to be a father, if that means anything to you, which it obviously doesn't.'

'You don't have to stop living, do you?'

'No, I have to go on living. All she's asking is that I find a job where I don't get shot at every other day.'

'What do you mean – every other day? Come off it! We haven't been shot at for months.'

'There was that business after the wedding . . .'

Mastino groaned. 'Jesus! What's happened to you, Poma?'

'I'm going to be a father, that's what's happened to me.'

'Well, get yourself a fucking ice-cream cart, then. You can push it round the streets of Florence singing *O sole mio* for the fucking tourists . . . Now what?'

'I'm pulling over. We can't go on in this.'

'Even driving's got too dangerous for you, has it? We can't

hang around in a lay-by, you know that. It's a security risk.'

'Do you want to drive?'

'That's your job.'

'And I'm telling you we can't go on. It'll ease off in a minute . . .'

They sat in silence, isolated by the streaming torrent that surrounded them. Mastino had drawn out his pistol and was checking it on his knee.

'He still sleeping?' asked Poma after a moment.

'Mm,' confirmed Mastino after a quick glance over his shoulder. He put the safety-catch back on and began polishing the barrel with a soft yellow cloth from under the dashboard.

'Can't we go on yet?'

'No.' After a moment he added, 'If you want to know, we're thinking of going back to Naples.'

'You're kidding! To do what?'

'I could work in my father-in-law's restaurant . . .'

'You'll get flat feet.'

'Fuck off, Mastino.'

'All waiters get flat feet. I read it somewhere.'

'So do all cops.'

'You'd still be able to sing *O sole mio* for the tourists, though.'

'Fuck *off*!'

'But with flat feet.'

'Don't you ever fancy going back up north?'

Mastino shrugged. He began to hum *O sole mio*.

'Pack it in.' But Mastino went on humming. 'Pack it in!'

There was no rancour on either side despite their words. They were both equally miserable at the thought of breaking up the old firm. It was only by keeping up their traditional exchange of insults that they could hide it.

'That's better.' Poma started up the engine. The road had become visible again and the torrent had given way to a steady downpour. The autotrain with the coloured lights went by. It, too, must have pulled in a little further back.

'Do you want to know something?' Poma said as they picked up speed.

'What?'

'I've already got flat feet.'

When Bardi got out of the car in the prison yard his limbs were stiff and his mouth unpleasantly dry.

He had woken with a start on the last stretch of motorway and a file had slid off his knee on to the floor of the car.

'Damn . . .!'

Mastino had swivelled round. 'Everything all right, sir?'

'No, it isn't. Why the hell didn't you wake me up? I've got work to do.'

'You were up at five-thirty, sir, after all . . .'

'And so were you two. If I'd been awake I'd have told you to stop for a coffee.'

'Don't worry about us, sir,' put in Roma, 'Only thirty-five kilometres or so before Rome.'

'And still raining,' Bardi had grumbled, reorganizing his papers.

'Nothing like it was.'

As a matter of fact, all the time he'd been asleep he'd believed he was still reading, which explained why he'd somehow kept the file balanced on his knee. He had been aware, even as he slept, of the noise of the engine, the continuing rain and the familiar rise and fall of the lads' voices. Perhaps it was just as well that he'd slept. He had started going over the Li Causi file because it was his habit to do so on the journeys he made to other prisons for interrogations. In this case there was no real need since he knew the file almost by heart. It was too late to worry about it now, in any event.

'Go and get yourself a coffee . . .'

He tucked his briefcase under his arm, opened a large umbrella and started to dash for the main entrance.

What had he been expecting from this confrontation with

Li Causi? He had told Corbi he expected nothing, that Li Causi wouldn't talk and the interrogation was only a matter of form. He had told himself that it was nothing more than an overt reason for going to Rome when in reality he had quite another motive. Nevertheless, he had expected something, some radical change in their relationship now that it had been proved, after all these years, that he'd been right. It was his disappointment that made him realize how much, after all, he'd been expecting. There had been a radical change all right, but there was no question of any satisfaction to be got from facing in new circumstances the arrogant young man who had once sat calmly beneath the gesturing angels giving slow, precise answers with just a touch of contempt in his voice. That man no longer existed.

He seemed smaller. Or was it just that the two guards who brought him in were tall? They took the handcuffs off him and he sat down without so much as acknowledging the presence of the lawyer provided for him by the State. The lawyer, on his part, had not even bothered to open the briefcase that stood on the floor beside him. That, and the look of boredom on his face suggested that he had been given similar clients before and had no illusions as to how things would proceed. A strong contrast with Chiari, Li Causi's own slick lawyer, who had been present at the interrogation six years ago.

Next to Bardi sat a clerk who now slid a sheet of paper into his typewriter and waited in silence for the Substitute to begin his interrogation.

'Name.'

'Li Causi, Antonio.'

'Date and place of birth.'

'31st December, 1948, Naples.'

Forty years old. His hair had begun greying slightly at the temples and there were lines around his eyes which hadn't been there six years ago.

'Residence.'

'Florence, Via delle Terme 18.'

The clerk was typing rapidly with two fingers. It was true that prison could change a man's appearance overnight. Without a tie the unbuttoned shirt collar made a man's neck look thin and vulnerable and one night without sleep was enough to produce a greyish pallor which bad air and claustrophobia would intensify over the months or years inside. But that, in Bardi's opinion, wasn't enough to account for the change in the man before him. More likely it was the six years that had gone before. Six years of clandestine living, of avoiding policemen in the street and avoiding even more any chance encounter with old friends or colleagues; not being able to go into a bar for coffee or into a restaurant for a meal.

'Civil status.'

'Bachelor.'

'Profession.'

'Professor of Sociology, University of Florence.'

Six years of virtual imprisonment in a tiny apartment, alone or with the same few people all with the same obsession. An atmosphere that was like a drug, cutting them off from the real world, from life itself, an atmosphere that Gori and those like him tried desperately to recreate by setting up a similar intimacy with their 'confessor'. Prison was nothing new to them after years of voluntary seclusion. But Li Causi was no Gori. He would fight the need to communicate with all the skill and knowledge which his particular field of study put at his disposal.

The clerk had stopped typing and was waiting, his two fingers poised.

The lawyer settled further back in his chair, cleared his throat and glanced at his watch.

Bardi opened Li Causi's file and looked across at the prisoner.

That was when he realized what had really changed. Li Causi met his eyes blankly and his gaze wandered away, indifferent. Was it possible that he didn't even remember? He was tempted to say something, anything, that would break through that wall of indifference, to say that Gori had talked and would go on talking, even to say that he was about to pay a visit to a certain ecclesiastical tailor. But all he said was: 'You were interrogated by me at the Procura of Florence six years ago, you may remember.'

'I remember.' But it no longer mattered. Bardi had once been a threat to him but that was before he went underground. It had no importance now. And before Bardi could speak again he made his statement.

'I refuse to answer any questions. I declare myself to be a political prisoner.'

And it was over.

The lawyer, with another glance at his watch, gathered up his briefcase. The clerk pulled the sheet of paper from his typewriter and pushed it along to Bardi for his signature. The guards moved forward with handcuffs. A scene that would be repeated over and over as magistrates from all over the country with cases against Li Causi arrived to interrogate him.

Without a word to the clerk or the lawyer, Bardi tossed the file into his briefcase, locked it and strode off down the long corridor towards the exit.

One of the guards on duty reached for his phone when he saw the magistrate, ready to alert his escort.

Bardi hesitated a moment and then said, 'No . . . or rather, find them and tell them to get an early lunch in the canteen. I'll be back in an hour.'

The guard stared at him a moment and then shrugged and picked up the receiver. It wasn't his responsibility.

It was still raining heavily but Bardi was reluctant to have a taxi called from the prison. Outside on the street there were few pedestrians, apart from a group huddled by a bus stop under shiny dripping umbrellas, but the wide road was blocked solid with traffic that moved along sluggishly for a few yards and then stopped again and set up a chorus of impatient hooting. Clouds of exhaust fumes hung in the rain and the occupants of the cars were invisible behind the streaming side windows. There were quite a number of yellow taxis dotted amongst the traffic but though many of them were empty they must have been on radio calls because the drivers shook their heads when Bardi tried to hail them. He soon gave up and began squeezing between the cars, making for a bar across the street that had a yellow telephone sign over the door. His shoes were already wet and the lower part of his raincoat spattered with dirty water.

'A coffee and a telephone token.'

'Looking for a taxi?' The barman must have been observing him before he decided to come in.

'Yes.'

Without further comment the barman dropped four telephone tokens decisively on to the counter and slapped a small cup under his steaming coffee machine.

Bardi used up all four tokens. Each of the radio taxi firms he tried kept him waiting an interminable time before telling him they had no cars available. One of them added by way of explanation, 'It's raining . . .'

'Coffee!' bellowed the barman, slapping the cup on to the waiting saucer on the counter.

'Your best bet,' he went on, as Bardi drank, 'is to get the number 58 as far as the piazza and try for a taxi at the rank – not that there's likely to be one but you'd have a better chance waiting there than wasting your time telephoning.'

Bardi looked out of the open door where the rain was bouncing up from the pavement. The traffic had barely moved and the huddled group at the bus stop was still there. He looked back at the barman, who shrugged.

'That's all I can suggest. You'd be quicker walking. How far you going?'

'As far as the Vatican.'

'Say hello to the Pope for me. Coffee!' And he turned his attention to another customer.

Bardi walked. At the empty taxi rank in the nearest big piazza he waited for eighteen minutes, his shoes now squelching and the lower part of his raincoat soaked. The taxi which eventually reached him had been visible for a good ten minutes, a yellow blur beyond a snarl of barely moving traffic. He settled into the already damp back seat and gave the address.

'You'd be quicker walking,' said the driver glumly as he tried to edge back into the crawling mass. Some time later, still in second gear, he added: 'I hope you're not in a hurry.'

Bardi, who had thought he wasn't, began to realize that he had been reckoning time and distance in Florentine terms and looked anxiously at his watch.

'I imagine they'll close at one . . .'

'If you want to get out just say the word. Most people do in the end.'

Bardi looked out at the pouring rain. On the banks of the Tiber with the Castel Sant'Angelo visible beyond the line of bare wet trees, he paid the driver, got out and began walking quickly. He concentrated on avoiding the worst of the puddles and glanced frequently at his watch, only vaguely aware of the noise and fumes on his left and the rain falling steadily into the steaming river on his right beyond the wet marble embankment. Every now and then a tram squealed past and he wondered whether it might be worth jumping on. Nevertheless, he continued walking like an automaton, his wits being more exhausted than his body. It occurred to him to be grateful to the lads for having let him sleep so long in the car. Walking distances couldn't be judged in Florentine terms either; the buildings were so much bigger, the distance between bridges so much longer. The round castle with its angel on top was a lot farther away than he had thought. When at last he reached it he had to ask for directions. Two tiny raincoated nuns insisted on accompanying him to the corner of a short street below the walls of Vatican City, chattering all the way in rapid Italian with a strong foreign accent.

'It's on your right, now, you can't miss it . . .'

'Thank you. You've been very kind.' And he watched

them hurrying back in the direction they had come. They must have gone out of their way for him.

The interior of the ecclesiastical tailor's shop was large, rather dark and very quiet. An old-fashioned bell tinkled as he pushed open the door. Immediately before him was a small haberdashery counter where two women, one youngish, the other middle-aged, were buying plain black socks, no doubt for some priest in the family. The assistant was a youngish woman in a neat black dress. All three speaking in subdued tones, almost whispering. To the left, down three carpeted steps was a much bigger room, equally gloomy, where rows of dark suits hung on racks. The only light came from an open doorway beyond the haberdashery counter where a glittering white cope encrusted with gold embroidery was draped on a stand beneath a brilliant spotlight. It was towards this glowing rectangle that the sales assistant turned on seeing Bardi and called softly:

'Signor Attilio . . .'

'Oh . . .!' came an anguished little cry from the interior. 'What is it, what is it?'

'A customer. I'm occupied!' She smiled gently at Bardi and went on making a parcel of the black socks.

'But it's almost one o'clock . . . it's *quite* one o'clock!' lamented the off-stage voice. 'Really, people these days have no consideration . . .'

A small, bustling figure appeared in the rectangle of light, rotund, smartly dressed, pixie-like ears protruding beneath a shiny bald crown, eyes dark and shiny as berries and so brimming with innocent friendliness as to make nonsense of the laments which nevertheless continued.

'It's quite one o'clock, what can I do for you? There's my lunch, you see, and it's been an appallingly busy morning, I can't tell you . . . I don't think we've seen you before . . .'

'No. May I –'

'I must say *right away* that if it's a question of an order you'll absolutely have to come back at three-thirty. I *hate* to say it and to a new customer above all but I have my timetable and if I didn't stick to it I'd never have a moment . . . do you understand?'

The little man was wringing his soft hands in such genuine distress that Bardi turned to the assistant for help but she was ringing up her sale on an ancient cash register and seemed quite indifferent to his predicament.

'People have so little consideration and at times I'm overwhelmed . . .'

Bardi couldn't help gazing round at the dark empty shop before interrupting as politely as could be managed.

'I just want a word with you, in private if possible. I don't want to order anything and I hope I shan't keep you from your lunch.'

'A word in private . . .?' And he, too, gazed about him at the empty rooms as though the impossibility of such a thing must be evident.

'I really don't see . . .'

'Perhaps you have a private office?'

This seemed to distress him still further.

'Quite frankly, unless it's of the utmost urgency . . .'

'It is of the utmost urgency. My name is Bardi. Substitute Prosecutor, Florence.'

'Oh . . .! Good heavens. Do forgive me. Then of course it must be urgent.' And the friendly brown eyes took on an expression of deadly seriousness. '*Do* forgive me. Now, how shall we manage . . .? Signorina! You must lock up everything and go to lunch immediately –'

'If she wouldn't mind staying a moment,' put in Bardi, 'we might need her help.'

'You think so? In that case . . . Signorina, lock up everything and stay right here! Don't let anyone in, I insist on that, you understand? Anyone at all. Stay right here . . . now, where would be best? I don't know, I really . . . let me see . . .' He was wringing his soft little hands again but now his earnestness and anxiety were certainly bound up with his pleasure at receiving someone of importance and authority. Bardi could well imagine him receiving a bishop or a cardinal with just this same fluttering solemnity, overloaded with respect but without obsequiousness.

'Your office perhaps,' he suggested again.

Attilio stopped his fluttering and flushed deeply.

Bardi was puzzled. He had every reason to believe that the tailor had something to hide but it was difficult to imagine that there should be any overt evidence of it in his office. It made no sense.

'If you wouldn't mind . . .' he urged, looking pointedly at his watch.

'Yes, of course, of course, my office . . . Come this way . . .'

They passed through the room where the spotlight flooded the gold and white cope. Other similarly cloaked shapes stood out in the shadows beyond reach of the spot, like silent figures observing their passage. A door at the far end of the room opened on to a small tiled area with a door on each side. Attilio opened the door on the right but before Bardi could step in behind him he found himself suddenly shut out and Attilio's voice on the other side calling softly: 'Just one moment! I won't keep you more than a moment . . .'

For a few seconds Bardi was too surprised to react. Then he bent and looked through the keyhole. A light was switched on. Only the tailor's back was visible. He was evidently scooping something hurriedly from the desk, talking all the while in low urgent tones. It was impossible to see who else was in the room. Without turning, Attilio stuffed whatever he had collected up quickly into the drawer of some sort of dark wooden filing cabinet. Bardi straightened up. There was more murmuring and a faint swishing sound. Then the door opened.

'I do beg your pardon, I just . . . I have my timetable, you see, I'm sure you understand. Oh dear, you're dreadfully wet, aren't you. Now, perhaps you'd like to hang your raincoat behind the door. You'll see there's a hanger . . . Here we are . . .' He hurriedly removed his own coat to prevent its getting dampened by Bardi's. A pair of outdoor shoes was placed neatly in the corner behind the door.

Bardi hung up his coat in silence. After the austere, almost ecclesiastical spaciousness of the shop this room came as a shock. It was small and, though not exactly dirty, decidedly dusty. It was filled to bursting point with undefinable pieces of furniture, all piled to an incredible height with every kind of office clutter. Some of the great mounds were discreetly shrouded in faded cotton cloths, others spilled on to the floor so that it was impossible to walk about the room without having to step over the tottering heaps. A large, coloured photograph of the Pope hung on the wall. There was no window. There was no third person in the room either but a sharp little yap from behind the desk explained Attilio's one-sided conversation of a moment ago. Two antique chairs were drawn up to the desk and on one of them a dishevelled little grey dog of indeterminate breed was sitting on a much battered cushion, his shiny eyes peering out from under a ragged fringe. He yapped again and then began whining softly, disturbed by the presence of a stranger.

'Hush now, hush, there's a good little boy. You must be very, very good because we have a most important visitor!

The little creature half stood, wagging the whole of its hind parts and whining more excitedly, its eyes fixed on its master.

'You understand exactly, don't you, of course he does, he understands perfectly that he has to be a *good* little boy and absolutely quiet, *absolutely quiet*!'

The little dog began yelping.

'Now! Fido! Hush! That's enough! That's enough or I shall get very angry! Come to Daddy! Come on! There's a good little boy. Now we're going to sit in your chair and this gentleman will sit in mine.' He settled the dog on his lap where it immediately covered his well-creased trousers with grey hairs. As he sat down Bardi spotted a clothes brush sticking out from the jumble of files and loose papers on the desk. No doubt Attilio retreated to this sacred den many times during the day, brushing himself off and reappearing as spruce as ever to greet his customers afterwards.

'Now then.' He turned his bright eyes to Bardi, looking for all the world like a deadly earnest pixie. 'I don't want to hurry you but I must be with the Cardinal at four – I go to him, you understand, he's extremely busy. A fitting, you see . . .'

'Of course.' He could hardly have feared that their interview would last three or four hours so Bardi put this down to a desire to mention the Cardinal. In this he was proved only too right. 'I doubt if I'll need to disturb you for very long – is the signorina your only employee?'

'Oh, goodness, no. I have a cutter and two sewers in the workrooms upstairs – they go off to lunch at twelve – and a very nice young man who helps serve but he's off sick today, a very nice young man indeed, excellent manners, he came to me highly recommended. So many young people these days have such distressing manners, don't you find? I must say I've been very fortunate, in fact, only last week when I was quite dreadfully ill with influenza I had to send him to the Cardinal in my place and His Eminence was very satisfied with him, very satisfied. Then of course there are my embroiderers, all ladies who work at home.'

'I see. Do you think I might smoke?'

'Certainly. I don't myself but please do. Oh dear . . .' He began to burrow among the papers on the desk with one hand, the other holding on to the dog. 'I *do* have an ashtray somewhere . . .'

'Don't worry, if you can't –'

'No, no. It's here somewhere, I know exactly where it is, just excuse me one second. You get down for a moment, Fido – No! No! You're not to bark. Stop it!'

'Please don't bother, it's not important.'

'That's *enough*! Daddy's going to get cross! That's better . . . that's better. Good boy – No! No! Get up on your chair! Get up! Good boy, now sit! Sit! Now, this area here, I think . . .'

'Could it perhaps be under here?'

'No! Please don't touch anything! I have my system and if anything gets out of place . . . there!'

The gold-rimmed ashtray bore a bad likeness of the Pope in gaudy colours.

Bardi took out a cigarette and broke it in two. The truth was he was playing for time, trying to come to some sort of decision about Attilio who had taken the little dog on his lap again, his bright eyes watching him gravely as he lit up. He looked as innocent as a child, sitting there amongst his chaotic 'system', gently stroking his dog and no doubt waiting for the next chance to mention the Cardinal. Nevertheless, the number in Li Causi's diary was undoubtedly his and there didn't seem to be anyone else in the place likely to be responsible for its being there. Unless . . .

'You must lead an extremely busy life; this is quite a sizeable business, I can see . . .'

'Oh, indeed. I manage well because I'm systematic and I do insist on keeping to a strict timetable.'

'It must leave you little time for your family, even so.'

'That is a problem. I only have my mother but she's almost blind and getting on in years. I try to spend as much time with her as I can because she can't leave the house – we're on the fourth floor and no lift, you see. To be quite honest . . . not that I want to hurry you . . . but I was hoping to spend half an hour with her before going to the Cardinal – we have a very kind neighbour, very kind indeed, who sees to her lunch, but Mother is expecting me to look in on her and old people, you know, are easily distressed by any unexpected change of plan. There's the question of time, too. I don't drive and the buses are quite hopeless. It's exercise for the dog so I walk everywhere, and then there's the signorina who ought to go to lunch, so . . . I don't want to hurry you, please don't think that, but I do have my timetable.'

'Of course. What I want is something very simple. I'm trying to trace a person in connection with a case I'm investigating. It's possible that this person may be one of your customers.'

'My customers . . .? Well, I do have some lay customers but as you can imagine most of my customers are in Holy Orders so I don't see . . . May I ask what sort of case – or is it confidential?'

'Highly confidential. In fact, although my visit is an official one I must ask you not to mention it to anyone.'

'Oh, of course not, of course not. You can rely on me absolutely. Now, would I be right in thinking that what you need is a list of my customers?'

'You would. The reason I wanted the young lady to stay is that she might be good enough to photocopy the list for me. You don't by any chance have a photocopier?'

'No. No, I don't but I can see to that for you right away. There's a room upstairs, you see, which I rent to a young solicitor – a very nice young man, he came to me highly recommended – and he lets us use his machine on the rare occasions when we have need of it. He will have gone to lunch but I have the key and I'm sure that in an urgent situation such as this he won't mind, I'm sure he'll understand.'

'Forgive me for reminding you,' insisted Bardi gently, 'but it's essential that you don't mention my visit to anyone.'

'Oh no. Quite. I wouldn't dream . . . now, the thing is to find the blue file . . . the blue file . . . the blue file – just give me one moment, I know exactly where it is . . .'

He did seem to know exactly where it was but it took almost ten minutes of excavation among one of the great shrouded heaps to uncover it. The little dog yapped frantically throughout the disturbance. When Bardi reached out a hand to quiet it, the nervous creature first snapped at him ineffectually, then changed its mind and jumped on to his knee, covering him with long grey hairs.

'There! That's the one we're looking for! Oh, has he made a new friend then? Has he? There's a *good* little boy, there's a *good* little boy! Now, I shall see to this for you right away.'

And he bustled off, full of zeal and self-importance, calling as he went through the empty rooms, 'Signorina! Signorina . . . !'

Bardi set the dog down on its cushions and extricated the clothes brush and got rid of most of the grey hairs. It was useless to try brushing the splattered lower part of his trousers because they were still soaking wet. He buried the brush where he had found it so as not to disturb Attilio's 'system'. Was it possible that the tailor's number had been used without his knowledge? To Bardi it was beginning to seem likely. Not that he wouldn't have been willing to cooperate. Authority was only too obviously sacred for him . . . the Pope . . . the Cardinal . . . his reception of Bardi himself and his solemn delight in helping him. But who would ever have trusted him, innocent chatterbox that he was? Only one doubt remained. Bardi stood up quietly and went to an ancient wooden filing cabinet. The top drawer was filled to overflowing with old letters and postcards. Bardi shut it without touching anything. The next two contained dusty cardboard folders with samples of cloth. Nothing had been thrown in there in a hurry. In any case, Bardi was fairly sure that Attilio had bent quite low to hide whatever had been on his desk. He found the hidden objects in the bottom drawer: a piece of brown paper containing two ham sandwiches, one of them half eaten, a quarter bottle of wine with a screw top and a packet of dog biscuits. The little dog whined and looked at him hopefully.

'Mother? Is that you? Yes, I know and I'm sorry but I shan't be able – Quiet, Fido, stop it! Daddy can't hear! Stop it – just a moment, Mother, he's making the most dreadful noise – no, I shan't be able to, that's why I'm ringing. Now, please don't get upset . . . have you had lunch? Yes, of course you did but I promise you it's not my fault, a quite unexpected visit – no, not the Cardinal – Stop it Fido! Mother, I shall have to leave you, I'm a good hour behind schedule and I must take Fido

out for ten minutes before I – no, no, Mother it wasn't a question of putting my pleasure before your comfort at all, I had a very important visitor, very important indeed, a well-known magistrate who'd come all the way from Florence on an urgent matter – now I'm sworn to secrecy and I can't say a word, not even to you –'

The voice became a gibbering, high-pitched squeak as the tape ran backwards.

'Shan't be able – Quiet, Fido, stop it! Daddy can't hear! Stop it – just a moment . . .'

This time the young man operating the machine let the tape run on to the end of the conversation. Then he switched off and picked up the receiver from the telephone at his elbow.

'Put me through to the General. Priority.'

CHAPTER TEN

Poma crossed the bridge with the big envelope under his arm, walking slowly. When he reached the centre he stopped, looking down at the river. He mustn't get there too soon. The weather had changed; the icy mountain wind was blowing and only a few clouds reflected in the smooth green water still swollen after the rains. Winter seemed to stretch endlessly ahead like the river, a winter full of problems that were overtaking him too fast so that he had no time to solve one before another presented itself. Just as he had begun to get used to the idea of his wife's being pregnant something had gone wrong and this morning she had been taken into hospital. He'd only seen her pregnancy as an abstract problem before but the thought that she might lose the baby had made him realize that he wanted it. Only maybe it was too late already . . . Was there any point in going to see that house this evening? Wouldn't he, in any case, have to go back to the hospital? What he needed was some time off. Below him a very old man was crouched over a fishing rod beside a battered overturned boat. To sit quietly like that for a day . . . And instead he was here running risks for his chief as usual. He turned and walked on, sometimes hurrying for a few paces, sometimes dawdling. He shouldn't arrive too early but on the other hand he didn't know how long a job it would be and he was supposed to be at the hospital at one o'clock.

As he turned left into Borgo Ognissanti a squad car passed him and he saw the gold insignia of an unknown colonel sitting in the back. And what if he got caught? He'd already decided to leave the army but getting kicked out . . . after fourteen years. He could neither remember nor imagine any other life. The squad car turned in at the main entrance to the barracks. Poma quickened his pace again. It was bound to take time. Bardi had no right to ask him, he was too used to always getting what he wanted.

'All you have to do is go through the names on the general file, which could take you some time because it doesn't just list known and suspected subversives but all agents and contacts too. We can't hope to get a look at anything more specific. If you find a name that's on the list I've given you, note it down. That's all I want. Except, of course, that you don't sign for it.'

'But I'll have to sign, sir. They won't let me in otherwise.'

'Come on, Poma, I don't know what's got into you lately.'

'You're right. Maybe Mastino would do a better job . . .'

'This is no job for Mastino, he's too much of a northerner.'

'Even so, he's got guts.'

'It's not guts I need, it's wits. He's as courageous as a bull and has about as much guile as one. If anybody can get away with this, it's you. Come on, Poma! You've pulled off trickier things than this in the past.'

'I'll never get away with it . . . unless Mario's on duty . . .'

'He is.'

'He is . . .?'

'I've just telephoned and hung up as soon as he answered. There's no mistaking his voice.'

'No . . .'

'Then you'll do it?'

'I'll do it.'

'That's more like the Poma I know. You've always enjoyed this sort of thing.'

That was true, too, or it used to be. But in the end it had only been pride that had made him accept because now things were different, and not just for Poma. Bardi was different, too, in a way that Poma was unable to define. He had said, as he always did when asking them to take this sort of risk, that if anything went wrong he would take all the blame. Poma had always trusted him without question but now he wasn't so sure. He had a lot of influence, there was no denying that, and on the surface he seemed the same as ever. But something was wrong. There had been that business of his dodging off in Rome, for a start. When Mastino had protested afterwards Bardi had winked and said, 'A man has to live.' The way he used to ages ago when he'd had that fancy woman and was forever dodging them so that life was one long game of hide-and-seek that had driven the two of them half crazy. But Bardi hadn't given a thought to that sort of thing for years and he wasn't giving a thought to it now, that was certain. Did he think they were half-wits? Maybe he did, at that . . .

He had slowed down again, his way sometimes blocked by luxuriously dressed winter tourists who paused on the narrow pavement to stare with delighted exclamations at the window displays of lace and embroidery, antiques and vastly expensive clothes. The entrance to the barracks was only three doors away. A group of schoolchildren dressed in track suits crossed the road in twos on their way to the gymnasium, shrieking and chattering. The happy indifference of all the people around him made the knot in Poma's stomach tighten even more. He turned in at the barracks.

The guard on duty only glanced at his uniform and nodded before turning away. It wasn't anyone he knew, which was a good start. He walked along the old cloister and began climbing the stairs.

'Hey!'

Poma stopped dead.

'Poma! What are you doing in these parts?'

'Just a message,' Poma mumbled, his red face half averted. It was a man who'd gone through training school with him and they usually stopped for a gossip on the rare occasions when they ran into each other.

'I'm going down for a coffee. Come and join me if you've only a message to leave.'

'Can't manage it. Another time . . .' He continued up the stairs.

'All right . . .' He was going on down but Poma heard the note of surprise in his voice and he knew he had made himself conspicuous. He should have said yes and then just not turned up and the other man wouldn't have given it a thought.

By the time he reached the Archives on the top floor his breathing was fast and shallow and sweat was rolling under his armpits. It wasn't the stairs though he tried to tell himself that it was.

'Well, look who's here!' Mario was at his desk in the ante-room and his bored face lit up at the sight of an old friend from his home town. 'What's wrong with you? You look as though you've seen a ghost.'

'Nothing. I ran up the stairs. How are things, then?'

'Can't complain. And you?'

'Oh, much as usual . . .'

'Concetta?'

'She's expecting.'

'No! Congratulations, and about time, too. Let's hope it's not born with a moustache like yours.'

'To tell you the truth, she's not all that –'

'And I'll tell you who else is expecting, Marcello's wife – you remember Marcello? Always sat behind you in the last year at school, had that accident and got a fortune in damages? Set himself up with his own workshop on the money and married what's she called . . . Lucilla, the one you used to go out with before you joined up and left. They'd been trying for over seven years and had just decided to adopt and now it turns out she's pregnant. Of course you can imagine the sort of gossip that's going the rounds. People saying it was him who couldn't and that she must have found herself a boyfriend, but whether that's true or not he's over the moon about it. I had a letter from my mother last week. She hears everything, of course. Want a smoke?'

'Thanks. Is she still working?'

'Still going strong. We tried to persuade her to give up when we were all home last August but you know what she's like. She won't give up cleaning for the chemist as long as she can stand because that's where she gets all her gossip. Still, she's had to give up the Senator. His wife closed up the house after he was arrested and moved into the flat in Rome. You heard about it?'

'I saw it in the paper.'

'Well, I suppose he had it coming to him, like all the others. I must say we were relieved because she was doing far too much and she'd never have given up of her own accord.'

'And Alberto?'

'Alberto? You mean you haven't heard? He's in America!'

'No.'

'Upped and left, when was it . . . over a month ago. I'm surprised you didn't know . . .'

Poma knew. But he let Mario chatter on. They had plenty more old friends to get through yet but it all depended on somebody coming in before they ran out of steam. The place was deserted.

'And since the state paid for his medical studies while he was in the army he was supposed to work in Italy for a certain number of years – I forget how many exactly – so he can never come back. You can imagine his mother . . .'

Still nobody came.

'– They've turned it into one of these hamburger places so nobody goes any more. Remember the hours we used to spend in there? Of course once the old man died . . . and now it's packed with tourists and they're shut all day Sunday. Remember Sunday nights?'

A plainclothes man came in.

'They're making a fortune, but even so . . . 'Morning, Inspector. Sign here, please. Going on where you left off yesterday? Section 2. B14 83 if I remember rightly . . . just let me check.'

Poma had edged away but Mario looked up.

'Hey, Poma, you haven't –'

'Carry on, we'll do it afterwards. I won't be a minute, anyway . . .'

And he was in.

In the narrow dusty passageway between grey filing cabinets he pulled Bardi's list out of the envelope. His hands were trembling. Before starting, he looked at his watch. Twenty to twelve. At twelve Mario would go off duty and the man on the next shift would assume that Poma had signed on his way in. That left only two possible risks: that Mario, when he came to say goodbye to him before going to lunch would bring the book with him to be signed, or that he would leave a message with the next man on duty. The first was unlikely because the register hadn't to be moved, according to the regulations. The second was possible but improbable because Mario had no reason not to trust him.

By the time he reached the names beginning with C he had stopped trembling though he had found nothing. He was even sufficiently collected to notice that Bardi's photocopied list was peculiar. All the names had some sort of measurements after them. He even cursed once or twice under his breath because it was all written by hand and some names were difficult to decipher, making him waste time. He struggled on as far as F, still finding nothing.

'Poma!'

Mario was watching him from the end of the passage.

'What is it?' His heart was thumping fast but his voice remained normal.

'In case I forget: a group of us are going out for a pizza next Saturday night, what about coming with us?'

This time he got it right.

'OK. I'll give you a ring before then.'

'Great. See you on your way out, anyway.' And he was gone. Poma worked steadily on. Listed under L he found what he was looking for. Lazurek J. According to Bardi's list he was a monsignor. The name was foreign. Did that mean he was supposed to be some sort of Communist spy? Well, it wasn't Poma's problem and the file indicated that the disc on which the information on the subject was stored was classified so that was that. He had what he needed and now he could get out as soon as Mario . . .

He looked at his watch. It was twelve-twenty. Mario had gone off without a word.

Poma felt himself begin to sweat again. He tried to think clearly, fighting against the instinct to get out at all costs in any way he could. Had Mario simply forgotten? And what if he had left a message with the man coming on duty who would then stop Poma on his way out? He took a few steps forward and then stopped again. It could be that Mario, having seen where he was working, had filled in the register for him. If that was what had happened there was nothing he could do. He'd done his best for Bardi and he was covered. The best thing that could have happened. He walked on between the grey cabinets at a quicker pace. He would stop at the desk, ask if Mario had left him a message and glance at the register. One thing he couldn't live with was the uncertainty, that on top of everything else was more than he could take. And if things had gone wrong he would resign immediately instead of waiting until the end of December as he had intended. He reached the ante-room and walked straight to the desk. The man there looked up at him.

'My mate who was on duty before you . . .' No, he shouldn't have said Mario was a friend. Too late. 'He didn't leave any message for me?'

'Not that I know of.' The man looked through the papers on the desk. 'Unless it's a written message. He didn't say anything . . .'

Poma's eyes scanned the register upside down. His name wasn't there.

'No, there's nothing here,' the other concluded.

'Wasn't important . . .'

The man shrugged, unconcerned. Poma turned and left the room.

From a bar well away from the barracks he telephoned Bardi.

'Why are you telephoning? I told you to come straight back here.'

'Just to say I found what you wanted . . .' Perhaps if he

explained about the hospital . . . but he didn't. He'd just have to be late.

'You didn't run into any trouble?'

'No . . . . I did it the way I said and he just went off without saying anything. He must have forgotten me. I'll be there in five minutes.'

Mario hadn't forgotten. He had followed Colonel Tempesta's instructions to the letter. It hadn't even occurred to him to be concerned about whether Poma had signed or not signed the register. If the Colonel had called him in it meant something big and it wasn't his friend Poma they were after.

The old man selling oranges from a stand below the walls of Vatican City eyed the two men on the corner speculatively. It was almost eight o'clock on a cold dark Saturday night and there were few people still about. He gave a last call offering the remaining fruit at half price but without much hope of a sale. The rest of the street was deserted. He folded up his stall and trundled it away.

The two men continued to stand there, watching a lighted shop window. One of them was carrying what looked like an overnight case. When the light in the window went out they began walking forward without a word. A young man and woman came out of the darkened doorway and walked off together in the opposite direction. As the men approached the shop an older man came out with a little dog on a lead. He reached up with a hooked pole to roll down the metal shutter to head height, went inside to replace the pole and came out again holding a bunch of keys. The two men stepped forward.

'Signor Attilio?'

'We're closed, I'm afraid. It's quite eight o'clock, past eight o'clock. Out you come, Fido, there's a good boy, Daddy has to lock up. We reopen on Monday at three-thirty.' He inserted the key firmly without looking up.

'We'd like a word with you in private.'

Attilio turned. They were holding out cards which he barely saw in the gloom before they were rapidly withdrawn.

'Oh . . .'

'I think you may already know something of what it's about. You've already had a visit from Substitute Prosecutor Bardi?'

'Oh, yes indeed, of course. Oh dear . . . It couldn't wait till Monday afternoon? Or even the morning? I'm usually here Monday morning, you see, although we're closed for business and at this time my mother . . .'

'We won't keep you a moment. Shall we go inside? It's rather cold standing on the pavement.'

'Well, yes, if you think . . .' He unlocked the door and the two men, much taller and heavier than the little tailor, ducked under the half-closed shutter and followed him inside. Attilio switched on the light and bent towards the dog.

'Now, sit still one moment and I'll take off your lead. Sit! Oh . . . did he think he was going home? He did, he thought he was going home – well, you be a good little boy and we'll be off home in a few minutes. There! Now I must ask you gentlemen to be patient just for a moment whilst I call Mother and explain –'

'We'd rather you didn't,' one of the men said firmly, 'For security reasons we'd prefer that this visit be kept between ourselves.'

'Oh, but of course I wouldn't dream . . . naturally some other excuse –'

'As we shan't keep you any longer than it would take you to get home it will be quite in order for you to telephone after we leave, inventing, as you say, some other excuse. The traffic perhaps, being a Saturday night . . .'

'Well, if you think that would be better . . . I always walk, of course, but –'

'You'll think of something. Perhaps you have an office somewhere behind. We don't want to be disturbed by people thinking you're still open.'

'Quite, quite. Please come this way.'

They followed him behind the haberdashery counter and one of them switched off the light in the front of the shop as soon as the spotlight came on over the gold and white cope. As they crossed the big room the man in the rear paused to look up carefully at the metal beam to which a number of these spotlights were attached. Then they went into the tiny office, Attilio chattering softly as he closed the door.

'I wouldn't be so concerned but I've been late home on a number of occasions this week. The Cardinal, you see, when it's fittings I always go to him and he very kindly offers me a glass of vinsanto when we've finished which I *can't* refuse. We chatted for quite some time on Thursday, quite some time indeed – quiet, Fido – no, not on your chair, there's a gentleman going to sit there. Now I'm going to give you a biscuit and you're going to be as good as gold. Hush! Now stop it. Biscuit! Good boy. Now we shall only be five minutes . . .'

They were in there for twenty-three minutes. During the first quarter of an hour the gentle voice of Attilio rose and fell, punctuated occasionally by a sharp question in deeper tones. It may have been the excitement of finding himself suddenly so important or perhaps the desire to hurry matters along so as to get home to an ever fretting mother that caused Attilio's voice to repeat several times, not very truthfully: 'That nice magistrate explained everything fully, everything, and I'm glad to say I was able to be of considerable help to him . . .'

During the last few minutes there were no voices, only a faint whine from the dog and the noise and the shuffle and tumble of objects being moved about. Then the door opened.

'Do we destroy the list here or take it with us?'

'Take it with us. Take too long to do it here. Damn nuisance that there's no window, this smell's going to stick.'

He lifted one of Attilio's eyelids and examined a glazed and sightless eye. When he let go the head lolled sideways and a little spurt of vomit trickled down one well-brushed lapel.

'Think he's queer?'

'I'm sure he is. Probably goes in for choirboys. Take the feet. That big room with the spotlight. There's a beam . . .'

They left the door open behind them to let the smell of chloroform disperse but the little grey dog didn't follow them. He remained standing in the middle of the office, trembling, one paw awkwardly treading on a biscuit. The whole packet of dog biscuits had been emptied on to the floor and he had gulped three of them down greedily before backing out of the way to stand watching, his head on one side.

When he heard the shop door close and the building fell silent he trotted rapidly out into the big room and into the circle of light where the gold and white cloak glittered. He looked up and gave three short barks. The black feet twirled slowly from side to side, brushing the gold embroidery lightly. He jumped up trying to lick them in encouragement but he couldn't reach them and after a few futile attempts he lay down beneath them beside an upturned chair and put his head on his paws.

The movement of the black feet diminished imperceptibly minute by minute until the three figures grouped beneath the spotlight became a tableau with an audience of cloaked and headless figures grouped about it in the surrounding shadows. Half an hour passed. The dog got up stiffly, trotted back to the end of the short tiled corridor between the office and the washroom where his water pot stood and lapped up all the remaining water thirstily. Then he went back through the big room to the shop door and sat down, looking back over his shoulder and giving a few short barks. After waiting a long time he padded back to the office where he finished the rest of the biscuits and jumped up on to his chair whining softly with pain. He lay very still for almost an hour. Then the pain became too great and he jumped down and crept into the most obscure corner he could find among the heaps of boxes and files. He sniffed and gazed anxiously about him before lifting a straggly little leg that quivered with shame and fear.

CHAPTER ELEVEN

On Sunday morning Bardi was woken by the telephone. He snatched up the receiver and his free hand groped for the switch on the bedside lamp. It was barely light.

'Yes?'

'Substitute Prosecutor Bardi?'

'Speaking.'

'Police Headquarters. I have a message for you, sir, from the chief of the drug squad. He thought you'd want to be kept informed . . . It's about the Marchese Acciai.'

Bardi sat up and reached for a pen. 'He's got something new?'

'No, sir, the Marchese's dead. He thought –'

'How?'

'I don't have any details, sir, it only happened a couple of hours ago, but I think a gunshot wound.'

'Where did it happen?'

'At his home.'

'Is your chief out there now?'

'He was, but he'll have left by this time, I imagine.'

'All right. I'll go out there. Thank you.'

'Then you'll need an escort, sir. Shall I –?'

'Don't bother. I'll call my own boys.'

'Forgive me reminding you but it's Sunday, sir. If you like, I can put you through now –'

'No. I'll call my boys. If there's any problem I'll ring you back. Thank you.'

Though he had no intention of disturbing Poma and Mastino.

While he was dressing Laura appeared in the doorway.

'What's happening? I heard the telephone.'

'Nothing. Go back to bed, it's early.'

'Do you have to go out?'

'As you see.' He was in shirtsleeves and buckling his holster.

'I could make some coffee . . .'

'No time. I'll get one on the way.'

During the drive out to the castle Bardi wasted no time on idle speculation before having all the facts. He tried, rather, to recall the details of that other Sunday when he had made the same journey with Corbi chattering beside him, but it all seemed so long ago now and the drive had more of the nightmare quality of that frustrating dream in which he had searched so long in vain for the right road only to find in the end that the castle was no longer there.

It was there now, a dark bulk on the horizon. He remembered the image of the Marchese suddenly appearing beside him in the car.

'Haven't you heard . . .?'

Two police cars were parked haphazardly in the courtyard. An ambulance waited by the main entrance with its doors wide open and near it was Corbi's battered car.

The two policemen who were talking quietly in the doorway recognized him at once and stood aside to let him pass. His footsteps echoed loudly in the tiled hall. There was none of the noise and bustle which habitually greeted him when he arrived at such a scene. But this time he was the last to get there rather than one of the first and no doubt the photographer and the technicians had already finished work. Two porters from the Medico-Legal Institute were smoking outside the billiard-room and they, too, made way for him in silence.

Although such people as were in the long room were at the far end of it, Bardi's attention was drawn first to the left where he had once stood drinking coffee at a big refectory table and looking out of one of the tall windows. The table was no longer there. Instead, a leather armchair had been drawn up to face one of the windows. The broad shaft of morning sunlight in which the chair now stood was broken by a great dark splash which had hit one of the panes and dripped down it to the floor. Bardi's glance progressed along five unbroken shafts of light in which fine particles of dust were revolving slowly. The last of them fell on the billiard table where four men were working intently on whatever was lying there. Bardi began to walk down the room. Two of the men were plainclothes policemen, Bardi recognized one of them as they picked up the polythene bags they had been labelling and came away from the table in his direction. The man nodded and gave him an odd look as he passed, probably because the Substitute in charge must already have been and gone. The other two, Corbi and Professor Forli from the Medico-Legal Institute remained by the table talking quietly. The body of Filippo Acciai was laid out before them. It was Corbi who glanced round first at the sound of approaching footsteps. He stared at Bardi without a word, then turned and murmured something to the professor, drawing him away to the right where a concealed door in the room's panelling stood slightly ajar. They withdrew and closed the door after them. Bardi was alone.

He moved forward and stood looking down at the body. Acciai was dressed in hunting gear with the same old leather jerkin about which he had talked with such enthusiasm. A thick towel had been placed under the head. There was nothing left of the face, only a gaping hole. There were powder burns under the place where the chin should have been and on one of the ears. Bardi stared at the burns for some time. The rifle he had seen them carrying away in a polythene bag was the one Acciai had used on the boar hunt.

'Good shot, well done!'

The body exuded the same odour of blood and gungrease that had mingled with the smell of rotting leaves when Bardi had stood in the dappled sunlight of the forest, his face splattered with gore and the bristly ears in his hand. In the closed dusty air of the billiard room it was an unpleasant echo. Bardi wiped a hand over his face in a remembered gesture. His skin was cold and dry. After a moment he turned and walked out of the room.

Granchi, the gamekeeper, was crossing the courtyard with a bucket in his hand and Bardi stopped him more from the need to speak to somebody than from any desire for information. Nevertheless he asked him:

'When is the funeral to be?'

'Tomorrow morning, at San Miniato. They're all buried there.'

'Has his son been informed?'

'His son . . .?' Granchi pushed his cap back and scratched his head. Then he shrugged and went on his way.

There was no one else in the sunny courtyard; even the two policemen had disappeared. Bardi got into his car and drove off.

'Kyrie Eleison, Kyrie Eleison, Kyrie Eleison.'

The one altar boy murmured the responses. There was no choir to sing the requiem and the chilly ornate church was in darkness except for the altar and the tall candles burning by the coffin. The mourners, presumably cadet branches of the family, were a solid black group in the first few pews with a few figures scattered here and there in the ones behind. Among these last was Corbi with the Count Manni close by him. Despite the amount of free space in the rear half of the church, Bardi stood apart beneath the great fresco of St Christopher where he had once had Acciai beside him whispering his commentary on the wedding. It was the same priest with the pale dry hands who stepped down from the altar now to bless the coffin, the little altar boy trailing after him with the aspersorium which gave a faint clink each time the priest dipped into it.

'May his soul and the souls of all the faithful departed through the mercy of God rest in peace.'

'Amen.'

When communion was given he saw Corbi rise and walk

forward, waiting respectfully behind the family. After him followed Granchi and the rest of the servants from the castle, all in tight Sunday clothes in a variety of darkish colours. When the black-clad mourners rose and returned to their pews Bardi searched their faces in vain for someone who might be Acciai's son. Since his attempt to talk to the gamekeeper he had made no further effort to find out exactly what had happened and nobody had contacted him. During the brief hour he had spent in his office before the funeral his phone had been silent.

'Let us pray . . .'

During the last silent prayer two gaunt and heavily powdered women in deep mourning at the end of the pew nearest to Bardi inclined their grey heads together and carried on a whispered conversation.

Every now and then Bardi lifted a hand to the scar on his cheek which had begun to ache with the cold. The scent of incense and beeswax mingled with a strong smell of floor polish was overpowering and he was glad to follow the coffin out into the winter sunshine, keeping a discreet distance between himself and the mourners. As they turned the corner of the church and entered the graveyard he caught a glimpse of the coffin being manœuvred rather clumsily near the entrance to a large marble tomb. Why was it that a detail like that, the sudden incongruity of manhandling what had once been a person as an inanimate object, should bring home the reality of death much more than the solemnity of the funeral rites? In that brief moment it came home to Bardi how easily it could have been his own remains being disposed of in Acciai's place.

'Remember, man, that thou art dust and unto dust . . .'

The bright wintry sun was strong enough to warm the surface of the tombs and statuary and Bardi himself began to feel less chilled except for his hands, which remained dry and bluish with cold. The thin voice of the priest went on murmuring inaudible prayers punctuated by cheerful birdsong.

When the mourners began coming away from the tomb Bardi stood aside on a gravel path in the shadow of a towering marble angel. His head was slightly averted from the approaching figures and he heard rather than saw Corbi pause at the junction with the main path and then move towards him.

'Well, are you satisfied with yourself?'

Bardi turned and met Corbi's eyes blinking unhappily behind the thick spectacles. 'Satisfied?'

'This is your doing, you must know that.'

'I don't know anything, as yet, except what I read in this morning's paper. They say it was an accident, that he was cleaning his gun. The sort of thing, to use the words you once used to me, that happens all the time during the hunting season.'

'He had the foresight,' said Corbi quietly, 'to have a cleaning rag by him and to dress himself for hunting before firing into his mouth. He trusted me to see to the rest, to ignore the fact that nobody goes out after big game alone or after small game with a gun of that calibre, and to ignore the burns, of course, that too.'

The mourners had disappeared from view and they were alone among the white marble figures and the cypress trees filled with birdsong.

'There must have been an autopsy,' Bardi said after a moment.

'Professor Forli agreed with me that there was no justification for . . . in short, he behaved as a gentleman.'

'Which I don't, is that it?'

'I begged you not to send that judicial communication.'

'I was doing my job.'

'Were you? Or were you just pursuing your trouble-shooter image as seen in all the newspapers?'

'I was doing my job. There was evidence against him and you've yet to tell me that it was false, that I was wrong.'

'It wasn't false.'

'Then he was trafficking in heroin.'

'Storing it, as you so cleverly guessed. He was dragged into it.'

'By some wicked Sicilian baron, no doubt.'

'More or less. He was desperate. He was in debt up to his ears and the entire estate was mortgaged. That's something I don't suppose you'd understand, that it wasn't a question of personal survival, or even or personal property. He considered himself as the custodian who had been handed the family property intact and who was duty bound to hand it on to the next generation intact, whatever the cost to himself.'

'It may surprise you to know that I do understand it. I just don't accept that dealing in heroin was the right answer to his problem any more than it's the right answer for the lowliest addict in the piazza. It was only there that I refused to differentiate and I still do.'

'Well, he found that out for himself. But he was frightened, of course. It wasn't easy to get out but he did get out.'

'After paying off his mortgages?' A sudden thought struck Bardi. 'How frightened was he? Frightened enough to ask for protection?'

'Of late, yes. With the Palermo gang operating from prison he was bound to be considered a danger to their contacts here. He was given some protection, certainly.'

'One of Tempesta's men.'

'You knew about that? Well, it was considered safer that way, anyone of sufficient experience in the drug squad would have been recognized. Filippo got out long ago, you know, and he told me everything. It was thanks to him that the Palermo gang was broken up. We owed him some protection for that.'

From beyond the church came the noise of car doors closing as the mourners left. They both turned towards the sound.

'Those people will inherit nothing but debts and death duties, though they may not know it yet.'

'I didn't see his son,' Bardi observed.

'He wasn't here. Didn't you say Filippo himself had told you he was in the United States?'

'In some college, yes. He told me the day we were out hunting.'

'I see. I think we'd better leave. I have an appointment at the Archbishop's palace, the usual lunch for the city authorities . . .'

They began walking towards the church. Before they reached it Bardi had understood.

'The son . . . of course, he became an addict. That was why Acciai –'

'Yes, that was why, not because he'd paid off his mortgage – but the trouble the boy got into was nothing to do with Filippo. Ironically enough, the boy never did know what his father was involved in, any more than Filippo knew about the terrorism episode.'

'You kept it from him?'

'By the time I found out the boy was well on the downward path with drugs. What was the point? The boy's a poor specimen, though Filippo always maintained that if his mother had lived . . . well, he may have been right.'

'Where *is* the boy?'

Corbi got into his car without answering but Bardi held on to the door. 'He's not in any college or he would have been here – he's in some fancy clinic for addicts, isn't he?'

'Nothing matters to you, does it, Bardi? Filippo lost everything, his self-respect, the property in his trust, everything except an old and respected name that he tried to protect even in his last despair to prevent you from dragging it through the courts for your personal satisfaction! But he escaped you in the end, even though it meant going through that grotesque pantomime of dressing up before shooting himself, he escaped you, damn you!' Corbi, red in the face, tried to wrench the door from Bardi's hands but Bardi held on.

'Everything? He lost everything? And didn't he still have a son which some people would consider a reason for going on? Didn't he still have something that others would give anything to have?'

'Did you see his son here today? For God's sake use the intelligence everybody thinks you have so much of!'

For a second Bardi faltered and loosened his grip on the door. Corbi slammed it to and started the engine. But his anger had boiled over and the wheels had barely begun to move before he stopped and wound the window down. Bardi stood where he was, staring down.

'His son –' Corbi stumbled over the words in his rage – 'will be dead within two months, his liver destroyed by drugs, and if it hadn't been for you his father would have been with him. Now you can splash that all over the papers and win the game!'

He stamped on the accelerator and the car lurched away, spraying gravel.

'Are you ready to leave, sir?' It was Mastino. They walked together to the car where Poma had already started the engine. Outside the gates they turned left instead of right and Bardi roused himself sufficiently to say: 'Where are you going? I have to go back to the Procura . . .'

'That's all right, sir,' Poma said quietly. 'We're just taking a different route, that's all, if you don't mind.'

'Ah, just the thing,' beamed the Archbishop expansively, as the tray approached. 'A small glass of something, Monsignor?'

Lazurek peered dubiously at the tray and murmured something incomprehensible.

'Bring some whisky,' ordered the Archbishop quietly and the servant disappeared among the other guests. 'You see, I haven't forgotten your tastes though you haven't honoured us with a visit to Florence for so many years.'

'You're very kind,' said Lazurek, gazing about him and automatically dusting off the front of his jacket, 'but I'm afraid I've chosen a bad day to impose myself on you.'

'Not in the least. I like to receive the civic authorities well before the round of Christmas engagements begins and you're a welcome addition at any time – nevertheless, I hope you'll stay on after lunch so that the two of us can have a quiet talk. You're not our only visitor from Rome, either, we have Binetti with us, vice-president of the Upper Council of Magistrates – I don't know if you've met?'

'Once, at dinner.'

'Not so unexpected as your visit, of course; we Florentines come home to roost as often as possible. Who's the young priest who accompanied you?'

'An American, McManus. He's been secretary at the American College for the last two years.'

'He looks bright.'

'Oh yes . . . he's bright enough. He's going home, though, at Christmas.'

'Pity. You must introduce him to me – ah, Binetti, we were just talking about you.'

Binetti joined them, baring his teeth at the Archbishop, and Lazurek excused himself as soon as possible, saying he wanted to keep an eye on young John McManus, which was at least partly true.

He had already seen the boy buttonholed by the *Provveditore*, a verbose and intense man who had insisted on giving him a rapid and detailed account of the seven-hundred-year history of the city's voluntary ambulance service, oblivious to the fact that less than a quarter of his monologue was comprehensible. Now McManus was trapped in a group of high-ranking military men and local politicians whose conversation was going well over his head and he shot a despairing glance at Lazurek in the hope of his coming to the rescue. Satisfied that the young priest was ill at ease and well out of his depth, Lazurek retreated and joined Colonel Tempesta who was standing alone looking out of the window with a drink in his hand.

For a while they were silent, observing the octagonal baptistery and the cars and people swarming about its base in the cathedral square.

'He hasn't arrived yet?'

'No.' Tempesta scanned the moving mass below in vain for Corbi's figure, 'but there's no reason to worry. They buried the Marchese Acciai this morning and he was sure to have been at the funeral. He'll be here . . . but that's about the only thing we can be sure of.'

'You think he'll oppose the transfer?'

Tempesta shrugged his heavy shoulders. 'Bardi's the best man he's got.'

'But surely it's a promotion . . .'

'Outside Florence. Bardi won't want it. And Corbi will know he won't want it. If he decides to oppose it he'll warn Bardi.'

'I suppose so. But if I've understood the process correctly he can't refuse promotion to Chief Public Prosecutor without destroying his chances of ever being offered it again.'

'That's quite correct.'

'Then what can Corbi do even if he is against it?'

'Warn Bardi before it becomes official.'

'And Bardi . . .'

'Will do the sort of thing we did in order to procure it. We are in Italy, remember, and Bardi's not without friends.' Tempesta glanced over his shoulder as a new influx of guests arrived. 'Odd . . . that's the Count Manni and he must have been at the funeral. I can't think what's keeping Corbi . . . Manni looks as if he's in a state of shock and I'm afraid Corbi will be just as badly affected which isn't going to help matters.'

'A sudden death?'

'A nasty one; face shot away with a hunting rifle.'

'Shot . . . nothing to do with our business, I hope?'

'No, no. A bad business, even so, but it's a long story and I won't go into it now. What's upsetting his friends is that it was almost certainly a suicide, according to rumours I've heard going the rounds, but nobody's going to say so. A nasty business altogether – ah, at last.'

Far below them, the small figure of Corbi was now visible,

crossing the cathedral square hurriedly and blinking up now and then in their direction.

'Well,' said Tempesta with a sigh, 'there's nothing you or I can do now except hope.'

'And pray.'

'I'll leave that to you. If he doesn't block us Bardi will receive official notice of his transfer by telex tomorrow morning.'

'And that will satisfy the General?'

'I hope so . . .'

'But you're not sure. Have you talked to him again?'

Tempesta didn't answer immediately and when he did it was with some reluctance.

'He talked to me, he telephoned me late Friday night . . .' Still he hesitated: 'You won't like what I have to tell you.'

Lazurek waited patiently.

'Bardi . . . Bardi has been to see Attilio.'

'Oh, dear God. But how did the General . . .?'

'That telephone's permanently tapped, you know that.'

'Even now?'

'Even now. And Attilio telephoned his mother. Well, you can imagine.'

'I can imagine. Poor foolish man.'

'How Bardi deciphered that number I'll never know. I only wish . . .'

'What do you wish?'

'I was going to say that I wish he were working with me instead of . . . Ludicrous, isn't it, when I'm doing my best to get rid of him.'

'You're doing your best to save his life.'

'Even so, we'll lose the best magistrate we have in Florence if this morning's work goes well.'

'And wouldn't you lose him anyway if it were left to the General?'

'Oh, indeed.'

The Colonel was silent for a moment, sipping at his drink.

'Why is it,' asked Lazurek, observing him, 'that I have a feeling there's something you're not telling me?'

Tempesta looked away from him, frowning.

'Well, there's no reason why you should tell me everything that's on your mind. Forgive me.'

The frown was replaced by a rueful smile.

'Would it offend you if I said I wished I had you working with me, too?'

'I have worked for you after my fashion, in the past.'

'But you never will again.'

'Not if I can possibly avoid it, no.'

'No . . . well, you're right, as usual, I haven't told you the full story. The fact is that Bardi's visit to Attilio must have been successful. One of his guards was in the Archives on Saturday morning, checking through the general index.'

'I see.'

A servant was holding out a tray for their glasses.

'Lunch will be served in five minutes.'

As they waited for him to move away the Monsignor fished out his handkerchief and dabbed at a few dark drops on his jacket.

'I suppose you informed the General immediately?'

'No. I haven't told him yet.'

'Then would it offend you, in turn, if I said that I wouldn't have thought you capable of taking such a risk?'

'It would be no more than I deserved. At any rate, if we fail this morning I shall have no choice but to tell him.'

'Then we mustn't fail.'

They turned to where they could see a rather breathless Corbi being greeted by the Archbishop.

'It depends on him now,' Tempesta said.

'And what about poor Attilio?'

'I don't know. I just don't know . . .'

'That his telephone should still be tapped after all these years . . . It isn't that someone else uses it now?'

'No. Nobody. But Li Causi had that number and he was under surveillance. The General is a very tenacious man. Much as I dislike him and his methods I have to admit he's efficient. Ah, Corbi! Pleased to see you. May I introduce you? Monsignor Joseph Lazurek of the Vatican Secretariat of State, Chief Public Prosecutor Alessandro Corbi.' His eyes were already casting about for Binetti, who soon caught his glance and came towards them with a fixed smile.

'Corbi, just the man I wanted to see! I have some good news for you, or rather for one of your Substitutes.'

'That means you're going to talk shop and we shall leave you. I think they're going in to lunch, anyway.'

'So they are. Well, I shall keep you by me, Corbi, we must talk . . .'

In the dining-room Tempesta found the young American priest beside him and had to concentrate on conversation more than he would have wished, apologizing frequently for his inadequate English. Lazurek was out of sight somewhere down the table on his left but he had Corbi and Binetti in view. It was difficult, even so, to judge how things were going there. Binetti was doing most of the talking while Corbi blinked fixedly at his plate, looking both depressed and annoyed.

'I've been trying to follow up on political events while I've been here and that's really been difficult. Things are so different from home. But I'm pretty satisfied that I've got a good idea of how things are by now.'

'Good . . .' Tempesta dragged his attention back to his neighbour who was, fortunately, too pleased to have found someone to speak English with to notice just how spasmodic that attention was.

Coffee was served in the small drawing-room where the situation was too quiet and static to permit Tempesta to approach Binetti without its being noticed. He settled instead by Lazurek who was seated a little apart from the rest of the company contemplating his coffee cup.

'What do you think?' the Monsignor asked him as soon as he was seated.

'I don't know what to think at this point, though Binetti, to judge by his expression, seems to think his news went down well – not that that's anything to go by.'

'You find him a stupid man, I think.'

'I do indeed. Don't you?'

'He's not a man I would want any dealings with, but apart from that I haven't given the matter too much thought. As a matter of fact, when you joined me it was my own stupidity I was thinking of. I'm afraid I've made rather a bad mistake.' He was looking across to where their host sat surrounded by a group of his most important guests. Beside him, on his right, sat Father John McManus and the two of them seemed to be having an easy and intimate conversation.

'Your young friend seems to be a great success with the Archbishop,' Tempesta observed, following his glance.

'I'm sorry to say you're right,' sighed Lazurek, 'and I had so hoped he would pass the most uncomfortable two hours of his life here. I obviously underestimated him; I certainly overestimated my own intelligence in the handling of him.'

'I can't begin to follow you.'

'Oh, it's of no matter. Saving souls, as you constantly remind me, is my business and doesn't interest you. When will you talk to Binetti?'

'Immediately, outside when everyone else has gone. I don't want him in my office; it would be indiscreet, apart from æsthetic considerations. Will you be with us?'

'That would be even more indiscreet. In any case the Archbishop expects me to stay on here and I can hardly refuse or he'll start wondering why I came at all. No, I'll telephone you as soon as I get home, late tomorrow morning. I think people are starting to leave . . . I would have liked to meet him, you know.'

'Who?'

'Your friend the good magistrate.'

'Bardi? You forget he's your deadliest enemy. He'll expose you if he can.'

'But I would have liked to meet him, even so. And now I suppose I never shall.'

The cathedral square in this quiet hour after lunch was almost deserted. Binetti was strolling to and fro beside the marble walls of the baptistery. Tempesta joined them and they walked on.

'The telex carrying the good news to Bardi will go off first thing tomorrow morning. I hope you're pleased.'

'I am. Very.' Tempesta didn't trust himself to ask anything though there was a lot he wanted to know.

'Bardi should certainly be pleased. Not only does he get the promotion he so deserves, he even gets the city he wants!'

'He does?' Surely not . . . Corbi could hardly have been so upset that he'd resigned . . . because of this? Because of Acciai? It wasn't possible –

'Bergamo!'

'Bergamo . . .?'

'Exactly. We had three positions open, one in Bergamo, the other two in the south. I rather thought Bergamo myself but I wanted to check with Corbi and he told me – I'm surprised that as a friend of Bardi's you didn't know, or didn't think to tell me – that he asked to be transferred there some years ago though nothing came of it. I couldn't say why, it was before my time. According to Corbi, there was some woman involved but I don't know whether there's anything in that. He's still with his wife, isn't he?'

'Yes, he's still with his wife.'

'Well, be that as it may, we'd better ask no questions, eh?'

'Did Corbi . . . He must be sorry to lose such a good man.'

'Odd that you should say that. I'd have thought so, too, but between ourselves, I got the impression that he was glad to have the man off his hands. Of course Bardi's known as something of a trouble-shooter. Probably not an easy man to deal with. Well, he's got what he wanted so he should be happy enough now.'

'Yes. He should be happy enough now.'

CHAPTER TWELVE

TAILOR HANGS HIMSELF WITH PRIEST'S STOLE

ROME: A tailor specializing in ecclesiastical vestments was discovered dead yesterday after having hanged himself with a priest's embroidered stole. Attilio Piccioni, 51, ended his own life in his shop in the vicinity of St Peter's Square. The body was discovered yesterday afternoon when a shop assistant in possession of the keys went in to re-open at 3.30 p.m. as usual. Piccioni, who had been missing from home since Saturday evening, was described by his employees as a nervous, lonely man dedicated to his work and the care of his elderly mother who is in poor health.

The mother alerted neighbours to his disappearance late Saturday evening and they in turn called in the Carabinieri on Sunday morning. No attempt was made to enter the shop since Piccioni was thought to have left the premises along with his employees at approximately 8.15 p.m. on Saturday. However, police say the suicide almost certainly took place that night. According to a reconstruction of events, Piccioni tied the stole to a metal beam in one of the shop's showrooms and then knotted it round his neck after climbing on to a chair which was found overturned on the floor beneath him. It is unlikely that death was instantaneous. The neighbour who came to the elderly Signora Piccioni's assistance and who knew the deceased well expressed an opinion that the use of the stole may have been symbolic; Piccioni studied for the priesthood when a young man but never took Holy Orders. A small dog, said to be the tailor's constant companion, was discovered in a corner of a room near that in which the body was found. Piccioni was unmarried and is survived only by his mother who is 76.

Lazurek let the newspaper fall into his lap and put a hand to his eyes.

'Is something wrong?' McManus put down his coffee-cup and leaned forward towards the Monsignor, who seemed not to notice as the paper slid down on to the floor of the study.

'No . . . nothing. I think if you've finished your coffee you should be getting along. Thank you for driving me home . . .'

'I'm the one to thank you for giving me such an opportunity despite all you said before about not –'

'Yes, yes. I'd rather you didn't thank me, even so, for my foolishness.'

'For your . . . Are you sure there's nothing wrong?' He glanced down at the newspaper but hazarded no direct question.

'Quite sure, except that I'm very tired. It's so long since I travelled anywhere and I'm feeling old all of a sudden . . .'

'Then I'll leave you to rest.'

He closed the door quietly.

Lazurek stared after him for a moment and then, as if he knew that once the effects of the article overwhelmed him he would be incapable of concentrating on anything else, he turned his chair back to the writing-desk and began a letter to the Archbishop of Chicago. He wrote rapidly in a firm hand hoping that, after all, they might be capable of understanding each other. When the letter was finished he sealed and addressed it and then leaned back, letting his eyes close and his chin fall forward on to his chest. It was his habitual position for the naps he took with increasing frequency during the day but he wasn't asleep. He remained so for a long time, the only sound in the room the faint ticking of a small clock on the desk. When, without moving, he opened his eyes, they fell on a small stain on the front of his jacket which was much crumpled after the journey down from Florence.

He heard the voice of Attilio clucking softly in earnest disapproval: *'I believe it's coffee, Monsignor, and I'm afraid there's a little hole here, too, yes,* quite *a hole – now I don't want to insist but I do think that while we're fitting I might send it upstairs to be mended and perhaps a little brush and press . . .'*

'Poor Attilio, you'll never manage to make me look elegant, but you mustn't despair. The new suit will work wonders, at least for a week or so.'

The new suit that he would probably never wear, and then the telephone call that would always interrupt the fitting.

'Now please don't apologize, I quite realise that someone in your position is never really free for a moment. You must take it in my office where you won't be disturbed . . .'

Followed by the inevitable scene with the neurotic little dog.

Poor Attilio. Only a child's vision of heaven could accommodate such a soul. A celestial hierarchy in which he could operate comfortably with St Peter to replace his beloved Cardinal . . .

'– So kind, he was saying to me only yesterday – I always go to him, of course, for fittings . . . someone in his position can hardly . . .' And the lower orders of angels to be clucked and tutted at for having rumpled wings.

'We must send them up immediately for a brush and press . . .'

The voice faded. Lazurek picked up the telephone and dialled.

'Tempesta.'

'Good morning, Colonel.'

'Ah, it's you. I suppose . . .'

'I've seen it, yes. But he didn't kill himself, Colonel.'

When there was no reply he went on: 'You never met Attilio, did you?'

'No.'

'And you don't want to talk to me, at least not on the telephone. I hardly dare ask you if this line, too –'

'You'll want to know about yesterday. We were successful. He'll have the news of his transfer and promotion by telex some time today.'

'Good . . . good. Then it's over.'

'I hope so.'

'You hope so? But surely –'

'Thank you for your cooperation.'

The line went dead.

Lazurek replaced the receiver slowly. No doubt Tempesta was right not to talk, though what the General could hope to learn that he hadn't already told him to his face was unclear. Perhaps they were planning to come for him too. An unlikely contingency, given his position, but that was little enough comfort. The thought of the General toying with an idea for some suitable 'suicide', though it held no terror for him, served to increase the oppressive sadness that weighed upon him like a physical pain. He leaned forward with his elbows on the desk and covered his face with his hands in an attempt at prayer, but the innocent chatter of Attilio filled his mind, light and fluttering as a bird, insistent as a guilty conscience. And hard as he pressed his fingers into his closed eyes, beyond the dazzling worms of light was an image of Attilio hanging from a beam like a dead bird caught dangling on a branch. He was part of what had killed Attilio.

The thought made him raise his head and uncover his face to his own guilt. The tiny clock ticked on and he stared at it as though the ticking contained some message for him. The image of Attilio retreated and blended with other images: Carlo Rota's feverish eyes watching him as he anointed the bound hands; the small, insignificant man with the big cigar sitting in this same room talking quietly; the General, many years before that, settling back into his chair after supper at the college and wondering if he might have Lazurek's cooperation in a small matter. Far back as he went, he could see no point at which he might have interrupted the chain of events that had led to the death of Attilio. And he had been a link in that chain himself. Only yesterday he had gently rebuked Tempesta for despising Binetti. But how much more difficult it was to refrain from despising oneself. It needed humility. But humility was something Lazurek had in good measure, and instead of condemning himself he got up slowly from his chair and went over to a corner of the room where there was a prayer stool, frequently polished but otherwise untouched.

When Sister Agatha tapped softly and came in to say that lunch was ready she stopped short and stared at a sight she hadn't seen in all of fifteen years.

'Lies and mystification!'

'Speak the truth! Condemn us for being militant Communists!'

'Lackey of the Imperialist State of the Multinationals, that's *you*, Bardi!'

'And Bardi, don't imagine you can frighten us with your squalid little repentants! Listen!'

Once again the presiding judge rapped briefly with his gavel.

Bardi, seated alone to the right of the judges' bench, could see out of the corner of his eye the threatening gestures being made through the bars of the cage containing the defendants. Still the noise did not subside completely and a scuffle could be heard as the carabinieri stationed inside the cage tried to get them all seated again.

The presiding judge waited in silence, flanked by the six jurors with their tricoloured sashes. He was sixty years old but his athletic build was evident even beneath his robes and he had a thick shock of waving grey hair. His austere face expressed neither boredom nor anger. He simply waited, his calm grey eyes turned towards the source of the disturbance.

When there was relative quiet his eyes dropped to the papers on the bench before him.

'The Public Minister will please continue.'

Bardi, who had sat down during the interruption, got to his feet and pushing back the wide sleeves of his gown reached for the microphone.

'With your permission, Mr President, I will repeat my last paragraph to avoid any confusion which might have been caused by this latest interruption.'

'As you wish.'

Bardi, stooping and leaning slightly forward with his hands gripping the sides of the table as was his habit, began to speak.

'As regards the shooting of the bank guard, we have heard three witnesses state that all three shots were fired by the female of the group, later arrested and identified as the defendant Patrizia Rossini, and that the third of these shots was fired at point blank range into the victim's neck when he was already lying on the floor immobilized by the first two shots which had hit him, the first in the abdomen and the second in the leg. Witnesses have also stated unequivocally . . .'

His voice, coming back to him from the speakers around the bare walls of the bunker courtroom, was as steady as usual but it sounded flat and lacking in its customary attack. Occasionally it almost lost its force altogether, though still audible, because he took a more upright position, too far away from the microphone which he had set to accommodate his habitual forward-leaning stance. Each time this happened the presiding judge, who normally listened with his head slightly inclined towards the speaker but with his eyes fixed on his notes to which he occasionally made an addition, would glance at him with the suggestion of a frown. Bardi had never before been conscious of himself, of his own voice and of the figure he was making in court. Normally his concentration on the content of what he was saying was such that he was oblivious of all else, but today his eyes constantly sought those of the journalists seated together immediately behind the lawyers near the front of the courtroom, aware that they were taking in his every gesture and no doubt making as many notes about him as about the progress of the trial. One of the journalists present was Marco Nesti, an overweight, sleepy-eyed man who looked perpetually bored but who missed nothing. It was Nesti who had once written of Bardi that his habit of leaning forward when prosecuting combined with his hawklike profile and the backward sweep of his full black gown, made him look like a huge bird of prey about to rip open its victim. His article had appeared under the headline *TERRORISM'S MOST PREDATORY ENEMY*.

'We come to the second victim, Alessandro Benigni, who was on the point of entering the bank when the masked raiders were leaving it. Benigni was hit from behind by a fourth accomplice who was stationed in a car opposite the bank . . .'

Again he was aware of his voice fading, and this time he overcompensated, leaning too far forward so that the microphone coughed as he brushed against it. And this time, besides being aware of the judge's sharp glance, he was convinced that Nesti's eyes, too, were fixed on him in surprise. The journalist made a note and Bardi, to his irritation, found himself imagining how that note would appear in print. It was ridiculous. He was, after all, only doing his job, prosecuting what was anyway a watertight case.

'Or just pursing your trouble-shooter image as seen in all the newspapers?'

The specially constructed concrete bunker, even though it was so bare and only a quarter full since there was little public, was much too hot. The day before, through some administrative oversight, it had been ice-cold. The journalists had sat huddled in their overcoats and afterwards an official complaint had been made by the presiding judge. As a result, the room was now so overheated that Bardi had felt his face beginning to burn only minutes after the Court's entry and the reopening of the debate.

He only had to deal now with the laundering of the stolen money which had been used to buy arms. When another barrage of threats and insults burst from behind the bars of the cage he sighed audibly and turned to the presiding judge. If this continued he would be unable to get through today's part of the summing up before an adjournment was ordered at twelve-thirty. He knew this judge well enough to be sure that the Court would rise at the hour he had appointed no matter what the circumstances, neither a minute earlier nor a minute later. And it was essential to Bardi that he clear up this section today so that tomorrow he would be free to concentrate on his prosecution of the leader of this Florentine nucleus of the Red Brigades who had not taken part in the bank robbery but who, according to the Bardi Theorem, was being tried for it along with the others.

'Mr President, I request the expulsion of all the accused from the courtroom unless I am able to proceed uninterrupted.'

Even with the speakers it wasn't easy to make himself heard clearly above their concerted shouting.

'Very well.' Another weary tap with the gavel and the judge leaned forward a little to speak into his microphone. 'I cannot tolerate insults and threats in the presence of the Court. The accused will remain silent during the Public Minister's summing up or be expelled from the courtroom.'

The group in the cage consulted among themselves, looked at their watches and then sat down in silence. One of them began writing in a notebook, the others watching and sometimes intervening. They ignored what was going on in the courtroom to which their backs were turned.

Bardi finished at 12.16. That meant that he had spoken too quickly and he was dissatisfied with himself. Despite the frequent interruptions, he had completed the day's summing up fourteen minutes earlier than expected, for he was noted for timing his discourse to the minute. He hitched up his gown and seated himself, hoping against hope that the judge would order an early adjournment since he has no wish to begin on tomorrow's speech and then be interrupted after only a few minutes.

He saw the judge look at his watch. Then the strident voice of Patrizia Rossini rang out from the cage. Bardi turned a little in his seat so that he could see her.

'Mr President! We have an announcement to make!'

'Pray make whatever announcement you wish, but I must ask you to be brief.'

'Thank you. It has been decided that we dismiss our defence lawyers on the grounds that we do not recognize the logic or validity of this court debate given that it is already a foregone conclusion that, as always, the exploiters will condemn the exploited, obliged as they are to do so in order to protect their privileged position obtained by force and maintained by oppression. We therefore deny any lawyer the right to speak in our defence.'

'Is that all?'

The group inside the cage retreated to consult in undertones. When Patrizia Rossini came forward again she had a printed leaflet in her hand. She was heavily pregnant with a child which might be Gori's and might be Li Causi's, probably the latter, but which was certainly destined to be born in prison. She seemed oblivious of her physical condition. Before beginning to speak she put on a pair of reading glasses.

'We have a statement to read, addressed to the proletariat.'

The rest of the group sat down and lit cigarettes.

'Comrades! The time has come for the organization of a new combatant force which, operating independently of existing revolutionary forces now isolated and impotent after a series of tactical and strategical errors, will take its rightful position in the historical context of the fight against the bourgeoisie and confront the real social, political and military problems which have emerged in recent years . . .'

Singly or in small groups the journalists gathered up their notebooks and shuffled towards the door, bound for the nearest bar or restaurant. The solid rank of carabinieri lining the courtroom opened to let them pass and then settled back in position staring straight ahead, sometimes imperceptibly stretching first one leg and then the other in their weariness.

A couple of photographers had remained behind and one of these, a woman, got up from her seat to take a flash shot of Patrizia Rossini. The presiding judge sat motionless and attentive.

Was it Bardi's imagination or had his colleagues avoided speaking to him in the Council room before the hearing began? The presiding judge was an old friend of Corbi's and would know about the Acciai business by now but the others surely had no reason to avoid him. Probably it was his imagination. It was true, at any rate, that Bardi himself was never in the mood for idle chatter before a hearing and once the clerk had brought him his robes he tended to sit apart smoking and studying his notes, oblivious of the conversation going on around him. Even so, it was usual for him to exchange some remark, however casual, with his colleagues and this morning he hadn't, though for once he felt the need to. What was worse, when he had first walked into the room one of the judges, an insignificant man whose name Bardi wasn't even sure of, had been speaking to the others who were listening intently.

'I assure you it's true. I heard it less than half an hour ago at the Procura, though it seems he may not even know himself yet . . .'

And he had stopped and looked embarrassed when he saw Bardi.

Well, if they had been talking about him it was of no importance. No doubt they often did. He was aware that over the last ten years his success had earned him some enemies. Did they imagine that he didn't yet know the truth about Acciai, was that it? Whatever they thought, there was no reason why it should bother him. Perhaps what really bothered him was the way the others had looked at him when the speaker had stopped short. A look that might almost have been of pity and which he couldn't explain.

'Our intention is not to set ourselves up in opposition to existing revolutionary forces but to inherit their place in the armed struggle, adopting methods which, while still based on a rigorous Marxist analysis of prevailing conditions . . .'

The photographer must have taken over a dozen pictures of Patrizia Rossini and now she approached the cage, almost pushing the camera between the bars to take close-ups. The defendant held her hand up to her eyes, blinded by the flash.

'Young woman!' The judge's voice was loud with the first sign of anger he had shown that morning. 'I cannot imagine what your purpose might be in tormenting the defendant in that manner but I am sure your behaviour is as distasteful and irritating to her as it is to me. Leave this courtroom immediately. Continue.'

'Which, while still based on a rigorous Marxist analysis . . .'

Did he really feel any remorse about Acciai? If that was what they imagined, if that was why they felt sorry for him, they were mistaken. It wasn't remorse but something more complex which he hadn't yet succeeded in putting into words. It had less to do with Acciai himself and the way he had died – it wasn't the first suicide of the sort he had dealt with and violent death was something he was long used to – than with Corbi's failure to tell him the truth beforehand. Yet, despite that, he knew he would have been incapable of acting differently even had he known but still it mattered to him that Corbi hadn't talked, that he had turned and looked through him that Sunday morning at the castle as though he were a stranger and then shut the door in his face in order to talk to Dr Forli. This morning, too, when Bardi had walked into the Council room they had stopped talking as though a stranger had entered rather than a colleague. And yet he had always got on easily with people, always been considered brilliant company, surrounded by friends and colleagues so that the chief difficulty had been escaping them all to get enough peace to work.

'All our comrades, all avant-garde elements, all revolutionary organizations, are every day faced with the problem of repression and that of the right to exist and fight for their needs. Only massed organized force can succeed in combating the mystification inherent in the rule of the bourgeoisie . . .'

Had he succeeded too well in escaping? It was true that there were many people he still automatically called his friends but whom he hadn't seen now for six or seven years. Giorgio Galli he had seen recently but only because he'd had need of Galli's expertise in deciphering a code. When had they last met for purely social reasons? Bardi had no idea. So many people had somehow got left behind and he had never had time to give it a thought. There was Laura to consider, of course, he could hardly expect her to put herself out entertaining for him in the circumstances. Galli had said, he remembered now, *'Haven't seen you for years – except in the paper, of course.'*

It struck him quite suddenly that people regarded him as a phenomenon rather than as a person like themselves. A freak even. Someone to be left to himself, to whom they never considered confiding human problems. Corbi hadn't considered it and Acciai, too, after a feeble attempt at it during the hunt, had soon given up.

'We have different ways of looking at things.'

Perhaps it was just the nature of his work . . . but Tempesta had once been his friend and now he, too, looked at him in that same odd way.

'Always the same excuse . . . Relax a little before it's too late.'

He thought of his father who had kept the same friends all his life, people who thought as he thought and had progressed slowly and steadily in their careers along with him. His father who had once sat where the presiding judge sat now – no, there had been no need for bunker courtrooms in his day, he'd presided in the dusty baroque elegance of the tribunal where no insults were hurled and no threats made to his life. What would he think if he were here now listening to a young pregnant woman who had shot more than one person at point blank range in support of the ideology she was now stridently professing though it fell on deaf ears?

'Multinational imperialism dominated by the capital of the monopolistic multinationals –'

'That's enough.' The dry, emotionless voice of the presiding judge superimposed itself from the loudspeakers.

'I haven't finished!'

'Sit down, please.' It was twenty-eight minutes past twelve. He signalled to the clerk who handed him up a list and he read out the names of three duty lawyers who would replace the defendants' own lawyers whom they had dismissed. The three were already present in court, this being a not unexpected development, and they stood to request an adjournment which would give them time to study the case. A seven-day adjournment was granted and the Court rose at 12.30 precisely.

Bardi was on his feet and getting his papers together. The judges were filing out at the back of the platform and handcuffs were being put on the defendants.

There was a sudden scuffle.

'Bardi!'

Patrizia Rossini was thrusting her face through the bars, laughing. Two carabinieri tried to pull her away but she held on to the bars with both hands.

'I wanted to ask you how you enjoyed the wedding!'

Bardi turned away and left the courtroom but not before hearing another voice shout, 'There'll be a next time!'

It was nothing new but for once it disturbed him and it was perhaps because of this that, once settled in the back of the car, he spoke only to say, 'My office,' and then buried himself in the newspaper that had lain untouched on the back seat all morning and tried to concentrate on reading it. Nevertheless, after they had been on the road only a few moments he looked up to say: 'It seems we owe the episode after the wedding to our friends in the Florentine nucleus.' Though by then he was thinking of the hunting accident which now seemed as though it might have been a genuine accident after all. He would never know for sure.

The two men in the front made no comment, only glanced

at each other in silence. When after a moment Poma spoke it was only to say:

'When we get back I'd like a word with you, sir, if it's convenient.'

When Bardi didn't answer he glanced in his mirror and frowned to see that he was again engrossed in the newspaper.

TAILOR HANGS HIMSELF WITH PRIEST'S STOLE.

'Sir . . .'

'I've changed my mind. Take me home.'

'Sir? I wanted a word with –'

'Take me home!'

'Yessir.'

His first instinct after dropping his briefcase and flinging off his overcoat was to call Tempesta, but he thought better of it. He needed to think first. Half way to the telephone, against which a letter was propped, he turned back, picked up his briefcase and took it upstairs to his study. More than anything he needed a drink, something strong that would drive off the jaded feeling that had been oppressing him all morning. He took a glass and a bottle of cognac from the cupboard, then changed his mind and poured himself a large whisky instead. His liver would probably suffer for it next day but he needed it. His forehead was still burning and he began to think he'd caught a cold at the funeral yesterday. If it wasn't 'flu.

'Damn!'

He couldn't afford to be ill, now when he needed his wits about him.

Had he been wrong to believe the little tailor an innocent dupe? Was this another suicide to be laid at his door? Suicides could be faked. Not by the Red Brigades, though, it wasn't their style. But there were others who could have found out that the tailor had talked to Bardi. The Grand Old Man himself, his friend the priest who had protection at high level . . .

'Monsignor Joseph Lazurek.'

If Poma or Mastino had been there he'd have heard a

murmured 'Yes sir' and he would have gone on thinking his disjointed thoughts aloud until they resolved themselves into some logical sequence. His voice sounded oddly resonant in the empty room. His throat was as dry and hot as his head and he poured himself another whisky half hoping to burn away the imminent infection, for he had no doubt now that he was coming down with something. His heart seemed to him to be beating a lot faster than it should and he put a hand to his chest. Men of his age had heart attacks . . . His chest was too hot and he was feeling weak. That might be because he hadn't eaten. He had no appetite now, and besides if he was feverish he surely shouldn't eat. He realized that he was pacing the room and that it tired him and he paused by the window. There was very little traffic because it was lunch-time. The stuccoed houses on the opposite side of the street were bathed in cold sunlight and the big leaves of the magnolia below him looked black in the shade. The reflected glare hurt his eyes and he partly closed the inner shutters so as to admit only a narrow slice of light. Then he removed his jacket and shoes, lay down on the smooth bed and lit a half-cigarette which he extinguished almost immediately because it tasted so unpleasant.

'Monsignor Joseph Lazurek . . .' He closed his eyes to try and conjure up an image to go with the name. After a moment he pulled down the counterpane a little so as to rest his burning head on the coolness of the pillow. He must have dozed off. Some time later, without waking completely but remaining in a pleasant twilight zone from which he could easily sink into unconsciousness again, he shifted himself slowly until he was able to slide under the covers, aware in a detached way that his whole body was shivering and that he urgently needed to get warm. Then he let himself sink again.

What mattered was to maintain a sort of equilibrium, to keep himself at a level of consciousness where he could resolve everything. And he was sure now that he could resolve everything in the simplest way possible. He mustn't let himself sink into total oblivion so that he could no longer move in the heavy blackness. If that happened they could easily start to manhandle his body and he would be helpless to prevent it. If, on the other hand, he rose almost to the surface of consciousness so that the narrow band of light touched his eyelids the terrible confusion that awaited him there would distract him from what he had to do. So he had to make a constant effort to stay at the right level no matter how much it tired him, and it tired him so much that he was aching all over. Dragging himself up from oblivion was the hardest thing but he had worked out a system for it; once he became aware of feeling paralyzed and suffocated he would concentrate on moving just one part of his body, usually a finger, a fraction of an inch. It required enormous force but once he achieved that tiny movement the spell was broken. Afterwards it was necessary to rest for a moment until the heavy feeling in his head eased off. Then he was at the right level. Coming down from the surface where the band of light intruded was easier. He only had to stretch his limbs slightly, luxuriating in the warmth, and then let himself sink slowly. At the right level everything was clear and simple. So simple that he wondered why he had struggled all these years without understanding what he had to do. He felt light and at peace with the world and his actions followed one another with a swiftness and ease that delighted him. He was going home to talk to his father and put everything right. That was all that was necessary. The idea had come to him quite suddenly at school and he chuckled aloud now at the simplicity of it. He had the perfect excuse since it was obvious that he had a fever. Even the pillow under his head was burning hot. If he hadn't done it before it wasn't his fault, he had been too young. Even so, it had taken him all this time to realize that he now had means at his disposal. He no longer had to wait at the gates until his father's chauffeur turned up, often long after the other boys had left. Didn't he have his own car with

Poma and Mastino to escort him? He was even free to take a taxi if he wanted to. It was exhilarating! And it was incredible that he hadn't thought of it sooner, that he had gone on suffering in silence instead of realizing that he was in a position to act. The simplicity of it all delighted him and he laughed softly, shifting his hot head on the pillow to find a cooler patch. Poma was driving him home. It wasn't very far. There was a lot of traffic, though, which meant that it was later than he had thought and the quiet lunch-hour was over. The band of light touched his eyelids. No . . . he sank slowly down until he was in the car again and they were passing familiar landmarks: the stationer's where he always bought the folded sheets of lined paper for his homework, the church, the pet shop with cages filled with brightly coloured singing birds hanging outside and puppies playing in the sawdust inside the window. He had spent hours as a child watching them tumbling about and the memory of it filled him with joy. The wide avenue, the house. He remembered that the servants were no longer there to open the door for him but now he had the keys. It was so easy!

He went straight to his father's study on the right. Why had he never thought of going in there in all these years? His father must have had the same thought because he looked up sadly from his papers in the shuttered room and asked him at once:

'Why didn't you come before? Where have you been for so many years?'

He had to think for a moment, searching for a reason for this long absence.

'I don't know . . . I think it was because I had to travel so much. You must realize that in my job I often have to be away. It's not my fault.'

'But when you're here you could spend some time with me.'

'I have to be in court. My responsibilities are very heavy, you're old enough to understand that.'

But his father only looked at him sadly and he felt a great

weight of sorrow inside him that had to come to the surface or it would burst his heart. It was enormous, swelling like a balloon, out of all proportion to what he had to say. Warm tears welled up in his eyes and poured down his feverish cheeks. He made no attempt to control them. The soothing endless flow relieved the pain and even afforded him a sort of sensuous pleasure. It didn't disturb him or prevent him from speaking normally. His father's face had changed and became much gentler and the expression in his eyes was warm instead of forbidding.

'Why are you crying?'

'I don't know. I think because I'm very tired.'

'It's not because of your mother?'

'It can't be, I don't remember her.'

'But you should. You weren't so very young when she died, you were old enough to remember.'

Hadn't his great-aunt said the same thing? He had been on his way to bed and had stopped to listen at the door, attracted by the solemnity of their low voices and knowing he wasn't meant to hear.

'It's not normal. He's seven years old and perfectly aware of what's happened. You should have him seen by someone.'

'By whom?'

'A doctor, perhaps.'

'He'll come round in time. He doesn't need a doctor, he's in excellent health.'

'Nevertheless, it's not normal. He hasn't shed a single tear. If you won't take him to a doctor, at least try to spend a little time with him.'

'You must realize that I often have to be away. The child's intelligent enough to understand. What's happened has happened and we each have to face up to it in our own way.'

His tears were flowing even faster now but still soundlessly. Hadn't Acciai said the same thing?

'If his mother had lived . . .'

But it wasn't too late, that was the important thing to remember. He could still make everything right. He must make his father understand that. He went closer to him and held his shoulders gently.

'It's going to be different now, that's what I've come to tell you. When I have to go away I can take you with me. I have my own car and there's room for you beside me.'

Did he understand how simple it was?

'And when I'm here I'll spend as much time with you as you want. You won't be alone in this room any more. I'll be here. Everything will be different. We could even change this room, it's so gloomy.' He began moving things, opening the double shutters that had been closed for years.

'This house is so dark, that's why you're sad.' A joyous thought came to him: 'I'm going to buy you a dog so that if I do ever have to go away you'll have company. There's room for a basket for it in this corner, look! You always thought it wrong to keep a dog in the city but we have a garden. You'll see how different things will be now that I can look after everything.'

He was smiling with relief and happiness though the tears still flowed down his cheeks. He could feel them trickling under his collar but it didn't matter. He'd found the solution and now there was so much to do, so much time to make up for. They were talking, he and his father. He couldn't hear what they were saying but it was warm and pleasant. Someone was trying to interrupt, shaking him by the shoulder gently but insistently. He ignored it, reluctant to leave the tranquil, radiant atmosphere he had created.

'I'm sorry.'

That was a woman's voice. He opened his eyes suddenly and was confused a little by the absence of the bar of light.

'I wouldn't have come in but I heard you talking.'

CHAPTER THIRTEEN

Reluctantly he turned his head. The girl who came to clean was standing by the bed wearing her coat and holding a polythene bag. He was unable to imagine why she should be there or what she could want from him.

'You must have been talking in your sleep.'

'Yes.' He put a hand up to his cheek, remembering the warm flow of tears, but it was quite dry. 'What time is it?'

'Just after six.'

Then he had slept for hours. His head was aching.

'I'm sorry,' the girl repeated, 'I came to ask you what you wanted me to do.'

'About what?' He still couldn't understand why she was there but he felt too drained to protest.

'Have I to come tomorrow?'

'I've no idea. You must ask my wife.' His head really hurt quite badly though the pain was sensuous rather than unpleasant. Even so, he should take an aspirin.

'Are you ill?' The girl was staring at him oddly. He could just make out her face in the half-dark.

'No . . . yes.' He saw her glance shift to the whisky bottle and glass on the bedside table. Had she come close enough to smell his breath? He could have said he had influenza but it didn't seem important enough to bother.

Since she still stood there he said again, 'You must talk to my wife.'

She looked at him uncertainly and then went out of the room, leaving the door ajar.

As soon as he was alone he got out of bed to get an aspirin from the bathroom. His body felt odd and very light and although he knew it must be because he was ill he didn't find it an unpleasant feeling. On the contrary, he felt a sort of excitement, a sense of arrival after a long journey, of finding himself in a new country where anything was possible. He slid back into bed quickly, finding the hollow he had left between the crumpled hot sheets and settling deeply into it, wanting to recapture the radiant atmosphere of his dream. He was convinced that it was possible, not in the way he had dreamt it because he couldn't remake the past, but in some way for the future. He could do nothing for the lonely child in the big dark house who no longer seemed connected to himself so that he was able to feel a detached pity for him, but despite the confused sense of time in his dream the blinding simplicity of the solution he had found, of breaking the pattern and taking charge of his own destiny, seemed just as valid now that he was awake. He would change everything. The possibilities tumbled through his head so rapidly that he could barely grasp them. He was impatient to see Laura, for one thing, as if he hadn't seen her for many years and needed to know what she looked like. Wasn't that how he had felt the morning she had opened his door to speak to him about the wedding? And she must have been aware of it because she had tried to cover herself. He had repressed the feeling immediately, ashamed of it, but now he realized that she had probably meant to provoke it and had been deeply embarrassed at his reaction. What a fool he'd been! But before he saw her again he needed a little time to think, to examine all the elements of his life in this new light.

The room was dark. He hadn't switched on the light for fear of dispelling the fragile new world he had created, but now he was anxious to look about him. He was curious to see everyone and everything as if after a long absence. He reached out to press the switch and sat up. A wall of leather-bound books faced him. Most of them his father's law books that were long out of date and no longer served any useful purpose. He would get rid of them and make space for new books. When had he last bought a book for pleasure? He must remember that . . . and pictures, too: all the paintings in the house had been his grandfather's and they were well worth keeping but that needn't prevent his buying something himself, something else he'd never thought of doing. But he must tread cautiously in this new world. He was over-excited, though that might only be the fever.

Someone tapped on the door and he looked towards it curiously.

The girl came in again. She was still wearing her coat but no longer carried the polythene bag. She came towards the bed holding a letter out to him.

'You'd better read this.'

'Is it urgent?' He didn't want the outside world intruding yet and he opened it reluctantly without even glancing at the envelope.

He had to read it three times before it made any sense. It seemed to him that it had been written to someone else and he had difficulty connecting it with himself. Even when he finally understood that Laura had left him there was only one sentence that sank in fully.

'If you had excluded me from your life because of another woman I could have understood it, or at least tried to . . .'

He almost held his breath, waiting for the blow to register, but nothing happened and he remained calm, buoyed up by a new sense of power over his fate. It wasn't final. She wasn't dead like the past and he would find her and put everything right.

'If you'd excluded me from your life because of another woman . . .'

It was astonishing. She had never known or even suspected about Giovanna and must have blamed their estrangement on the sudden pressure of work that had immediately followed the affair. Perhaps there was even some truth in it. In any case, he could put it right now . . .

Nevertheless, his fingers were trembling slightly as he

folded the letter and pushed it back in the envelope out of sight.

The girl was standing there, waiting. He looked at her.

'When . . .?'

'This morning. She left that by the telephone downstairs.' She was watching him anxiously as if she expected something from him. She had asked him a question the first time she came in and he tried to remember what it had been. He must pay attention to everything now, even to this slight girl whose name he couldn't remember. He had to learn to concentrate on one detail at a time, to move step by step until he found his feet. But he needed help.

'What did you want to ask me?'

'I told you. Have I to come tomorrow?'

'Do you want to?' It was strange. She had been working in the house for at least two years and he had no idea what she thought of him or whether she would be willing to work for him. It was important now. She was the first test of his new life and the relief was immense when she shrugged her shoulders and said: 'If you want.'

'I do want you to.' It was a small success but it gave him enough confidence to add: 'I think I have influenza.'

'Do you want me to get you something?'

'Will you bring up a bottle of mineral water?' It was the only thing he could think of. The important thing was to ask for it.

While she was out of the room he decided. He must convince her to stay with him, at least for an hour or so. He wasn't ready to be alone yet. He felt too confused and tender, like someone just recovering from an operation. His eyes followed her as she came in with the dark green misted bottle and opened the cupboard to get a clean glass. He would have liked to ask her, humbly, to pour it for him but before he could speak she had done it automatically and handed him the full glass. He drank thirstily. The water was deliciously cold and he realized that he had really needed it. She filled the glass again and placed it with the bottle near the bedside lamp.

'Shouldn't you go to bed properly if you're ill?' She was staring at him and he noticed for the first time that he was still wearing his clothes.

'I suppose so . . .' Wasn't she going to go out of the room? He wasn't in charge of the situation and could only wait to see what she would do.

'If you want, I could change the bed. I should have done it anyway this afternoon but you were in here.'

He got undressed in the bathroom. He never wore pyjamas but now he found some, anxious to go back into the bedroom before the girl had a chance to leave. In the few seconds it took to put them on he began shivering and his skin felt flammy and unhealthy. He was vigorous but no longer young. Would she accept him? The question, or rather what it implied, surprised him but he wasn't shocked by it. There was no moral reaction because the old rules of his life no longer applied. He knew he needed help and that was all.

She was still there. She had taken off her coat and made up the bed and now she was changing the pillow cases. He stood apart, watching her brisk movements as she plumped the feather pillows and then smoothed them, a lock of light brown hair falling over her forehead as she leaned forward. Although he had barely noticed her in the past he was aware that for some reason she looked different from the way he remembered her. Perhaps she usually wore some sort of overall which was now in the polythene bag he'd seen her carrying. She was wearing faded jeans and a thin woollen sweater that showed her nipples when she moved. That didn't arouse him; on the contrary, he felt only a sad ache in his chest that made him want the hand that was smoothing the pillows to smooth his head as though he were a sick child.

'You can get in.'

The sheets were cool and made him shiver more.

'I think I have a temperature.' Would she touch his head?

'Haven't you got a thermometer?'

'There should be one in the bathroom.' He didn't move and she went to get it. When it was in his mouth she stood looking down at him, not quite smiling but looking amused. His eyes remained fixed on hers as she removed the thermometer and looked at it.

'Thirty-eight point five. Not as bad as all that!'

'Why are you laughing at me?'

'I don't know. Because you're different. Maybe because you're sick and I've never seen you sick before.'

How could he explain that he really was different, that everything was different now?

'What was I like before?' He had to know what she thought of him. Sooner or later he had to find out what everybody thought of him. It was important.

She shrugged, her eyes still merry.

'Tell me.'

'I don't know,' she repeated, 'You were strange. You always seemed to be thinking about something else, as if you were never really there . . . So nobody could talk to you.'

'Did you want to talk to me?'

She didn't answer.

He ran his eyes slowly over her body and then looked at her, questioning.

'You're sick . . .' But she didn't move or protest when he reached out a hand towards her and felt her warmth through the soft sweater. He withdrew his hand with his eyes still fixed on hers.

'Take that off.' She wasn't going to refuse him. Now that he was at peace with himself he had only to ask for help when he needed it and it would be given to him. He no longer felt any anxiety.

She had taken off her sweater and stood watching him a little uncertainly, clutching it against herself but letting him see her breasts. There was still a trace of amusement in her eyes.

'Do you want me to get in bed?'

'Take it all off.' He wouldn't help her or even move to

touch her. He wanted her to uncover herself to him simply. For some reason that was essential. There were to be no games, no dishonesty, no pretended relinquishing of responsibility. It had to be simple and pure.

She slipped off her shoes and turned a little away from him to unfasten her jeans.

'No. Turn to me.'

She pulled off her jeans, woollen tights and pants all together and left them there on the floor.

With a little sigh of contentment he drew back the covers and pulled her towards him as she slid into the bed, feeling the warmth of her all along his body. How long had all physical contact been absent from his life? A long, long time. As her warmth seeped into him he stopped shivering and took off the pyjamas, pushing them away down the bed. Turning to her, he took her head gently on to his shoulder and began stroking the soft front of her body tenderly as though she were a kitten.

'Like silk . . .' he said softly, parting her thighs a little to caress her.

After a moment she murmured against his shoulder, embarrassed:

'You don't need to wait for me, I take a long time.'

'You can take all the time you want.' He was still cradling her head and she relaxed against him. When he felt her begin to respond he leaned down to kiss her, first on her forehead and eyes and then on her lips with more sweetness than passion. He remembered the warm tears flowing over his cheeks in the dream and the same feeling was welling up inside him now though he didn't cry, only went on kissing her slowly and tenderly. He wasn't thinking of her. The image fixed in his mind was of Laura covering her breasts in that protective gesture which made him ache at the recollection of it. But he wasn't really thinking of Laura either. This was an atonement for all the sensitive life he had crushed out of others and most of all out of himself. Only when he felt her body begin to move in soft convulsions did he enter her, holding her head gently as she clung to him. He was filled with a deep and thirsty desire which he had never experienced before and which had no frenzy in it even at the end.

Afterwards she lay clinging to him for a long time, still trembling slightly. When the trembling stopped she murmured something which he barely heard, he felt so far away. He only became conscious of her when she drew apart a little. Then he looked down at her.

'Tell me your name.'

'My *name*?' She had come to herself and was laughing at him again. 'It's Mariangela.'

'Mariangela . . .' He kissed her forehead lightly as he might have kissed a child.

'I didn't expect . . .'

'What didn't you expect?'

'That you'd be like that. You don't feel ill?'

'Not very. I took some aspirin.' He turned back the covers. 'You're not cold? I want to look at you.' Her nipples were childish and rosy. It was a long time since he had seen such young breasts and he found their immaturity touching. Her skin still had a fading tan from last summer except for the paler triangle. He stroked her firmly all over, smiling.

'What are you smiling at?' She was watching him, quiet and trusting, her eyes still slightly dilated.

'Nothing in particular. Just for the pleasure of looking at you. You're so young and healthy.' A frown crossed his face at a sudden memory. Every detail . . . 'Why is it that you're so often ill?'

'I've never been ill in my life!'

'But . . . when you don't come to work?'

'Is that what you thought? You don't know?' She was laughing.

'There's very little I do know. Tell me.'

'It's because I have exams to take.'

'Exams?'

'Of course. I'm enrolled at the University but I only go

there every so often, mostly for exams. I have to work.'

'Don't you have parents?'

'My dad's been ill for years, only my mum works. It's not enough to keep me studying. You are funny!'

'Why am I funny?'

'Because I've been working here for years and you've never so much as noticed me and now you're so curious.'

'Why do you work here?' he insisted, 'You could surely do something better or at least easier.'

'Like what? I could do supply schoolteaching but they only call you once in a blue moon. That's for middle-class students who want to earn their holiday money. And if I worked in some fancy shop I'd have to spend a fortune on clothes. I have to give what I earn to my mother.'

'Do you have brothers and sisters?'

'Two younger brothers. What else do you want to know? Who I vote for?'

'If you like.' But he had noticed the remark about the middle classes. 'You vote Communist?'

'Of course.'

He hadn't the courage to ask her what she thought of him, or of his work, at least not directly.

'Tell me what you think of the Red Brigades.'

'Of *what*?' She laughed aloud.

'Why is that funny?'

'Don't you think it's a strange question to ask someone when you've just made love?'

'If you say so. But I really want to know.'

'Well, I don't think about them at all. I've got other things to do with my time.'

'You must have an opinion, even so.'

'Well then, I suppose I think what everybody thinks, that they're a pain in the neck.'

'Is that all?'

'That's all.'

He had to have more courage. 'I suppose what I really want to know is what you think of me.'

'I don't know. I told you, you're different today, somehow.'

'Before, then.'

'Before . . . I suppose I only really noticed how you treated . . . her. I mean, you hardly even spoke to her.'

What else had he expected? Some reflection of his newspaper image? Anything but this because he had always thought that, given the circumstances, his behaviour to Laura had been punctiliously correct. Only the 'circumstances' hadn't existed except in his own mind. He felt humiliated.

Misinterpreting his silence, she said: 'I'm sorry. I shouldn't have mentioned her. I know you must be upset or you wouldn't have . . .'

'What do you mean?'

'Well, it's a standard reaction, isn't it? Jumping into bed with the first person who comes along. Don't worry about admitting it, I'm not offended. It was nice.'

A standard reaction. He wanted to cry out against it but he only lay back on the pillows, his face like stone.

'I suppose you want me to go now. Can I use the bathroom?'

'Yes.'

She gathered up her clothes and took them with her. To his relief she must have gone through Laura's bedroom for her coat and only called out as she passed his door on the corridor: 'I'll be here at eight in the morning.' So there was no need to answer.

A standard reaction. It was the first blow to his new confidence. But wasn't that more or less his own reaction to the behaviour of someone like Gori? And Corbi and Acciai, too? And they, too, thought their reasons unique just as he did. It was a humiliation he deserved and would have to accept. He must still go on with what he had to do, knowing that nobody else would ever understand, he couldn't turn back.

He got up and put on a dressing-gown. He had to take more aspirin, the last ones must have worn off. As he started down the stairs he began sneezing and his ears rang in the silence of the empty house. In his hand he carried the key of his father's study. He opened the door of the dark room and stood there a moment, hearing his own shallow breathing. Then he snapped on the light. He hadn't known that the furniture would all be shrouded in dustsheets and they angered him. He went round the room tearing them off and threw them in a heap in an empty corner. The study seemed just as gloomy with the lights on. Perhaps the shades were all dusty. At any rate, when he went out he left the lights on and the door open. Should he eat something? The kitchen was so empty and tidy that he was reluctant to touch anything. He opened the refrigerator door and shut it again without coming to any decision. In the end he turned on all the lights on the ground floor and wandered from room to room as though he were looking for something, his restlessness increasing. What he really wanted to do was to go into Laura's room and he realized that he was trying to avoid doing it because the phrase 'standard reaction' was still in his mind.

'Why shouldn't I have a standard reaction?' He spoke aloud and his voice, muffled by the feverish cold, sounded resonant in the silence so that he barely recognized it as his own. Nevertheless, he started up the stairs, switching more lights on as he went as if nothing would dispel the suffocating gloom.

The big bedroom was tidy, the silk bedcover smooth and still. She hadn't left hurriedly, then, but calmly and deliberately, the way she always did things. He drew the long curtains closed to shut out the bluish light coming from the streetlamp at the gate and then went to open the wardrobe. There was an almost empty section where most of her winter clothes had been removed but her summer dresses still hung in their compartment and he fingered these lightly. Next he opened the drawers of her dressing-table, a thing he had never done even in the days when he had shared this room. He was reluctant, even now, to touch anything but one of the drawers fascinated him and he began to take things out of it one by one, replacing them carefully just as they had been. A porcelain pot with a broken string of pearls and one earring, a pair of white kid gloves in a polythene bag. She hadn't worn gloves like that for many years but they still smelled faintly of her perfume. A box with a calf-bound missal inscribed for her First Communion. He had never seen that before. A bigger carved wooden box full of old photographs of herself, her sister, her parents. More First Communions, Confirmations, family holidays and Christmasses. There was nothing more recent, no photographs of their wedding or their holidays. Did that mean she had taken them with her? He paused and looked about him. Everything that was personal to Laura was in this room. The pictures and photographs on the walls, too. He tried to think whether there was anything of hers anywhere else in the house. There wasn't. It was true that when she had moved in here after their marriage his father had still been alive and the house run by his servants. Laura had confined her personality to one room and must have gone on doing so even after the old man's death, caring for the rest of the house in a detached way. It had remained the Bardi house. He picked out another photograph of the two little girls. The sister was married to a businessman in Milan. It was the one place she might have gone. He went back to his own room and looked up the number, still holding the photo.

It was the sister herself who answered and he knew immediately from the tone of her voice that Laura was there.

'Oh, it's you.'

They met only rarely and had little enough to say to one another. This was another humiliation he had to accept.

'Will you let me speak to Laura?'

'She's asleep. I had to give her something, she was in such

a bad state. She won't wake up until tomorrow, I hope.'

'Then I'll ring again tomorrow.'

'If you like. But I can tell you now that she doesn't want to speak to you. She's already said so.'

'She may feel differently tomorrow. Tell her –'

'I'll tell her you rang, but as far as I'm concerned I think she's done the best possible thing and not before time.'

He understood that she wanted to quarrel with him and was disconcerted by his lack of aggressiveness.

'Tell her . . .' What?

There was silence at the other end. After a moment he said: 'Tell her I'll write to her.' And he rang off.

He wrote at once, rapidly, without stopping to seek the right words or to try to explain himself. Perhaps he would never explain himself. He only told her that he agreed with everything she was thinking, that from now on things would be different, that he would go to Milan to bring her home the moment she gave him permission.

Was that what all husbands said when their wives left them? Another standard reaction? He was too exhausted to care. He was still shivering and he felt dizzy and sick. He knew that he should go downstairs and turn off all the lights that were burning there but it was more than he could manage. It was all he could do to get himself back into Laura's bedroom and into the double bed where he huddled waiting for enough warmth to bring sleep and oblivion.

Tempesta picked up the telephone receiver, hesitated a moment and then replaced it without dialling. One of his men tapped and looked round the door.

'Not now.'

'You're not ready to go out, sir?'

'No. Is the Colonel-in-Command in his office?'

'I think so, sir. He was a moment ago.'

'Come back in fifteen minutes.'

The door closed and Tempesta sat still, his face heavy and

expressionless. The office of the Colonel-in-Command was only a few steps away down the corridor but he had already been there once and there was little he could do now except await his call. He swung round in his chair and opened the window. It was real December weather, bright and freezing. There was probably a fine dusting of snow on the hills around the city. Turning back, he settled deep into the leather chair and placed his hands solidly on the desk before him. Waiting was something he knew how to do. He stared at the door, his eyelids slightly lowered. When the telephone rang he reached for it without shifting his gaze.

'Tempesta?'

'Yes.'

'Well, I'm afraid I haven't been able to do anything. It looks as though you were right.'

'I was never in any doubt about that.'

'Well, I was, frankly. Could well have been coincidence. You must see how I was placed. Poma's request for compassionate leave was quite genuine. Wife's in hospital.'

'I know.'

'Hm. You checked, of course . . .'

'I did.'

'And he's leaving us, in case you didn't already know that too, so on the face of it . . . Well, Bardi officially ceases to hold his position here as of today so that without orders to the contrary his car and escort are automatically withdrawn.'

'In this case there should have been orders to the contrary.'

'Not necessarily. Normally the police would provide an escort to cover the interim period.'

'You've talked to them?'

'That was the first thing I did.'

'And?'

'He's been taken off the list. There's nothing they can do. I also telephoned General Command in Rome to make a recommendation that something be pushed through from scratch and a new escort assigned. You know the way of it, it could be done in twenty minutes.'

'Unless somebody doesn't want it done, in which case there'll be a bureaucratic tangle that somehow won't untangle itself until it's too late. Who did you speak to?'

'A number of people. They were passing me round like a hot potato. Eventually someone admitted with considerable embarrassment that the order came from outside the army. Big stuff.'

'There was actually an order?'

'That's my own phrase. I imagine it was no more than a suggestion, certainly nothing written, but we can take it as read that nobody's going to push anything through in a hurry, which means the answer's no. It's either political or your people, or both.'

'Yes. Thank you for trying.'

'Did what I could.'

Your people. It wasn't difficult to recognize the General's unseen hand.

He pulled the telephone a few inches closer and dialled Bardi's home number. There was no answer. He rang the Procura and was told that the Substitute Prosecutor hadn't been seen since he left to go into court the previous morning.

In that case did he even know about his transfer? The telex would surely have been sent to his office.

'Put me through to the Chief Public Prosecutor.'

'Immediately, sir.'

Corbi was weakly jovial. Tempesta cut through the cordialities firmly.

'I'm trying to reach Bardi but they say he hasn't been in his office since yesterday morning.'

'No, I don't believe he has. The hearing was adjourned, of course . . . I think you'll find him at home.'

'I've already tried his home.'

'That's odd . . .' Corbi was plainly embarrassed. 'He was there earlier this morning.'

'You spoke to him?'

'Not personally . . . You've heard the good news, of course, that he's been promoted?'

'I have. I was hoping to congratulate him, apart from anything else. He does know, I take it?'

'Oh yes, indeed. It's odd that you didn't find him at home. I understood he was under the weather. Influenza, I think. Perhaps he's just not answering, not feeling up to it.'

'Perhaps. Excuse my being persistent but it's rather urgent. If you didn't speak to him yourself . . .'

'No, no. I sent somebody over there. There's been a bit of confusion because of his not coming into the office – hadn't seen the telex, you see, so of course he rang in about nine-thirty or so this morning . . .'

'When his escort didn't arrive?'

'It's all rather complicated. I sent someone over right away with the telex . . . rather an unfortunate muddle.'

'And whoever you sent said he was ill?'

'So I understand.'

'I see. I'll keep trying, then. Excuse my disturbing you.'

'Not at all, not at all, my dear Colonel. Always glad to be of help.'

Tempesta pressed the receiver rest and dialled Bardi's number, letting it ring interminably. Then he called the switchboard.

'Colonel?'

'I want you to ring Substitute Prosecutor Bardi. Take down the number.' He dictated it clearly. 'Try him every fifteen minutes and keep on trying until you get him. I have to go out and I'm already late.'

'Yes, sir. What shall I tell him when I do get him?'

'That I'll be in touch with him. Above all, that he should stay where he is.'

CHAPTER FOURTEEN

'Express number 705, the 11.30 from Milan for Arezzo, Terontola, Chiusi, Orte and Rome Terminus is leaving from platform ten instead of platform twelve. Express number 705, the 11.30 from Milan for Arezzo . . .'

It was difficult for Bardi to make out the announcement, his head was so muffled and his ears ringing, but he was carried along by the crowd as people rushed to change platform, pushing in front of each other and banging their luggage against his legs. Their panic was needless since the train was a long one and mostly empty and it didn't leave for a further ten minutes after they had all climbed into it. He had to walk almost its entire length before finding a first class non-smoker and sinking wearily into the window seat of an empty carriage. He felt too ill to smoke and doubted whether he could even tolerate the smell of other people's cigarettes. He realized that he was probably too ill to travel, too, but it was easier now to go on rather than make the mental effort of changing his plans. A trolley clattered along the platform and he signalled to it to stop, winding down the window and leaning out to reach for a bottle of mineral water. His mouth was dry and hot and he needed to take more aspirin. He took two immediately, washed them down with three cups of water and lay back with his eyes closed to fight down a rising nausea. When the train pulled out of the station with an almost soundless jerk he kept his eyes closed and drifted close to sleep, the voices from the next carriage confusing themselves in his head. When he opened them briefly winter fields and an old man digging in a cabbage patch near a ramshackle shed slid drunkenly past his gaze. The door of the carriage was open and a young couple stood in the corridor with their backs to him, smoking. He stirred and looked at his watch. Less than half an hour had passed but his limbs and neck already ached from being blocked in one position. He moved his head carefully and rested it on the wing of his seat away from the window. After a while his eyes closed again and the rhythmic noise of the train took over in his brain, the snatches of muffled conversation fitting themselves to it like words to a song. Once or twice, though aware of being asleep, his hand moved to his breast pocket checking that the letter he had carried there had been posted to Laura. The pocket was empty. He was doing all he could as fast as he could. A small sigh escaped him each time his hand fell.

When the train stopped at Arezzo the slamming of doors along its length awoke him properly and he drank a little more water. The couple in the corridor were embracing each other despite the people pushing past them with luggage. Nobody came into his carriage for which he was thankful. Then they moved off again and he saw the guard interrupt the embracing youngsters to clip their tickets and got out his own. It was a three day return because he wasn't sure he would have the strength to travel back that night. It seemed to him that the guard looked at him oddly when he handed back the ticket, sliding the door half closed as he went out. Did he look as ill as he felt? It was true that he had been shocked by his own reflection in the mirror when he had shaved himself with a shaky hand, hardly recognized the expression in the eyes that looked back at him. Even so, he hadn't been disconcerted. Nothing surprised him any more. He was content to accept whatever might happen to him next. He had slept until almost nine o'clock and woke in Laura's bed to lie still gazing at a watercolour of storm clouds over a pasture, knowing that he would not be dressed when Poma and Mastino arrived but not moving even so. Perhaps because of that it only seemed logical that they didn't come. He had put on a dressing gown and wandered through to his own room to stand watching the cold sunny street beyond the magnolia tree and the big iron gates. Half past nine came and went but no familiar car drew up. He went on standing there observing the traffic and the movements of a man in a Fiat 500 parked across the street smoking and reading a newspaper. After ten minutes or so the man folded his newspaper and drove away and Bardi roused himself from his reverie and called the Procura. He asked for Corbi and they kept him waiting an interminable time without ever putting him through. In the end it was the switchboard operator himself who said: 'They're sending someone round to you in a few minutes.' And something about the voice told him that things were not as they should be. The voice had reflected someone else's embarrassment, but he hadn't troubled to ask himself why. He would wait and see. He had faced the strange reflection in the cold light of the bathroom mirror and then showered and dressed. Before going down to the kitchen where he knew the girl would be working he had hesitated but only for a moment. He would face that, too. The phrase 'standard reaction' no longer upset him. On the contrary, he even found it comforting. Didn't it mean, after all, that things were taking their natural course, the way they did for other men and never had for him?

'Good morning.'

'Good morning. Are you feeling any better?'

'A little.'

'You're still pale, though. Haven't you had any breakfast?'

'I thought I'd make some coffee, if I'm not in your way.'

'Why should you be in my way? I'm cleaning out the fridge. You'll have to tell me if you want me to do any shopping.'

'I don't know . . . No.'

'Will you eat out?'

'I suppose so.'

'Well, if you intend to go on taking aspirin you shouldn't drink coffee. I'll make you some tea. Do you know you left every light in the house on?'

He had carried the tray himself up to the study and sat by

the window. The traffic seemed to have slowed down and the street was quieter. A woman wrapped in furs came out of the big gabled house across the way, opened the high gates, got into her car and drove off. Inside a maid was balanced on a ladder polishing the windows, sometimes lifting one hand to shade her eyes from the bright winter sunlight. He couldn't remember ever having been in the house at that hour on a weekday before and found the unaccustomed atmosphere fascinating. He had taken two more aspirin and was grateful for the sweet tea which washed the sourness of them from his mouth but after a brief attempt he gave up trying to eat the rolls which stuck in dry lumps in his mouth so that he couldn't swallow them.

A small car drew up, double parked outside the gates and a porter from the Procura got out and rang the bell. He watched the girl go down the gravel drive and take something from him, glancing up at his window as she came back towards the house. He listened to her steps coming up the stairs. She knocked and came in without waiting for his answer but it didn't disturb him.

He took the envelope from her and she began preparing to take away the tray.

'You haven't eaten anything.' When he didn't answer she straightened up and looked at him. 'Is it bad news?'

'No.' And he had gone on staring out of the window, the telex held loosely in one hand.

The train was slowing down. They must be approaching the station of Chiusi.

What he had said was true, it wasn't bad news. He had even smiled at the irony of it. Bergamo! He'd almost reopened the letter to tell her but had quickly changed his mind. It would have been proof that their life would be different from now on. He hadn't done it because he wanted her to believe in him without that. He would tell her later, when she came home. Everything was proceeding as it should and he felt an immense relief. So many problems that he hadn't known how to eliminate from his new world had simply been removed. No speech on the Bardi Theorem would have to be made. As Chief Public Prosecutor he would never again be the one to stand up in court and demand another man's condemnation. He was no longer capable of it. He wouldn't have to see Gori who would be transferred to a special prison and eventually be freed and helped to remake his life by the state he had attacked. Once that would have angered Bardi but now it would be all he could do to gain enough forgiveness to go on with his own life. The last thing he had done before going out had been to telephone the prison Governor to urgently recommend Gori's transfer. What good would it do for him to be killed by his ex-companions now? That sounded like Corbi's apologia for Acciai. Would he become like Corbi? He would have to wait and see.

He smiled again as the whistle blew and the train slid forward again. They thought they had beaten him but the man they were trying to crush no longer existed.

When he had dressed and left for the station it had almost seemed like a parody of his old life, except that he had gone out the front door without a glance at the portrait in the dining room. The other door had been shut, the girl must have shut it. And except that the familiar feel of the smooth leather holster under his jacket was absent. He had no further need of that, or of the armoured car and Poma and Mastino. In future he would travel like this, on a train with normal people. Beyond the half closed door of the carriage the young couple stood looking out of the window, their arms around each other, their foreheads against the glass as the bare winter vineyards sped by them. One lock of the girl's blond hair hung over the collar of the fur coat slung over her shoulders. She wore big fur boots, too, of the sort people wore in the mountains. Perhaps they had been skiing. Laura had wanted him to take her to the mountains. It was the first thing he would do when she came home. He would take her to the Dolomites where they had once used to go. The man's hand was caressing the soft fur on the girl's shoulder. Yesterday seemed years away. The sudden flood of relief at feeling a warm body against his . . . But it was better not to think of that yet. He had one more thing to do. Then he could walk away from it all. First he needed to know what had really happened to the little tailor who was somehow the only person from his old life who was connected with his new one. If Attilio had been entirely innocent and his death was Bardi's fault then he would learn how to live with it. But he needed to know for sure.

He leaned back and closed his eyes again. Was he deceiving himself? It was so difficult to be sure. Was there still a trace of the old Bardi who wanted to look one man in the eyes for his own satisfaction before walking away? He could sense the danger of it but he had to go on and find out or he would never be free of it. And it had been so easy, now that everything was different, now that it no longer mattered the way it had before. Just a telephone call. A telephone call . . .

He slept. When the train drew up at the Rome Terminus with a long squeal of brakes he opened his eyes, dazed. He would have liked to stay in the corner of the train indefinitely, letting it carry him along, all life suspended, and it took an enormous effort to get himself off and down the platform. He would have to get a coffee and try and eat something. When this was over he had an appointment at Palazzo dei Marescialli to accept and discuss his promotion. Once in the queue at the cash desk of the bar he remembered the girl's words: 'If you intend to go on taking aspirin . . .' and ordered chocolate instead of coffee for the comfort of following someone's advice. The chocolate reminded him of Poma and the way he had suddenly stopped drinking coffee. Had he, too, been sick? Something had been wrong, he realized, looking back. Poma had wanted to talk to him about something the other day. Perhaps it was too late to put that right. He wondered what the two of them would do now.

There were no windows in the long half-empty bar and under the fluorescent lighting the faces around him had an odd, cadaverous colour and the dazed, vacant look of people lost in a limbo between trains. Some of them, old people, looked as though they spent all their time there. Nobody spoke much and the only noise was of the clank and hiss of the coffee machine and the desultory repetition of orders. He got up and left, blinking in the roar and brightness of the vast station square. In the taxi that edged its way down the Via Nazionale he felt too hot and let his overcoat slide down off his shoulders. He made no conversation with the taxi driver who swore continuously under his breath and occasionally leaned on his horn to add his noise to all the rest. They crossed the Tiber by the Vittorio Emmanuele II bridge and queued to enter the broad Via della Conciliazone, swarming with people approaching or leaving the great marble basilica, filling the shops on each side selling postcards and guidebooks, rosaries, medals and big coloured photographs of the Pope. He got out at the obelisk where the first wooden barrier marked the beginning of the great upward sweep of St Peter's Square and walked to the right to follow the curved arcade that sheltered his eyes from the brilliant winter sunlight. At the second barrier he came out into the centre and joined the crowd that was filtering through a small opening guarded by two policemen. When his turn came they waved their metal detector in a cursory way around his middle. He remembered the absence of his gun with satisfaction and passed through with the rest to climb the marble steps. Most of the people were going straight on into St Peter's where a distant amber light glowed softly in the gloom. Few of them turned right with him to enter the museums which would shortly close. His pace became so rapid as he reached the first floor that the tourists dawdling around cases of Etruscan pottery turned to stare as he cut a path through them. At each junction his eyes scanned the signs indicating the different routes, seeking the shortest, but he never paused. As fast as he walked the marble corridors stretched endlessly before him as he passed under arch after decorated arch, past walls hung with tapestries and then with gigantic maps. The blind gaze of countless marble heads followed his progress. Harpies and cherubs, birds and grotesque animals grimaced, beckoned, writhed and cavorted on either side of him. The corridors went on and on. At the last turn by the staircase the sign saying 'Sistine Chapel' was covered by another saying 'Closed' in four languages. He stopped. There was no one in sight but he could hear footsteps approaching in the distance behind him. He tapped rapidly but softly at the polished door and a key turned in it on the other side. The door opened just enough to admit him and was locked again.

It was necessary to duck at once under boards crossing immense and complicated scaffolding that was hung about with rags, discarded white overalls and big cans of water. With head bowed he trod carefully between electric cables lying across splattered dust sheets, following the small dark shambling figure until they came out into an open space where Monsignor Joseph Lazurek stopped and turned, holding out his hand. It was such a natural gesture that Bardi, though surprised at himself, took it.

Somewhere, high up on the scaffolding that reached to the ceiling, a drop of water fell every few seconds, echoing in the silence. Bardi looked about him at the great rectangular room where, despite the tall leaded windows, the light seemed to emanate from the colours of the figures painted on the walls and ceiling.

'Why here?'

'Today they've been putting up new scaffolding. The workmen and restorers are at lunch now so no one will disturb us. You understand that I could hardly have received you, even privately, in my office.'

'Then you're afraid.'

'Yes indeed, very much so.'

Bardi took out a handkerchief. His forehead was beaded with sweat and he felt weak after hurrying so far. Or perhaps the fever was breaking. He had to try and concentrate but images and ideas were drifting and blurring in his mind and nothing was as it should be. For so many years he had imagined the dark and enigmatic figure of the man who had performed the last rites before an assassination, who had seen the Grand Old Man of terrorism and kept his own counsel. And now he was facing a small and shabby priest whose stature and significance were further diminished by the powerful gigantic patriarch gesticulating on the wall behind him, and who admitted he was afraid.

'And yet you agreed to see me.'

'Yes. I wanted to see you. I'm an old man and the old are often selfish. And besides, we can hope that you are safe now.'

'Don't you mean harmless? It's you who are safe from me now.'

'No, no. Do you think I'm afraid for myself? Perhaps I should be . . . But though there's a lot you can't have understood you must at least know that you have enemies.'

'Not any more.' He wanted to say, 'You were my enemy.' Wasn't it true, after all? But he felt so tired and the sleepy little eyes watching him were so calm that they hypnotized him and all he said was: 'It's true that there was a lot I didn't understand.'

The colours around him were shifting and dissolving. He needed to sit down but there was nothing other than the paint-splattered scaffolding in the big room.

The little priest was coming closer to him, an arm outstretched.

'You're sick.'

'No . . . Yes, but it's not important. What's important . . .' But what was it . . . ?

'Is it Attilio?'

'Attilio, yes . . .' Was this just another dream? The great swirling figures on the walls had more reality than the two of them and that wasn't right. How could he have known that Attilio was what had brought him here?

'I imagined it might be that.' The priest went on apparently answering questions that hadn't been asked and reality was sliding further and further away. His brow was wet again and cold and he dabbed at it with the handkerchief as the quiet voice continued.

'You talked to Attilio so you must have seen at once that he was innocent of anything except chattering too much about his beloved Cardinal. The rest of us are all guilty in some measure, if not of wickedness, of stupidity or ambition, but he was the one to die because I used his telephone. And yet he couldn't have told you anything. There was no need to kill him but either they didn't realize, didn't trust me enough, or they didn't care to risk it. He knew nothing at all. And I was sure you'd understand that, at least, from what I'd heard about you.'

The colours and images were settling into place again but he felt ill, very ill, and he had need of the arm that was now supporting him.

'If I hadn't gone there he would still be alive.'

'You couldn't have known that.'

'Nevertheless, it's true. It's over, now. I just need to know how much blame I have to live with.'

'No blame. No blame at all. You couldn't have foreseen it. If anyone should have foreseen it, I should. It's over for you but it will never be over for me. Do you know that I've often wished you might succeed and somehow put an end to it all? If you could have done it without its costing you your life. It wasn't worth that. Nothing would have changed ultimately. Nothing ever does. It was a selfish wish. You must go right away from us all and live your life peacefully. Do it for me, since I can't. Go away and rest.'

Another drop of water fell high above them with a soft plop. Another similar noise came from beyond the scaffolding behind Bardi at the door where he had come in. He saw a frown of surprise cross the priest's face as he stepped aside to see better.

'It's early for them . . .'

But somewhere in his subconscious Bardi had recognized that second sound for what it was. He turned slowly, even so, reluctant to obey the unwelcome signal. Even when he saw the young couple running towards him under the scaffolding he didn't react at once. The girl was in front. He recognized the fur coat that was swinging open and the blonde hair and saw that she was laughing and that the gun had a silencer on it. Still he was making the wrong movements, stretching out his hand to hide from himself the face of Mariangela beneath the blonde wig. Only when the man's voice said, 'Christ, he's not alone!' did his hand whip back and plunge in the familiar gesture under his lapel where there was nothing. The man spun round to run away, crashing his head against a metal pole. But the girl was still laughing and he suddenly had the sensation of something having sliced him in two.

'You were warned there'd be a next time!'

He was still standing so she couldn't have hit him. As long as he kept hold of his stomach he wouldn't fall. But it was happening anyway. The marble floor was bumping against his face and although he felt nothing he knew his teeth had been smashed loose and that the spatters of blood on the marble pattern came from his mouth. Even so, it was his stomach he went on holding. He saw a fur boot and the gun being pushed down inside it, then the red again dribbling along the smooth pale marble.

Why should she have bothered to say that about the aspirin? People said things automatically. Laura would have to find a new cleaner. Perhaps she would sell the house . . . it would be better. His body was moving very slowly, curling up on itself. He was conscious of it without willing it to happen which was strange since he was perfectly lucid. Perhaps it was so that it would be easier to keep his stomach closed tight. He could feel something hot and welling like the tears in his dream. He wanted to smile but he knew he wouldn't be able to because of his teeth and the warm saltiness in his mouth. Even so, he was smiling inside himself because he knew exactly how to cope with this. Hadn't he been preparing for it all along? Only they didn't know! All he had to do was to keep very still and maintain an equilibrium so that he could think clearly. They mustn't start manhandling him because that would mean he was dead. Would they understand that? It bothered him that they might not and then he remembered that the odd little priest was there and that he was the one person who would understand. He opened one eye a little to make sure. He was there. A black sleeve and an outstretched hand across the marble pattern quite close to him. He let the eye close again and relaxed. Everything was going right. He had posted the letter to Laura, Gori would be transferred and he had opened up his father's study. He'd done everything he could. He wasn't to blame and he must go away and rest. He let himself sink lower. When he rose again it was because of the light, a blinding light that tried to prise his eyes open but he wouldn't let it. There was too much noise in the room and he needed peace. His mind was quite clear and he even remembered the big cables crossing the floor and knew that the light came from the restorer's spotlamps. It made him feel sick but he could still maintain his balance as long as they didn't move him. The priest would explain.

But it was the priest they were moving. He didn't want to open his eyes but perhaps they were already open because he saw a brown shoe spotted with paint go by and then two black shoes that stopped and turned away close to his face.

'Take him first. The other one's dead, by the look of him . . .'

He smiled again inside himself. Because they were wrong! Only someone must tell them not to manhandle him and now the priest was gone. Laura would have to tell them. Of course! She'd be at the funeral. She'd have got his letter and would be there to tell them that the coffin . . .

But it was too late. He could feel himself being lifted and his stomach was tearing apart with terrible dagger-like pains. He tried to tell them but his mouth was full and he only managed one word.

'Don't . . .'

But even to him it only sounded like a faint rattle.

EPILOGUE

'Monsignor . . .? He's sleeping. He sleeps a great deal.'

'Then I'll just sit with him a while and leave a note.'

Father McManus went and stood by the bed looking down at the much diminished figure beneath the white counterpane. When the nurse had shut the door sharply behind her Lazurek opened his eyes a fraction and said: 'That woman is worse than Sister Agatha. A thing I wouldn't have thought possible. Sit down, you're towering.'

'Then you weren't asleep.'

'I was. Until I was sure it was you. You stayed away long enough.'

'I came the first day but they wouldn't let me in.'

'I never doubted it. But once you knew I was going to live you stayed away.'

The young man didn't answer. Lazurek closed his eyes for a moment, his breathing laboured and too audible in the small bare room. A small black crucifix hung at the head of the iron bed and the young priest stared at it, then at the hands lying limply outside the counterpane. Hands that had once been plump and sleek and were now thinner with the bluish white tinge of the sickbed.

'You've grown so thin.'

'Oh, indeed.' The small eyes opened and scowled up at the drip feed. 'Whatever they put into me through that thing it is not champagne and caviar. I take it you've come to say goodbye.'

'Yes.'

'When do you leave?'

'Tomorrow morning.'

'Then you certainly left me until the last minute. You must

have been very angry indeed. So the good Bishop refused to let you stay, despite your not unsuccessful efforts at rounding up support here.'

The young man flushed deeply. 'I had a telegram from him. He refused even to discuss the idea of my staying.'

'A sensible man.'

'Even so, had you wanted to, I'm sure that you –'

'Coming, as I do, from Chicago. Yes, I remember you thought that. Well perhaps, after all, you were right.' A faint smile crossed the Monsignor's face and faded quickly. His cheeks were sunken and the skin across the bridge of his nose was taught and mottled after days of pain. 'And what news do you bring me apart from your own departure? You always brought me news.'

'And you always knew everything beforehand. I bet you do now even in here.'

'That's more like you. You mustn't feel sorry for me, you know, though I'm sure, even without having seen myself, that I must be a dreadful sight for a healthy young man to look upon. I was never a great beauty, if you remember, and at least here they keep me cleaner and tidier than I ever kept myself. Tell me how the Great Schism is going.'

'There you are, you see! You do know.'

'You're not my first visitor. His Holiness himself was here, though he very kindly spared me the details. I imagine the vultures flew away in confusion at the news that I intended to live.'

'They did, but not before some very heavy financial commitments had been made, though that's only hearsay.'

'And according to hearsay they were made in my name, is that how it went?'

'More or less. I don't know the truth of it but they say there's a new bank involved and it's been claimed, on their side, that you made certain promises . . .'

'Which the vultures in my absence were only too happy to pretend to believe in.'

'It was said . . .'

'Go on.'

'It was said that you were seen dining with their representative . . . and at his expense.'

'I see. And now?'

'And now they say you'll be back in your office within another two months. You know who's been appointed temporarily?'

'I do. And he's by no means capable of dealing with the vultures.'

'Surely His Holiness, himself . . .'

'His Holiness is in many ways a saintly man. But an ingenuous one.' Lazurek sighed. 'One should never consider oneself indispensable but I'll have to be the one to fight that battle as soon as I emerge from here. I only hope it won't be too late. We can ill afford another scandal.'

'Is it true you'll be back in your office within two months?'

'What's left of me will. I may be minus half a stomach, or three-quarters of it. They haven't been too clear about that as yet. I suppose I ought to be grateful to those two young people for ridding me of my two prevalent vices. I have little enough taste for a Cardinal's hat now, and I doubt if a quarter of a stomach will permit me to indulge myself in Sister Agatha's offerings. I shall probably become a saint. You'll be able to pray to me.'

'I shall like that.' The young man laughed.

'In the meantime you can pray *for* me. It's good to hear you laugh. Don't ever get too serious in Chicago, or wherever they send you. You'll need a sense of humour.'

'I'll do my best.'

They fell silent but the young man sat on. After a moment Lazurek said with a touch of astringency:

'I imagine they told you not to tire me, not to stay more than ten minutes or something of the sort.'

'Yes, they did.'

'Then I'll tell you that I've enjoyed your visit very much but that you have tired me . . . So you'd better say what you came to say and then I can go back to sleep.'

'I'm sorry.'

'So you should be. The sooner you leave Rome and give up your newly acquired habit of diplomacy the better. What's bothering you?'

'I suppose . . . the newspapers.'

'I wasn't aware that I'd become a hero in the newspapers.'

'You haven't. That's . . .'

'I see. You find that strange.'

'Not just that.'

'What, then?'

'Some of the things in the newspapers are just not true.'

'You surely don't find that strange.'

'If you'd rather not talk about it I'll go.'

'I'd rather you said what you want to say.'

'I suppose I'm not sure. I only know that despite your refusal to help me stay, in all my time here you . . . you've been the most important person . . .'

'And now you're afraid your idol has feet of clay. There you're wrong. I'm clay all through like all God's creatures. Now tell me just what you read in the paper that made you so unhappy.'

'A series of things.'

'Such as?'

'The magistrate who was killed . . . they say he may have known he was being followed and took refuge in the Vatican, trying to hide in the crowd, but that they followed him there. And they say that a priest – they didn't even publish your name but it got out here, of course – was an innocent bystander who was injured . . .'

'Perfectly true. You don't imagine the Red Brigades would bother themselves with me?'

'No. But it's not true, even so. The chapel was closed; the restorers swore they locked it when they went to lunch. The terrorists shot the lock off to get in. But the magistrate was already in there . . . and so were you.'

'Anything else?'

'They say the magistrate should have had an escort, that

his life had been threatened repeatedly. Some people are demanding that there should be an official inquiry.'

'Very little will come of that, I imagine.'

'So I gather. Anyway, the man's dead . . .'

'Yes, the man's dead. John, have you spoken to anyone about this?'

'Of course. For a week no one talked of anything else.'

'I thought the usual thing was nine days. No, I mean about me.'

'No one. I wanted to ask you.'

'Good . . .'

Lazurek lay silent for a long time. At last the young priest stood up. 'I had no right to expect you to trust me. I'll go now.'

'I was wondering, on the contrary, how much you feel you can trust me.'

'Completely.'

'Despite my not helping you?'

'Yes. I know you felt it was in my best interests.'

'And despite the newspapers?'

'Of course. How could you imagine otherwise? I'll believe without question whatever you tell me.'

'And if I tell you nothing at all? If I ask you to trust me without giving you any help?'

'I think . . . yes, I suppose even that. Now that I've seen you, face to face and you've asked it of me. Forgive me. You're entitled to call me a Doubting Thomas.'

'I am not!' snapped the Monsignor. 'You are not, if you remember, speaking to Christ but to one Joseph Lazurek, one-time glutton, not above telling a lie or two in his time and quite capable of telling one to you. Now go away. Fly off to America and never, if you trust me, open your mouth to anyone again about any of this. Promise me that.'

'I promise.'

'Good . . . good. I shall miss you. Before you go . . . lift these pillows up a little, the pain is less if I'm straighter.'

He suffered himself to be moved and then lay back. When

Father McManus opened the door his eyes were already closed, waiting for the pain to subside.

Outside, the icy December afternoon was already growing dark. In a little while he would switch on the lamp and enjoy the sense of isolation it gave him to be in a small lighted room in a great hospital. As long as it lasted . . .

He wasn't ready yet for the world outside, for the moment when he would be a small red-clad figure joining an army of other small red-clad figures under the gaze of the patriarchs where he and the good magistrate had once lain side by side. And nothing changes . . .

'My faith,' he whispered to himself, 'is as weak as my quarter stomach, may God help me.'

When the worst of the pain subsided his head fell forward and he slept.